LETHAL
AFFAIRS

What Reviewers Say About Kim Baldwin's Books

"In a change of pace from her previous novels of suspense, Kim Baldwin has given her fans an intelligent romance filled with delightful peeks at the lives of the rich and famous...the reader journeys into some of the hot dance clubs in Paris and Rome and gets a front row seat to some very powerful sex scenes. Baldwin definitely proves that lust has gotten a bad rap. *Focus of Desire* is a great read, with humor, strong dialogue and heat." – *JustAboutwWrite.com*

"With each new book Kim Baldwin improves her craft and her storytelling. *Flight Risk*...has heated action and vibrant depictions that make the reader feel as though she was right in the middle of the story ...fast moving with crisp dialogue, and effective use of the characters' thoughts and emotions...this reviewer could not put the book down. Baldwin outdid herself with *Flight Risk*...her best storytelling to date. I highly recommend this thrilling story." – *Independent Gay Writer*

"A hallmark of great writing is consummate characterization, and *Whitewater Rendezvous* does not disappoint...Captures the reader from the very first page...totally immerses and envelopes the reader in the Arctic experience. Superior chapter endings, stylishly and tightly written sentences, precise pacing, and exquisite narrative all coalesce to produce a novel of first-rate quality, both in concept and expression." – *Midwest Book Review*

"Nature's fury has nothing on the fire of desire and passion that burns in Kim Baldwin's *Force of Nature*! Filled with passion, plenty of laughs, and "yeah, I know how that feels..." moments, Force of Nature is a book you simply can't put down. All we have to say is, where's the sequel?!" – *Outlookpress.com*

"'A riveting novel of suspense' seems to be a very overworked phrase. However, it is extremely apt when discussing...*Hunter's Pursuit*. Look for this excellent novel." – *Mega-Scene Magazine*

"*Hunter's Pursuit* is a...fierce first novel, an action-packed thriller pitting deadly professional killers against each other. Baldwin's fast-paced plot comes...leavened, as every intelligent adventure novel's excesses ought to be, with some lovin'." – *Book Marks, Q Syndicate*

Visit us at www.boldstrokesbooks.com

LETHAL AFFAIRS

by

Kim Baldwin & Xenia Alexiou

2008

ISBN10: 1-60282-022-8
ISBN13: 978-1-60282-022-7

THIS TRADE PAPERBACK IS PUBLISHED BY
BOLD STROKES BOOKS, INC.
NEW YORK, USA

FIRST EDITION: JULY 2008

CREDITS
EDITORS: JENNIFER KNIGHT, SHELLEY THRASHER, AND J. B. GREYSTONE
PRODUCTION DESIGN: J. B. GREYSTONE
COVER GRAPHIC: SHERI (graphicartist2020@hotmail.com)

Books by Kim Baldwin

Hunter's Pursuit

Force of Nature

Whitewater Rendezvous

Flight Risk

Focus of Desire

Acknowledgments

The authors wish to thank all the talented women at Bold Strokes Books for making this book possible. Radclyffe, for her vision, faith in us, and example. Editors Jennifer Knight, Shelley Thrasher, and Julie Greystone for making every word the best it can be. Graphic artist Sheri for an amazing cover. JLee Meyer for taking the author photo. Connie Ward, consulting publicist and first-reader extraordinaire, and all of the other associates who work behind the scenes to make each BSB book an exceptional read.

We'd also like to thank our friends and first readers Jenny Harmon, for your invaluable feedback and insights, and Sharon Lloyd, whose keen eyes seem to catch every typo and careless omission.

And to the readers who encourage us by buying our books, showing up for personal appearances, and for taking the time to email us. Thank you so much.

≈ ≈

Co-authoring a book with someone who lives on another continent can create some unique challenges, but Lethal Affairs was a labor of love from start to finish. My dear friend Xenia, thank you for entrusting me to help bring your stories to life on the page. I'm honored.

For Marty, for always going above and beyond to support my writing. You rock.

For my Father, your love and encouragement knows no bounds.

I also have to thank a wonderful bunch of friends who provide unwavering support for all my endeavors. Linda and Vicki, Kat and Ed, Felicity, Marsha and Ellen, and Claudia and Esther. You are family, and near or far, I hold you always close to my heart.

Kim Baldwin, July 2008

≈ ≈

There are so many people who believed in my ability to do this that I literally don't know where to start or who to thank first.

Kim, thanks for having faith in me and in this series. Claudia, for being my rock, and for telling me as long as I can remember that I'm a born storyteller. Dorien, Esther, Nicki, Miriam, Ro (Zus), for your constant encouragement and enthusiasm. Maria, for helping Manny sound so authentic. Dennis, for your dedication and endless supply of patience. And most of all, my family, for their support and for being my number one fans.

Xenia Alexiou, July 2008

DEDICATION

For my sister Anastasia. Thank you
for always believing in me.
Είσαι η καρδιά μου.

Ξenia

PROLOGUE

Istanbul, Turkey
Twelve Years Earlier

Sweat dripped from Domino's forehead into her eyes, making it difficult to focus. She'd been cooped up in this stifling room across the street from his hotel for four days, sitting at the curtained window with a view of Hamad Omar Hasan, the founder of an extremist group making life difficult for the American and U.N. Forces in his native Kuwait. Legal authorities had located him but didn't have enough evidence to arrest him, so the Elite Operatives Organization had the task of neutralizing him.

Though exhausted from the heat and lack of sleep, she watched his every move through a telescope. Years of training enabled her to shut out all distractions that might compromise the operation. This first time in the field she was strictly surveillance, so she had to notice everything. It was fourteen hundred hours—two p.m.—Hasan's usual nap time. He was lying on the couch today, though.

One of his men stood in front of the window to look out on the street, his long-standing hourly ritual.

Domino followed his gaze down three floors. Istanbul's Grand Bazaar was busy with tourists seeking handbags and rugs, colorful woven fabrics, or some type of handmade curio or piece of jewelry from one of the thousands of vendors and shops. The noisy midday traffic stirred up a haze of dust that covered everything.

A dark, four-door, late-model Audi stopped in front of the hotel. Most vehicles in the city were either rundown or older models of once-expensive cars, so this one stuck out. The guard in the window spoke into his cell phone while he continued to stare down at the street. The driver of the car appeared to be on the phone too. Was the son of a bitch finally leaving the hotel room?

The guard awakened his chief, then another of his men wrapped his turban—black, the same color as his beard. Since the owner of the car hadn't come up, Hasan must be going down. Domino took out her cell and dialed. "Take your positions. Rabbit leaving the hole." The three Kuwaitis headed for the door.

Letting go of the scope, she pulled a long robe over her clothes and wrapped the *hijab* around her face. Once on the street she climbed into the back of a nondescript, older car, one of her own behind the wheel, also dressed appropriately. A Muslim woman could not enter the car of a Westerner without drawing attention. The third EOO operative was a few cars ahead.

Years of training, pain, and no personal life all led to this moment. She was to keep low, follow the target, and update the others. No one would notice a local woman.

They drove for almost an hour in heavy traffic, the male operator cursing at their frequent stops to let people cross. Domino tried to stay focused. In the city of Esenyurt, the other operative in the car ahead called. Hasan was about to get out.

They stopped, too. *Never lose the target.* She grabbed a couple of transparent plastic bags next to her, filled with fruit and vegetables, got out, and caught up with her quarry as he exited the car. The street was jammed because of the open-air market.

A rivulet of sweat ran between her breasts. How did women endure such heat dressed in these things? *Stay focused and you won't feel the heat.*

The target appeared to be there for the market. She followed him, ignoring the stench of the dense crowd and overripe fruit. At one stall, he leisurely picked out the ripest watermelon, which one of his men then carried. They strolled on and finally entered a small Turkish café, which promised air-conditioning, coffee, and *lokum.* Hasan sat inside the café's large front window and peered at the passersby.

In the welcome shade behind a column of a nearby mosque, another good vantage point, Domino made the call. "Café Lokum, end of the market. Rabbit appears to have settled."

Less than ten minutes later, the window of the cafe shattered. One of the other EOO ops had fired from the balcony across the street.

The first bullet missed completely. One of Hasan's men jumped in front of his boss and took the second in his ear, which oozed blood before he dropped. How had the other operative missed? *It happens. Keep your focus.*

Someone fired another shot, from her left, and her confederate fell off the balcony to the street. *Fuck! Is he dead?* The shooter was screaming in Arabic something about Allah. *Damn.* Hasan had more men on the street.

Now Hasan and his remaining man opened fire from inside, and they apparently didn't give a damn who got hurt or killed. Civilians started to go down, and people screamed as they scattered for cover behind the market stalls. A woman shot in front of the café lay on the dusty ground, her toddler crying in her arms.

Amid the shots, Domino focused on the little girl trying to free herself from her dead mother's weight. She would walk right into the middle of this. *Assess and resolve.* Only two of them remained now, fighting God knew how many, and she didn't have a gun. One of Hasan's guys was firing nonstop at the other EOO operative, and the little girl wandered toward the line of fire.

Domino shook herself into action and retrieved the knife strapped to her calf. In a crouch, she silently hurried toward the shooter who'd killed the other operative, still firing from behind a tree. The adrenaline pouring through her filled her ears and drowned out even the sound of the guns. Her heart jackhammered so loud she wondered whether it might give her away.

The knife in her right hand would be fast and quiet. Behind the shooter now, Domino grabbed his hair, pulled his head back, and cut cleanly through the carotid. He dropped like a stone. Without hesitation, she sheathed her knife and hid his MP5 submachine gun under her robe, then started toward the café through the flying bullets and panicked civilians.

She still had an operative on his own who must be running out of ammo. They had yet to accomplish the mission, and she had to prove herself. *Don't hesitate. You can do this. Remember your training.*

Though concentrating on the café window, she saw the little girl on her knees, back beside her dead mother, crying while bullets flew over her head. The sight propelled her through the gunfire and past the

Turkish police, who were busily trying to arrest every local Turk and Arab. She had to act, now. *Don't overthink. Overthinking makes you hesitate. You hesitate, you go home in a box.*

Domino crept to the back of the café, intending to work around to the front as quietly as possible. But there she spotted the toilet window. She jumped with the submachine gun slung over one shoulder, hung on to the window frame, and pulled herself up. Once in the men's room, she put her hand on the door handle.

Failure is not an option. She took a deep breath and shut out everything in her head, until she could no longer hear the shooting in the next room or the cries of the little girl or the shouting of the people.

Swinging the MP5 up into position, she pushed the door open. Hasan and his man were hiding behind an overturned marble table, shooting at whatever moved. She pointed the gun around the wall and pulled the trigger, then stepped out, exposed. She fired until she couldn't hear them shoot back.

Hasan and his guard were limp, piled on top of each other on the floor, surrounded by hundreds of shells, their blood all over the place. Or was that watermelon…or both?

In a haze, she rushed back to the toilet, dumped the MP5, and shed the robe and hijab. She had to look like a lost, scared American tourist because men in robes had done the shooting. If she wore Muslim clothes, the police would question her before she made it halfway through the market.

She lifted herself up the way she had come in and was hanging from the window on the outside, about to let go, when a man shouted and pointed in her direction. He was forty feet away, yelling in Arabic for her to stop.

"*Antezer kef!*" He wore a robe—another of Hasan's men—and he held a rifle.

Cursing inwardly, she released her grip and dropped, and when she faced him, he fired. The bullet hit the wall beside her head, and she grabbed the knife strapped to her calf. From a crouch, she threw it in his direction.

They both watched in silence as the blood started to spread across the front of his robe. He tried to lift his rifle in her direction but an instant later was on the ground. She ran to his limp body and dislodged her knife from his chest. About to push her hair out of her face, she froze at the sight of his blood on her hand—a hand that seemed foreign.

More gunshots sounded from the near distance. Domino drowned out the noise and her surroundings and wiped her hands clean on his robe. She pulled out her cell to call the remaining operative. "Rabbit's down," she said without emotion.

CHAPTER ONE

Malta
Present Day

Dawn was still an hour away, so relatively few souls were already at work in the sleepy seaport capital of Malta on this cool June morning. Bakers, of course, and vendors at the open-air market, and fishermen returning from another night of casting their nets into the warm azure waters of the Mediterranean. In the Co-Cathedral of Saint John, five priests prepared for Sunday morning mass.

The massive sixteenth century cathedral was Valletta's most important historical monument. Its lofty baroque interior and priceless art brought in tourists and had inspired Sir Walter Scott to proclaim it the most magnificent place he had ever seen.

As the eldest of the priests replaced votive candles in the chapels, he stopped occasionally to admire the ornately carved stone walls and the inlaid marble tombs of knights that comprised its floor. Stooped and balding, except for the fringed crown of gray around the back of his head that he now scratched at absently, the monsignor had been at St. John's for thirty of his sixty-four years, longer than any of the others.

In the nave, the monsignor looked up to admire Mattia Preti's masterpiece, the vaulted ceiling with its vivid scenes from the life of Saint John painted directly onto the plaster in fresco. He was drawn to the scaffolding around one scene and the intense concentration of the woman at work there.

Like most priests, he was a good listener in the way most people are not. He'd heard tens of thousands confess their sins and so was wiser than most in the nature of men and their ability to hide what was in their heart. And he had grown adept at hearing beyond words, at understanding from someone's sighs and silences, postures, and expressions what they loved, or dreamed, or feared, or needed to confess.

But the young American was an enigma. He had tried on several occasions to strike up a conversation with her about her life or her work and had found her always well-mannered, almost uncommonly polite, but guarded. And her answers to his questions seemed practiced. Never spontaneous.

He had learned she was thirty-three, unmarried, and that she never knew her parents. She traveled a lot and loved her work, she said, particularly when it involved cathedrals, and she told him her time at Saint John's had been very rewarding.

And she certainly was a dedicated and capable artisan, always there even before he was, working tirelessly, often late into the night. And the result of her painstaking efforts thus far, in the neighboring scenes, was breathtaking.

But there was much she wasn't saying. Intense, he thought. Very earnest. He wondered why such an attractive young woman always appeared so lonely. Vowing to try again soon to draw her out, he resumed his preparations for mass.

Luka Madison paused to unzip the top of her navy coveralls, shrugging out of the sleeves to tie them around her waist. Beneath, she wore a black, long-sleeved T-shirt and jeans, both molded to her five-foot six-inch frame. Comfortable sneakers completed the ensemble. Standing for long hours, day after day, seldom bothered her. She was in excellent physical condition, trim and athletically toned but not overly muscular, with dexterous hands used to long labor.

Her medium brown hair needed cutting. She generally liked to wear it only to her shoulder blades, with long bangs she could pin back while she worked, but she lacked the obsession with hair and makeup of most women and had let her usual trim slip by a few weeks longer than normal.

She preferred working in the quiet before dawn, when she heard only the occasional muffled prayers of the priests and their soft footfalls as they carried out their duties.

In an hour, the parishioners would arrive and, later, the tourists, whose constant, whispered conversations created a dull white noise to mar her sense of peace. The smell of burning candles, old and new, grew pungent high on the scaffolding, and the incredible acoustics allowed her to make out snatches of conversations from below. The families—the loving parents and patient grandparents with strings of children in tow—saddened her, because they represented memories she had never had.

But at this time of the morning, in her solitude, she was content. For the last few hours, she had been restoring an auburn-haired angel to her brilliant, almost garish former glory, carefully removing years of candle soot and the previous restorer's handiwork to reveal what the artist had intended. The lovely face, the only area still unfinished, beckoned to her.

Luka checked her latex gloves for rips before she reached for another bottle of saturated calcium hydroxide and carefully dipped her swab. She brought it over her head once again and applied the solution to the angel's peaceful smile. As it became more vivid it drew her in.

The sudden vibration of the cell phone in her pocket broke her concentration. She checked the caller ID and sighed. Keeping her voice down, she answered. "Good morning."

The woman's voice on the other end was maternally tender. "Hi, honey. It's me. How's everything with you? Are you working?"

"I'm doing fine," Luka responded. "And yes, I'm at work. You know me, I always start early."

"That's nice, dear. I hope you make time for breakfast, though."

"I will. I have it right here with me."

"Oh, before I forget about why I called. We want you to join us for dinner tomorrow."

She frowned. "Dinner plans tomorrow? That's short notice."

"Thanks, honey, I knew you'd understand," the voice said, as though she had just readily agreed. "Don't forget breakfast. See you soon."

Luka flipped the phone shut and stared wistfully at the angel another minute before she packed up to leave.

❖

Baltimore, Maryland
Monday

Hayley Ward maneuvered through the throng of television, newspaper, and radio reporters, positioning herself so she would be standing in the hip-hop artist's direct line of sight as he left the recording studio. She knew every way possible to gain an advantage and didn't hesitate to do whatever she needed to get a story. For this one, she'd put on a red blouse, because it was the man's favorite color, and red lipstick.

She'd spent a lot of time on her makeup and hair, though she didn't need to. Beautiful parents had blessed her with unbeatable genes. She had full, kissable lips, a million-dollar smile with dimples, warm hazel eyes; high cheekbones; and shiny, shoulder-length auburn hair with natural wheat-gold highlights.

Hayley was only five-four, and most of the other media reps towered over her, so she compensated with three-inch heels. And when she interviewed men, she always wore clothes that showed off her perfect hourglass figure to best advantage. The blouses and tops displayed a little cleavage, and the skirts were short enough to allow a good view of her legs. Today with her red blouse, she wore a charcoal skirt and blazer with matching pumps.

She was striking, and it was hard not to notice her. Hayley counted on that fact. The crowd of media came alive as the singer's entourage emerged, and she elbowed past the *Entertainment Tonight* correspondent just as the rapper himself appeared.

Her voice was only one of many shouting his name, but she was in exactly the right spot to catch his eye, which was enough. He headed straight toward her.

❖

Southwestern Colorado

The campus sprawled over sixty-three acres and consisted of several squat red-brick buildings, dormitories and classrooms, and larger structures that housed administrative offices and training facilities. The remote location gave it much-needed privacy from outside scrutiny, and best of all, it was adjacent to the nearly half-million-acre Weminuche Wilderness Area, which provided it with the diverse ecological environments necessary for comprehensive field training.

It looked much like the private boarding school it was purported to be, except for the extraordinary security. High razor-wire-topped fences surrounded the campus, security cameras appeared everywhere, and the sign on the guard gate read *No Trespassing. Admittance Only With Proper Identification.*

At night, armed guards patrolled at irregular intervals. And in the administration building, a massive neo-Gothic structure with bell towers evocative of medieval cathedrals, nearly every door required a coded key card. The complex was the home of the Elite Operatives Organization, a specialized school that, in its fifty-sixth year, was still as unknown to the world as it had been in its earliest days.

Montgomery "Monty" Pierce, the EOO's chief administrator, studied the school's latest acquisitions as they romped on a massive wooden playset outside the junior dormitory. His fair Scandinavian complexion turned blotchy when he spent too long in the sun, even in June, so he kept his suit jacket on and chose a bench in the shade of the building.

The three boys and three girls he was inspecting ranged in age from four to six, and all were healthy, unusually bright children. But if the past was any harbinger, at least half of this current crop would end up in foster care or be privately adopted out before the age of twelve because they fell short of EOO requirements. And only one at most would have the exceptional qualities necessary to place him or her in the ranks of the school's top graduates, the ETFs, shorthand for Elite Tactical Force.

David Arthur, Director of Training, jogged toward Pierce from the gymnasium in his customary combat fatigues. Like him, Arthur had just passed his fifty-eighth birthday, but with his lean, muscled body and dense, copper-colored crew cut, at a distance he could pass for a student.

Though Pierce had kept his weight in check, his own body, by contrast, bore the fleshiness of his years behind a desk, and his face revealed the deep creases of his frequently dour expressions.

Arthur settled onto the bench. "Any obvious standouts?"

Pierce pointed to a dark-haired boy atop the monkey bars. "Him, for sure. Agile. Fearless. From the Ukraine." Nodding toward a red-headed girl jumping on one of the trampolines, he added, "And perhaps this one, from the Stockholm orphanage. Exceptionally high I.Q."

"Joanne will be pleased. Speaking of whom here she comes."

Pierce straightened his tie and sat up straighter.

Joanne Grant, the third member of the governing trio, was the least recognizable from her days as an ETF. Since she'd become Director of Academics she'd gained ten pounds, and her once-ebony hair was now entirely white.

Only Pierce and Grant dealt with the outside world, contracting with EOO clients and making contact as necessary with the myriad high-level resources the Organization had cultivated. But when they determined how and when to utilize their valued ETFs, Arthur took an equal role. In order to ensure its elite operatives were not unnecessarily put at risk to settle a personal vendetta, at least two members of the Governing Trio had to sign off on any high-level assignment, which was the reason for today's meeting.

Pierce and Arthur rose when Grant reached them, and they set off in the direction of the obstacle course, talking as they walked.

Arthur asked, "This about the Guerrero affair?"

"Yes," Pierce confirmed. "Our contact in Cuba called over the weekend. Guerrero's moved up his return home and is leaving tonight. We're still trying to nail down the particulars."

"Tonight?" Grant increased the length of her stride to keep up with them. "I thought Allegro was unavailable until Thursday."

"She is. We can't pull her off the case she's on," Pierce said. "It's taken two weeks to get her into position to obtain the information for our Seattle client, and it all goes down tomorrow morning."

"We can't send Mark alone to get Guerrero," Arthur pointed out, quite unnecessarily.

"No. Not on his first assignment." Pierce pictured their most recent graduate. Mark Johnson, aka Sundance, was a clean-cut young man with sandy blond hair and blue eyes. "Especially since things are in flux. We need a senior ETF with experience. That's why I sent for Domino as soon as we got the call. We don't have much time, and she's the only one available."

"I hate to use one of our best on such a high-profile assignment," Grant said. "Especially since it involves so many unknowns now. It's too risky—the cops and the media will be all over this. Surely there's someone else."

They were passing the ball field, where some students were playing baseball. Grant, without looking, quickly raised her left hand and caught a hard-hit ball coming from that side that otherwise would have hit Pierce, walking half a step ahead. The demonstration of her well-honed reflexes would have stunned anyone else, but neither man blinked.

"I know you have a soft spot for Domino, Joanne, but this job is too important to leave to someone less qualified," Pierce said. "And tonight will be our only opportunity. I'll have a support team in place in case they need it."

"I don't know…" Grant frowned, and her steps slowed, forcing the men to pause also.

"Domino is the best suited. You have my vote," Arthur declared, ending the debate. "Sundance needs a strong second. He has the skills, but he hasn't been tested yet. And Guerrero might present unseen difficulties. The man's cocky and unpredictable."

Two votes was all it took, so the trio disbanded, Grant and Arthur returning to their offices as Pierce reached for his cell phone to set things in motion.

CHAPTER TWO

D omino applied vivid red lipstick as the van paused at a traffic light, then continued to peruse the file folder on her lap. Reno, the driver, a taciturn twenty-something brute of a man with shiny black hair, was familiar. Less so was Blade, the attractive Latino woman seated with her in the back.

"It's a break for us he's decided to take this deal before he leaves," Blade told her. "It's at a hotel not far from here. Easy in and out, not one of the busier, high-end places. Good for his business, and ours."

Domino looked down at a color photo of the target. As Cuba's Information Minister, Juan Carlos Guerrero had diplomatic immunity, though his real work as the country's premiere drug kingpin had been well documented. It was no surprise that he was marked for liquidation—he was a self-serving, corrupt dictator who didn't hesitate to silence his opponents with death or imprisonment. Helpfully, his arrogance had provided them an opportunity to get to him in a much less risky environment than Miami International Airport.

For five days, Guerrero had been conducting his cocaine deals poolside, behind the fortress-like walls of his sister's Miami mansion, within view of his eleven-year-old niece but well protected from prying eyes or interruptions. That he had decided to risk arranging a final deal in a public hotel revealed both his unmitigated greed and sense of invulnerability.

"Sundance is already in place, but has instructions to wait for you," Blade told Domino as she flipped past Guerrero's picture and profile to a crudely drawn floor plan. "They're in the hotel lounge. Four ways in and out—the elevators and stairwell, here…" Blade pointed with a well-manicured fingernail. "Which lead to all floors and the underground parking garage. This way to the lobby and front desk… and this, to the alarmed fire exit to the street."

"Two more blocks," Reno said.

Domino fitted a wireless earpiece snugly into her right ear and ran a hand through her long blond hair to cover it. It was both a transmitter and receiver.

Blade handed her a plain dark tote bag to complete her preparations. "Guerrero arrived in a black Mercedes SUV. It's parked in the hotel's underground garage. The driver is the shorter of the two guys with him in the lounge."

"Security cameras?" Domino asked.

"Yes," Blade replied. "Above the exits, in the lobby, and in the garage."

"We're here," Reno announced as the van began to slow.

Full dark had come upon the city during their drive, and they were in a quiet alleyway, away from traffic, with no one about. Domino jumped out and waited for the van to be well away before she headed toward a nearby taxi stand. It was only six more blocks to the hotel, so she was in the lounge within ten minutes.

Within a few seconds, she unobtrusively took in the entirety of the place and its inhabitants.

The lighting was subdued, as she expected, and the Sharksfin Lounge had the dark colors and Caribbean kitsch decor that seemed to be all the rage in these middle-of-the-road hotel bars in Miami. The round tables were low and black, and the padded stools and comfy seats surrounding them were deep bordeaux, the same shade as the carpet. Live tropical plants were scattered about, and a baby grand piano in one corner hinted at live entertainment on the weekend. In the back, a mirrored wall above the bar reflected four long, neat rows of bottles, their colored contents illuminated by track lights from above.

It was an unremarkable place that fell short of its attempt to be trendy and tasteful, but it was comfortable and quiet, and the low Latin music in the background provided a pleasant ambience for businessmen turning a deal or tourists looking to unwind over a fruity drink and coconut shrimp. This early in the evening, only a few tables were occupied.

Guerrero was off to the left and toward the back, with his bodyguard and driver flanking him and his business contact sitting opposite. Four men in business suits, speaking too quietly to be overheard. Domino knew the bodyguard would be watching all new arrivals, so she skimmed her attention over them and on, without making eye contact.

Near them, a young Latino couple too intent on each other to notice much else seemed to be the only locals. Two other tables held tourists—a young Asian couple speaking Japanese close by to Domino's right, and, farther on, a bored-looking middle-aged couple whose sunburned faces told of their naiveté of the south Florida sun, even in April.

Sundance sat by himself near the abandoned piano, nursing a beer and reading the sports page. He looked exactly like the picture she had memorized, except for his deep tan. Blond hair, blue eyes, and casual preppy outfit, with the look of a college student on spring break who might be killing time waiting for friends.

Beyond him, a baby-faced Cuban barman in black pants, white shirt, and vest the same bordeaux as the carpet watched them all as he polished glasses.

She heard Blade's voice in her earpiece and knew Sundance could hear it, too. "Domino, flag down the waiter and order a ginger ale if everything is in order."

As she crossed to a table in the back where she would have a good vantage point, she caught her reflection in the mirrored wall behind the bar. Her attire was well suited for her task and environment. The simple dark navy dress was stylishly appropriate, without showing so much skin she attracted undue attention. It was cut to just above the knee, its V-neck modestly shallow. And her matching pumps had enough of a heel to be fashionable, but not so much she couldn't move fast if she had to.

Settling comfortably into a seat, she set the tote bag on the chair beside her and signaled for the barman, satisfied the situation was as expected.

"What can I get for you?" he asked.

"A ginger ale, please." She spoke loud enough for Sundance to hear.

Blade's voice sounded again in her ear. "Sundance, when the lady gets her drink, clear your throat."

The baby-faced barman returned with her ginger ale, and as he set it in front of Domino, Sundance dutifully cleared his throat.

When he did, Domino glanced his way in discreet acknowledgment. She could only hear him in person, not through her earpiece. When their eyes met, she felt her first niggling of disconcertion to see relief cross his face. She had once been a rookie too, and nervous, but also anxious to prove herself, as Sundance should be.

"Proceed as planned," Blade told them both.

The wait began.

Sundance kept to his newspaper, while Domino played the I'm-waiting-for-someone-and-they're-late attitude for the benefit of any interested parties. She checked her watch, stirred her drink, and acted bored, while inconspicuously keeping tabs on Guerrero and his party.

The Cuban's bodyguard was a hulking thug, and vigilant. He watched everything, glancing her way frequently. Guerrero's driver was a head shorter and only slightly less broad in the shoulders. The blond-haired man Guerrero was meeting with looked every bit the typical businessman, in his neat blue suit, polished oxfords, and leather briefcase.

Twenty minutes into their wait, when the barman returned to see if she wanted something else, Domino made sure her response was loud enough to carry to Guerrero's table. "Yeah, sure, I'll take another. And would you keep an eye out for my boyfriend, let me know if you see him come in? He's six feet, short dark hair, cute..." She checked her watch again. "And in serious trouble if he doesn't get here soon."

The barman laughed. "Sure thing."

After another ten minutes of waiting, she plucked a cell phone out of her tote bag and pretended to make a few calls, all seeking the whereabouts of her boyfriend.

It was twenty minutes more before the blond businessman sitting opposite Guerrero started putting things into his briefcase, while the bodyguard signaled the barman for their bill.

Out of the corner of her eye, Domino watched Sundance stand and fold his newspaper, then pull out his wallet for a tip, busying himself until his target was on his feet and ready to depart. Her disquiet increased when she saw his hand tremble.

As soon as Guerrero and his goons headed toward the elevators, Sundance went that way too, walking ahead of them. The businessman veered off from the rest, toward the lobby.

Domino forced herself to remain seated, observing the four men wait for the lift. As the primary operative, Sundance was supposed to stick with the target at all costs. She assumed they were all headed to the underground parking garage, since she knew Guerrero had a car waiting there and a flight to catch.

And indeed, when the elevator arrived, she watched the down arrow above it illuminate.

As soon as the elevator doors closed, she rose and headed quickly to the back bar, where she tossed the barman a couple of bills. "If he ever gets here," she said petulantly, "tell him he can go to hell, huh?"

While she was pounding down the stairwell beside the elevator after them, the voice in her ear relayed a disturbing development. "Domino, Sundance may be made."

CHAPTER THREE

Sundance steeled himself and tried to remain focused on his training and objective. But he couldn't help sweating, and the bodyguard had noticed.

The sudden change in plans had unnerved him. Although this was a much better setting for his first job than Miami International, he had memorized the airport layout, not this hotel's. There were too many unknowns here. And he hadn't expected to share an elevator with the man he was about to kill and the goons assigned to keep him from doing it.

Everything had gone smoothly until now.

He had proceeded to the elevator ahead of his target and pushed the down button with some confidence it was Guerrero's destination as well. To keep his backup apprised of the situation, he had hesitated by the elevator's control panel after pushing the round, white, *P-for-Parking* button and asked, "Which floor?" of the others as they got on.

Then he got the first hint he may have been made.

The bodyguard studied him a little too closely before peering at the panel and replying, "We're good."

Things unraveled further when the bodyguard positioned himself in the back of the elevator beside him. And when Sundance glanced his way, the man purposefully opened his suit jacket so he could see the gun beneath it.

This close, the guy was massive and intimidating.

"*Que pasa*, amigo?" the hulk inquired. "What's your problem?"

Sweat ran down his back. "No problem," he said, with as much nonchalance as he could muster.

The elevator braked to a stop, and he hesitated, intending to let Guerrero and his goons take a few steps toward their car. To his dismay, the bodyguard put his hand inside his jacket on his gun as he stepped out and glared at him. A warning.

To further complicate matters, the three men did not turn left toward the SUV they had arrived in as Sundance expected, but walked straight ahead, down the main parking aisle. He had no choice. He had to follow them, and he couldn't do so as discreetly as he would have liked. *Fuck this*, he thought, as he stepped off the elevator.

❖

Domino eased open the stairwell door to the parking garage and listened as she slipped on a thin pair of latex gloves from her tote bag. She could hear low voices, speaking Spanish, and the sound of footsteps, but everything was moving away from her, so she slipped out and took cover behind the nearest concrete column to ascertain the situation.

Guerrero and his goons were headed down the main parking aisle, and Sundance was walking right behind them, fifteen feet away, and had the perfect opportunity for a shot.

Domino paralleled their movements from a row of cars away, keeping down, diagonally tracking them, mentally urging Sundance. *Come on! Take the shot! You'll never have a better one.* But she could see his hesitation clearly, and their window of opportunity was about to close. The three Cubans were headed toward a dark sedan instead of a SUV. Soon they would be in it and headed to the airport.

Sundance had his hand on his weapon but wasn't drawing it. Guerrero was only a few feet from the vehicle and Domino had a clear shot.

As she reached for the holster strapped to her inner thigh and withdrew a Glock G33—a subcompact, semi-automatic pistol whose magazine held nine rounds—she spoke quietly to their backup. "He can't do it and I have a clear shot. Tell him to get the hell down."

She raised her hand to fire, her focus entirely on her target, as Blade's voice relayed her warning: "Sundance! Get down!"

Her first shot nailed Guerrero in the side of the head and he crumpled.

Both the bodyguard and the driver whirled around, reaching for their weapons. Sundance, though, moved too slowly and was too visible as the culprit, with Domino positioned off to the left and half-hidden behind a car. As she took her second shot, killing Guerrero's driver, the bodyguard got Sundance in the chest as he dove for cover, and he went down, too.

The bodyguard noticed her then, but it was too late. Her third bullet was already on its way. It buried itself into his temple and he fell like his boss.

She hurried to her target and fired another shot into Guerrero's head, though the blood pooling beneath him indicated it was unnecessary.

"Target is down," she relayed to her backup. "Everyone is down, Sundance included. What a fucking mess." Sundance had the keys to their escape vehicle, a dark coupe parked not far from where he had fallen. In a crouch, she ran to him.

He had a growing blossom of red on his shirt, right over his heart. He looked up into her eyes and weakly gripped her arm. "Don't leave me."

"I'm here."

"I screwed up, didn't I? Jesus, I'm hit bad." He tried to sit up, but his strength was gone. She watched him take in the pool of blood, his blood, on the concrete. His hand relaxed, releasing her arm.

She took the hand and squeezed it. "You did good."

His gaze became fixed and his breathing more shallow. "Domino, are you still there?"

"I'm here." She squeezed his hand again.

"I'm tired. It's cold. I need to…" His whisper tapered off and he lay still.

She patted down his pockets and retrieved the keys, but as she fumbled for his earpiece she heard the roar of an engine—a car entering the lot, approaching fast. She darted behind the nearest vehicle just as a Jeep came into view, braking abruptly when it rounded the curve from the entrance to find three bodies blocking the way, with a fourth lying not much farther on.

The front doors of the Jeep flew open and a pair of middle-aged men jumped out, tourists from the look of them. One was focused on the bodies, the other more cautious—he was looking around for the person responsible. A woman inside the Jeep started to scream.

Domino couldn't possibly make it to the coupe without being seen. Besides, the Jeep was currently blocking the only way out by car. She quickly backtracked, keeping low and out of sight. "I need another way out of here," she whispered into her transmitter.

"Take the stairwell again, up one floor," her backup replied in her ear, but Reno was talking this time, not Blade.

She noted the security camera above the door to the stairs and kept her face down as she approached. It was positioned too high for her to do anything about it. She didn't have time.

"There's an air vent in the stairwell on the floor above the garage. Use the screwdriver in your bag," Reno said, as she took the steps two at a time. The small battery-operated tool was fast, but two bolts remained in the grill that blocked her escape when she heard running footsteps on the stairs above, heading her way. Clipped voices. Anxious, and she couldn't hear the words. Security guards, most likely.

Working quickly, she removed the final screws and slipped into the narrow space as quietly as possible, fitting the grill back into place behind her and hoping it would stay put long enough for her to get the hell out of there. It was precariously balanced on a small ledge of metal.

She didn't have much room to maneuver in the square ductwork, but she'd been in worse places. She shimmied forward a few feet to a wide junction. Vents led forward, left, right, and up. "I'm in the vent at the first juncture," she informed her backup in a hushed voice. "Which way?"

"Keep straight, then up," he replied. "Then forward again a short way. You'll find the vent in the women's public restroom on the mezzanine of the hotel. Blade's headed there now to get the screws off for you."

Domino elbowed forward to the next juncture, then into the duct that led up. She didn't have enough room to change, but she stuffed her wig into the tote bag and paused to remove her heels. Bare feet would give her better purchase against the slippery-smooth metal walls of the vent.

Bracing her back against one side and her feet against the other, knees bent, she had to strain for every yard she gained upward. But in less than three minutes, she reached the next level of ductwork and followed it to the restroom. Peering through the grill, she could see Blade primping in front of the mirror.

Domino remained where she was, quietly waiting.

Soon a toilet flushed and a young woman appeared beside Blade at the sinks to wash her hands. When she left, Blade pulled a screwdriver out of her pocket and hurried over to the vent.

"Turn left out the front door," Blade whispered as she removed the final screw and lifted off the grill cover.

"Right. Now go." Domino hustled into one of the stalls and jerked on the change of clothes provided in the tote bag. When she emerged a couple of minutes later, she was wearing shorts, a T-shirt, and sneakers. Everything else was tucked in the small red nylon backpack she slung over one shoulder. She paused at the mirror to hand-comb her brunette hair into place and wipe the lipstick and rouge off her face with a wet paper towel. Then she plucked out her brown contacts. Blue-gray eyes stared back at her; she looked like herself again.

She emerged onto the mezzanine, which overlooked a lobby abuzz with people, harried hotel employees, worried-looking guests, and a handful of police passing through to the crime scene, appearing single-minded in their purpose and destination.

Domino strolled casually through the chaos, simply a hotel guest out for a day of shopping and sightseeing. After exiting through the front door, she turned left and had taken only a step or two before Reno said in her earpiece, "Turn right at the first corner, Domino. Then, halfway down the next block, you'll see an alleyway next to the Starbucks. We'll pick you up there."

CHAPTER FOUR

Senator, it's time to upgrade the glasses. And we need to darken your hair a shade and add some highlights."

Senator Terrence Burrows had employed an image consultant long before he decided to run for president, so he needed only minor tweaks these days to keep him in maximum photogenic form. Hair transplants had given him thick brown hair, dermabrasion removed the evidence of his chronic adolescent acne, and all his suits were tailor-made.

"Call my aide in the morning," he told the consultant, "and have her set up the appointments. Thanks, Seth."

When he disconnected, Terrence reached for his remote and turned on CNN. He wanted to catch their story on the energy bill, because they'd interviewed him for the piece. Though the rest of his staff had gone home, he was still in his plush Capitol Hill office, tying up loose ends.

When CNN interrupted its regular broadcast with breaking news of the Guerrero assassination, he turned up the volume to listen but gave it only marginal attention.

Only when he received a phone call from EOO Chief Montgomery Pierce while soaking in his bathtub at home two hours later did he begin to realize his entire political future might hinge on Guerrero's misfortune.

He was already upset with the EOO for their increasingly outrageous demands. Joanne Grant, the other Organization chief he dealt with, had called earlier in the week, asking for sensitive information regarding the upcoming visit of a Chinese diplomatic delegation.

"I don't have the China info yet," he told Pierce after he identified himself. "It's going to take some time."

"I'm not calling about that," Pierce said. "Miami police have a hotel security tape of the Guerrero assassination. We need you to make it disappear. Tonight, before they get it to their lab for analysis. And copies, if there are any."

"Are you insane?" He sat up so abruptly water sloshed over the side of the tub and onto the mat. "Do you know what you're asking? I can't do that. I *won't* do that. Don't you have people for such things?"

"Yes," Pierce said patiently. "People like you."

He forced himself to bite back a response he might regret. "How do you expect me to do this without jeopardizing myself?"

"I don't know, and I don't care," Pierce said. "Make it happen. Soon."

The line went dead.

Terrence cursed as he flipped the cell phone closed. His quiet peace had disappeared. He got out of the tub and threw on a plush burgundy robe, cinching the belt so tight in his aggravation he had to immediately loosen it. Dripping water onto the carpet, he padded in bare feet down the hall to the bedroom, where his wife Diana, a blond former Miss Connecticut, was reading in bed. "I have some things to attend to, honey. Don't wait up," he told her from the doorway, gracing her with the perfect, boyish grin cosmetic dentistry had provided him.

They lived with their six-year-old twin boys, Andrew and Austin, in a stately Tudor-style mansion in suburban Virginia, a seven-thousand-square-foot behemoth that boasted six bedrooms, five baths, a pool, sauna, fitness room, and other luxuries. But Terrence spent nearly all his time in one spacious, masculine room on the second floor—his private domain, part office, part den. In addition to his desk and books, it featured a giant plasma TV, cozy fireplace, well-stocked bar, and comfy leather couch long enough to accommodate his six-foot, one-inch height when he needed a quick nap. The windows along one wall provided him a view of his landscaped, terraced gardens.

Flipping on the TV to CNN, he poured himself a whiskey while he considered how to satisfy Pierce's demand. The network soon aired its next update on the Guerrero matter.

"Miami's police chief has confirmed a hotel security camera captured the assassination this evening of Cuban Information Minister Juan Carlos Guerrero," the news anchor reported. "Chief Marcus Thompson says the tape of the shootings and evidence gathered at the scene indicates the murders were the result of a well-orchestrated plot by two or more persons—a still-unidentified man, found dead at the scene, and a woman who escaped through an air duct into the hotel. Thompson says the female suspect did the actual shootings. The male suspect was reportedly killed by one of Guerrero's men. There's no word yet on whether the tape of the incident will be made available to news organizations."

Terrence knew from personal experience that Pierce had a well-trained cadre of female operatives. He should have realized it was an Organization hit.

Pierce had asked him for a lot of favors, but never anything so risky. However, this trend had recently become his biggest headache. The EOO was squeezing him too hard, long after he had paid his debt in full.

He had tried to get out from under them. He had called in every possible favor with his contacts in the CIA, FBI, and Secret Service, attempting to uncover something he could use as leverage against Pierce's demands. Terrence was powerful, with powerful friends, some of whom had regular dealings with the elusive EOO. But only a rare few individuals knew anything about the group except for its capabilities and an untraceable contact number. He had managed to learn only that it was based somewhere in Colorado.

Then it dawned on him that Pierce's phone call might be the break he'd been waiting for, that he might be able to squeeze them back.

He sipped his whiskey and considered the possibilities. He had to plan. No one could gain access to the tape for a few hours, anyway. The police would be all over it.

Pierce had been right about one thing. Senator Terrence Burrows knew how to obtain information and make things happen outside ordinary means.

He'd been a nobody and still naïve when he'd contracted the EOO to do his dirty work for him. Things were different now. Now he had his very own take-care-of-anything-and-everything contact. Jack. And Jack took care of all his needs very capably and quickly, without making the demands the Organization did. He dialed the number from memory, and it was answered on the third ring.

"It's me, Jack," Terrence said. "The Miami PD has a tape of the Juan Carlos Guerrero assassination. Get it for me, tonight, before the high-tech whizzes get to work on it. And find out if any copies exist."

"Doable, but expensive."

"Whatever it costs. Do it right away."

"Understood." The line went dead.

He poured himself another drink and stared out at the starlit night. Within an hour, he had a plan. The tape would set it in motion.

At the very least, it would get those assholes at the Organization off him for a while. Keep them too busy watching their own backs. And they'd think he'd done his best to fulfill an important and risky request.

Best-case scenario—this could sever the link between them permanently.

All he needed now was the right accomplice. Someone with the same drive and ambition he had, that hunger to succeed, whatever the cost. Someone willing to take risks.

It came to him. That bright young woman he'd met before he came to Washington. She was perfect.

❖

Domino returned to her condominium after the job to take a long, hot shower and unwind. She had no television, so she didn't learn of the Miami police chief's press conference until ten minutes after it occurred, when the EOO called her. The tape of the incident didn't surprise her, but she wondered what was on it. Whatever it was, they'd have to take care of it. Even though this had been a nightmare of an assignment, she'd done her part.

When she'd chosen her code name, a few of her classmates had kidded her about it, presuming she was paying homage to the Marvel comic-book character of the same name, a lethally trained mercenary with mutant powers that helped her escape dangerous situations.

But even then she had the gaming tiles in mind, though sometimes, like today, she wouldn't mind having some of the other Domino's talent to turn luck in her favor.

Her music helped her decompress, but she was too edgy to sleep, so she started a new layout, carefully setting up her dominos on the smooth, polished hardwood floor.

The spacious condo in suburban Washington had been hers for six years, though she spent vast amounts of time away from it for work.

But except for her books and CDs, it retained a still-moving-in austerity. No paintings or posters hung on the immaculate, off-white walls, no photographs sat on the coffee table.

She regretted the last part and wished she could steal some of the places she'd visited on film. Her assignments had taken her to locations worldwide, and even though she was there for a mission, whenever possible, she would stop and admire the beauty around her.

She could turn off all emotions during a job, and she could turn off the job for a few moments of peace. Only the feeling of surrender without consequence could provide that type of peace, the same sensation she experienced when she was in churches and cathedrals. But snapping pictures while on assignment wasn't an option. Never take any proof of where you've been with you—that was the cardinal rule.

Her bedroom furniture consisted of a mattress and box springs, end table, and dresser. A couch in the living room, set in front of her massive floor-to-ceiling windows, looked out on the DC skyline. In the kitchen were only a refrigerator and sink, because she never cooked. No mirrors, except the one on her medicine cabinet. Simple track lighting, always turned low.

The bookcases dominated—floor to ceiling, and filled. Hundreds of CDs fed her state-of-the art music system, and thousands of books fed her mind, for she was always learning. Reading was for knowledge, never pleasure, so her library consisted almost exclusively of nonfiction titles and covered such diverse fields as science, sociology, psychology, photography, and other cultures.

Her barren accommodations reflected who she was and provided maximum floor space for her dominos, though she never called them that. They were her *bones*, a player's term.

Four hundred thirty-seven bones into her new layout, shortly before dawn, she received another call from the Organization, notifying her the only copy of the Guerrero assassination tape was missing from the Miami police department.

She was instructed to remain close and available.

❖

Tuesday

Terrence Burrows was napping on the couch in his den when he received his first call back shortly after four a.m., informing him the tape had been successfully retrieved and was in safe hands, awaiting further instructions. It cost him ten thousand dollars. He thanked Jack and made another request, which took an additional forty minutes.

"I found her," Jack reported. "Want me to fax the info now?"

"Yes, that's fine." He put Jack on hold while he scanned the document. Under the heading Personal, it read Age: 29. Height: Five feet, four inches. Hair: Auburn. Eyes: Hazel. Single. Lives alone in a two-bedroom apartment. The address followed. Scottish-American. Both parents alive. Mother does charity work. Father is a retired banker. One brother, Ted, thirty-seven, a sergeant in the army, married with two kids. One sister, Claudette, thirty-four, doesn't work, married, also with two children. The names and addresses of the family members were included.

The next section covered education and employment. The subject had gone to nursing school, then worked in a hospital in Baltimore for two years before she switched careers. She had returned to college to get a degree in journalism, then been employed at a small weekly newspaper for several months before she was hired at the *Baltimore Dispatch*, where she'd been for the last two years.

"Good work, Jack." Terrence set down the fax and reached for a handwritten note. "Now, arrange to have the tape mailed to her at her home address, along with a message I'll dictate to you. Get it there as soon as possible, but be sure she can't trace it back to me." He didn't care whether the EOO could track the tape to Hayley; it would only make them more paranoid. But he had to make sure he was well insulated from discovery.

"Of course. Everything done by phone."

"Excellent. All right, here's the message." He would burn the note he read as soon as he hung up. "Got all that?"

"Yes. Anything else?"

"Nothing right now. I'll let you know."

It was five a.m. by the time he finished with Jack. He knew Miami authorities would likely discover the tape was missing when the day shift reported for duty, so he called Pierce immediately. He needed to get back to him before the media got wind of it.

"I'm calling about the tape," he said when Pierce answered.

"Yes?" Pierce sounded groggy.

"Someone beat me to it," he lied. "I tried right after you called me, but my contact couldn't get close to it then. The detectives assigned to the case were viewing it constantly. When he tried again a little while ago, it was missing."

"Damn!" Pierce suddenly sounded much more awake. "Anything else? Any copies?"

"My contact said none were made. That's all I know."

"All right. I'll be in touch if I need you for something more," Pierce said before signing off.

Terrence set down the phone, then ran a hand along the back of his neck to free a knot of tension there. Pierce certainly never neglected an opportunity to tug on his leash. Reminded him every chance he got they would always be nearby, looking over his shoulder, ready to ask for the next favor. Well, hopefully, not for much longer.

CHAPTER FIVE

Hayley Ward threw her keys on her kitchen counter, next to a pile of unopened junk mail and on top of a stack of articles clipped from newspapers and magazines, all of which had prompted ideas for potential off-shoot stories of her own. The clippings were everywhere—on her nightstand, bulletin board, coffee table, refrigerator. Nearly every waking hour, which was twenty or so out of every twenty-four, Hayley searched for page-one material, though so far her stories hadn't made it above page three.

And you never knew. The right investigative report might send her into the big leagues, net her a job on an influential paper with a wide reach, like the *New York Times*, or at some national publication like *Newsweek*.

For the time being, she had to expend her energy during her work-day hours on whatever Greg, her editor, handed her. And as second lowest on the office totem pole, that was often something for the Lifestyles section, which wasn't even worth saving for her scrapbook. Sometimes he threw her a bone, but she enterprised most of her meatier stories herself, working on them in her off-time.

The red digital readout on her answering machine told her she had three messages waiting. Her mom begged her to come for dinner soon, her sister Claudette wanted to see the latest Susan Sarandon flick, and an old friend from her nursing days offered gossip about mutual acquaintances.

As Hayley played the messages, she ran through her usual after-work routine.

While her laptop booted up, she turned on the TV to CNN and started a pot of decaf, then changed into comfy clothes. She chose sweatpants and a favorite well-worn T-shirt because she didn't expect to go out again.

Her apartment was warm, cozy, and colorful, cluttered with mementos. Framed photographs in small groupings—family, friends, pets, vacation snaps—adorned several surfaces. An enormous glass jar full of matchbooks from the restaurants and hotels she'd visited sat in one corner. Postcards from friends' journeys and drawings by her nieces and nephews crowded the clippings on her refrigerator, all tucked under kitschy magnets she'd picked up in airports.

She'd just nestled into her favorite chair with a mug of coffee and her laptop when her doorbell rang. Expecting a family member because almost everyone else would call first, she was surprised to see a stranger through the peephole in the front door. Mid-twenties, clean-cut, holding a large manila envelope.

"Yes?"

"Hayley Ward?"

"That's me." She opened the door.

He handed her the envelope. Her name and address were neatly typed on a stick-on label, and that was all. No return address, postage, shipping instructions, or tracking numbers. The deliveryman had already turned away and taken several steps before she suspected anything.

"Hey," she called as he neared the stairs that led to the parking lot, one floor below. "Who sent this? What delivery service are you from?"

But he disappeared as though he hadn't heard.

She walked back into her apartment and cautiously opened the package. It contained a VHS tape and a typed note—no signature. The note read:

Dear Miss Ward,

Enclosed you will find the only copy of the security-camera video of the assassination of Cuban Information Minister Juan Carlos Guerrero in Miami on Monday. It was removed from the Miami Police Station in an effort to ensure that the truth about the assassination would be told. If I had not worked to protect the tape, Miss Ward, it would have disappeared within hours or been altered or damaged.

The assassination of Guerrero was carried out by a member of the EOO, the Elite Operatives Organization, whose training facilities are located in a remote area of

Colorado. This covert organization has far-reaching, illegal influence in the government, law enforcement, the media, and elsewhere. No one can be trusted. They are expert at covering their tracks.

You must not show this tape to authorities, either state or federal, or a cover-up will follow and the people responsible for Guerrero's death and countless others will remain at large to kill again.

I am sending you this tape, Miss Ward, because I have been following your career, and I know you have the tenacity and talent to do this story the justice it deserves, to ferret out the truth about the EOO and expose it. Consider it a gift.

Hayley had to read the note twice before the enormity of what she'd just been given began to sink in. The missing tape had been all over the news since late that morning, and now she held it in her hand. Turning it over, she studied the label, which certainly looked authentic. A variety of markings covered it, including a Miami PD evidence number, the words Guerrero assassination, and yesterday's date.

As she slid it into her tape player, questions assaulted her mind. Who could have sent this? And why did they select her?

Like most surveillance videos she had seen on television, the quality of the tape wasn't great. It was black-and-white, grainy, and a bit out of focus. And the sound was weak and mostly unintelligible. But though the tape lacked clarity, it oozed significance.

The camera showed a wide-angle view of the underground garage's main aisle, so it had captured all four of the victims going down. The female assassin was out of view, however, during much of the incident, and when she *was* in the frame, she was maddeningly indistinct.

In the woman's first appearance, Hayley briefly saw the top of her head and her back as she crossed the bottom of the screen in a crouch. She reappeared after the others had fallen, and she shot Guerrero up close. Then she crept to her apparent accomplice and knelt over him, almost tenderly—holding his hand and exchanging a few words, none of them audible. When he slumped back and lay still, she took some things from him, then disappeared briefly again when a Jeep appeared on the scene. Finally, she reappeared, crouching again, and left the way she came. Hayley never saw her face clearly.

The person who'd sent the tape wanted Hayley to expose the group that trained this woman. The Elite Operatives Organization. She picked up the letter and read it again while the tape played for the tenth time.

This covert organization has far-reaching, illegal influence in the government, law enforcement, the media, and elsewhere. No one can be trusted. They are expert at covering their tracks.

If the note was accurate, if this organization existed and was able to buy or threaten or deal its way out of something this big, if it had politicians and cops and who knows who else in its pocket, then someone *should* bring it out in the open. And why shouldn't that someone be her?

Whoever had managed to send her this tape was certainly resourceful, or powerful, or both. She had to know this informant, because she didn't believe in coincidence. He couldn't have picked her randomly. If they had met, and that seemed most likely, she must have made an impression on him. Or her.

But she had interviewed hundreds of people, including celebrities, dignitaries, politicians, and law-enforcement officials. She wondered how her mysterious benefactor knew about this organization, and why the hell he hadn't given her more to work with.

What should she do with the tape?

She needed to make a copy, so she popped a blank DVD into her dual VCR/DVD player and recorded a backup duplicate, labeled it *Madonna HBO Special 2003,* and hid it among her hundreds of music CDs. The original needed to be somewhere more secure, like her safe-deposit box. Or maybe at her brother Ted's house—he had a big heavy gun safe in his basement.

Hayley decided not to tell anyone at the *Dispatch* about the tape. Aside from the note's *No one can be trusted* warning, if she alerted her bosses, they would assign a more senior reporter to the story, and she couldn't let that happen. So what if she didn't have the connections and years of experience some of the others had? She more than made up for those advantages with her determination, hard work, and resourcefulness.

She wouldn't sleep much tonight, not like that was anything out of the ordinary. First stop: the Internet. She didn't expect to find anything about the EOO online, but she could begin by searching for other cases of unsolved murders of a national or international political figure.

Hayley allowed herself to imagine her page-one headline and how the story would play on the evening news if she could pull this off. "A tenacious Baltimore newspaper reporter has solved the murder of Cuban Information Minister Juan Carlos Guerrero...while uncovering evidence of a covert training school for assassins located in Colorado..."

❖

Thursday

Monty Pierce paced in front of the large picture windows of his office, impatient for an update on the latest developments. He couldn't see anything but the lights of the campus below; the sun wouldn't rise above the Rocky Mountains outside for another half hour. But he couldn't sleep.

The EOO was all he knew. One of its first students, he had been raised within its environs, watched it grow and prosper. And his lifelong devotion to duty had earned him his position and a one-third share of the Organization along with Arthur and Grant, which its founder had presented to them when he retired.

He could allow nothing to jeopardize its future. But for the first time in its history, the Organization seemingly faced a serious threat. It had taken two days to discover what had happened to the security tape of the Guerrero job, and the news wasn't good.

One of the detectives on the case had accepted a ten-thousand-dollar bribe to switch a blank tape for the real one just before it was sent to lockup for the evening. Though his anonymous contact had advised him against it, the cop foolishly deposited the entire amount of cash in his wife's bank account the next day, which led the EOO to him. He gave them what they wanted when they threatened to expose him, but the trail had ended there.

Pierce stared down at a folder marked *Strike/Hayley Ward.* It contained a wide-ranging profile of the reporter and a color photo—the one on her Maryland driver's license. Inside was also a copy of the dictated note the cop had sent her along with the tape.

His greatest concern was the author of the note. Clearly, a powerful person who knew about the EOO and wanted to bring it down.

An inside job, he wondered. Arthur, or Grant, or perhaps someone else from within the Organization, ready to offer him up in a deal with a foreign government or some Boy Scout federal prosecutor, in exchange for immunity? He prayed it wasn't Joanne. *No one can be trusted*, the note said. Probably good advice. It was best to be prudent. For the time being, he decided not to brief Grant and Arthur about what was going on.

He glanced at his watch. It was eight a.m. in Baltimore. Their most immediate problem should be leaving for work any time. And once she did, an EOO team would search her apartment and plant listening devices on her phone and in every room.

From the logos on their van and carpenter's coveralls, any nosy neighbors would think Hayley Ward was getting new floor tiles from a firm called Absolute Renovations. But with luck, the Organization would profit from their labors.

At two p.m., Pierce received confirmation that the sweep of Hayley's apartment had been completed. Her computer files showed she'd been digging for information about the Organization and unsolved political murders, but the crew did not find the missing surveillance video. Hayley Ward was a pack rat—a sentimental collector with so much crammed into her two-bedroom apartment to search, they had no time to open every CD case and scan every DVD to see if it contained a digital copy of the tape.

Five hours later, the tap they'd placed on Hayley's phone gave Pierce his first usable information. In a call to her sister, Hayley revealed that she planned to attend an AIDS benefit in Washington the next night. There they could attach an operative to her, and since their intelligence indicated Hayley was a lesbian who favored blondes, Pierce sent for Cameo.

As he waited for her to arrive for their briefing, he mulled over other options for the evening.

The benefit would draw movers and shakers from all over Washington, a lot of whom Pierce knew personally, and he considered it entirely possible Hayley might try to ask some of them questions related to the tape. He might also be able to determine if she had solicited a colleague to help her.

He didn't often go out in the field any more, but he *was* the best person suited for this task. And he preferred to brief as few Organization people as possible about this whole affair until he was certain it wasn't an inside job. His paranoia was running overtime.

So they'd need two invitations. No, *three*, he realized. If everything went according to plan, he wanted to accomplish one more objective tomorrow night.

CHAPTER SIX

Domino's layout was one of her most inspired yet, with bridges, drops, curves, and stairways composed of neat stacks of dominos. She was always careful to insert securities as she built—gaps or wooden barriers—to prevent the premature toppling of a work in progress. And for some time in her setups she had used colored dominos, which made for more spectacular and eye-catching effects than the ivory or black bones with pips used for gaming.

Three days of meticulous work and she still hadn't finished the piece. While some modern-day enthusiasts strove to create layouts that mirrored real-life objects, she always produced abstract patterns—complex, colorful designs that sometimes filled nearly every inch of her condo's available floor space.

The precise meticulousness required for such an elaborate setup demanded her full attention, so when she needed to escape mentally, she used her dominos as a routine and welcome distraction. Especially after a hit, she needed something to engage her mind and free her from the haunting images of blood and death.

Her extensive music collection, heavily weighted with alternative rock and independent labels, also helped her flee the violence of her profession. On this particular night, Pink Floyd's "Comfortably Numb" was playing so loud her cell phone rang three times before she heard it.

"Good evening. I need you to join me at a benefit in DC tomorrow night." The caller didn't identify himself because he didn't need to. Monty Pierce had been a part of her life for as long as she could remember.

"Business?" As she spoke, she absently twirled a domino between her fingers, like a magician keeping limber with his disappearing coin.

"Undetermined. Dress up. It's an AIDS fundraiser. I'll pick you up at six thirty." The line went dead.

She stood still, staring at her cell. His unusual request made her curious. She rarely accompanied Pierce on a purely social outing.

❖

Friday

A late-model limo awaited Domino, its driver a young man she guessed to be one of the Organization's current crop of senior students—dark-haired and about seventeen. When he opened the door for her, Pierce was seated in the back, handsome in formal black tie. Beside him sat another ETF op named Cameo—an attractive blonde, close to her own age—dressed to seduce in a low-cut red cocktail dress and stiletto heels. Though this development surprised Domino, she revealed no trace of her reaction in her expression or greeting.

"Good evening," she hailed them both, as she slipped into the empty seat on the other side of Pierce. Her own black dress was only slightly less provocative than the other woman's; both were standard fare for female ops assigned to a social event where they might have to extract information or make an impression. And that morning she'd finally had her straight, medium brown hair trimmed to just below her shoulders, the long bangs styled to sweep away from her oval face in soft waves. Her makeup was understated,—a bit of rouge, a hint of eye shadow and mascara to enhance her blue-gray eyes, and a shimmery bronze lipstick. She had designed her entire appearance to convey tasteful elegance.

"You remember Cameo?" Pierce said as the limo pulled away from the curb and headed toward their destination.

"Yes, of course. Nice to see you again."

"Good to see you, too," the blonde answered. "Long time."

She wanted to ask Pierce whether he had learned anything about the Miami tape, but now wasn't the time. Although the car was a safe environment, they all knew not to discuss any specifics of their assignments—past, present, or future—with other operatives. "What brings us together tonight?" she asked instead.

Pierce plucked a trace of lint from the crease in his trousers. "Cameo is going to make a new friend."

"Why am I joining in?"

"You will arrive separately, avoiding contact with either of us," he replied, handing her an invitation to the event. "Mingle with other guests until Cameo signals you. You're to make sure her new friend has no problems with you."

"If they do?"

"Then you are to leave ASAP and contact me from somewhere safe," he replied. "Cameo will introduce herself as Michelle tonight, and I want you to use the name Jennifer."

"Understood."

The gala affair, in the candlelit ballroom of the Washington Hilton, had the formal ambience required when soliciting generous donations for a worthy cause. Crisply starched white linen covered the tables, the wineglasses were fine crystal, and one of the city's leading chefs was supervising the preparation of the five-course gourmet meal.

But the attendees didn't include the usual mix of big-money conservative businessmen who so often dominated fundraisers in the nation's capital. This benefit to help fund AIDS programs always drew an eclectic mix of guests—hip Hollywood stars, conservative politicians, trendy artists, flamboyant queens, rock legends, preppy students, medical professionals, and nearly everyone else imaginable. The cause united them, for a red AIDS ribbon was pinned on nearly every lapel and gown.

"Good evening. May I see your invitation?" The young man at the door was representatively dressed in a black tux with a whimsical pink cummerbund and tie that said the evening should be a lively, fun affair.

Once inside, Domino scanned the area like a predator looking for a vulnerable stray. Though solitary by nature, she had learned to fit in, to make light conversation, to observe. She grabbed a glass of wine from the tray of a circulating waiter and headed for a distinguished-looking man about her age who stood nearby staring at his drink.

"Interesting crowd, don't you think?"

After a brief, superficial conversation, she moved on to an older woman, a doctor with the Centers for Disease Control, and from her to a budding young artist with a mohawk. As she nodded politely to his discourse on the state of federal funding for the arts, she sensed she was being watched and looked beyond him at an attractive redhead studying her from across the room.

Nice. She favored this type—the right age and height, with appealing curves displayed to perfection in a clingy, low-cut, lavender dress.

When their eyes met, the redhead smiled, conjuring up wonderful dimples, and Domino smiled back. As she decided to strike up a conversation with this woman next—and perhaps mix a little pleasure with the business at hand—someone called her name, her *real* name, all too loudly. "Luka. I thought that was you."

She turned to find the assistant director of the Smithsonian American Art Museum, her contact for a lengthy art restoration project she'd tackled a year or so earlier. "Madeleine. It's been a long time."

"Yes, it has. Too long," the woman agreed before she acknowledged the young mohawk-artist Domino had been talking to with a tilt of her head. "Hello…Bernard, isn't it? I saw your exhibit at the Anton Gallery last month. You have a unique perspective." Domino had heard the line often when someone had to acknowledge an artist whose work was lacking.

"Thanks." The young man grinned. "Some people don't get my stuff. I know it's kind of out there…" He clearly planned to continue, and probably for a long while, but Madeleine cut him off.

"Would you excuse us, dear? I need to talk business with Luka, see if she has a place in her schedule to work on a painting for us."

"Oh. Sure. No problem."

As he ambled toward one of the open bars and Domino tried to decide how to cut short this conversation, the attractive redhead she'd been staring at earlier suddenly appeared at her elbow.

"Luka, is it? And you're an artist?"

"Art restorer," Madeleine curtly answered for her, obviously perturbed to lose one competitor for Domino's attention only to gain another. "And we were about to discuss some private business." She smiled as though this explanation compensated entirely for her rudeness.

"Let me give you a call tomorrow, Madeleine." Domino said, finding it difficult to keep from staring at the redhead's cleavage. "I have your number, and tonight should be about pleasure, not business."

"Indeed it should," the redhead flirted back, addressing her response exclusively to Domino.

Madeleine frowned, clearly outnumbered. "Of course. I'll look forward to hearing from you." Her tone was pure pout, but she took the hint and left them alone.

"Luka's an unusual name. What's the rest of it?" The dimples made another appearance, and Domino had to keep reminding herself she was here on a job, which she'd better get back to. But this woman was too damn attractive to brush off for good. She'd get her number, and perhaps they could meet later for a drink and an evening of fun. It had been too long since she'd been out with anyone.

"You have me at a disadvantage," she replied. "How about giving me your name?"

"Hayley." The redhead offered her hand. "Hayley Ward."

"Nice to meet you, Hayley. And I'd like to get to know you better, but I actually *do* have to work some tonight. I'm supposed to be looking for a friend." Domino looked around for Cameo but didn't see her immediately. The crowd was getting thick as people continued to arrive. "Perhaps we can get together later?"

"Oh, I'd like that. Very much," Hayley replied.

A cluster of partygoers dispersed, and Domino finally spotted Cameo standing by one of the bars, alone. And she was staring at the two of them. *What the hell?* What was she doing?

"Well, come find me." Hayley sounded disappointed, and her body language as she departed spelled reluctance, which Domino found immensely encouraging.

I'll find you. As soon as she could determine what she was doing here and how fast she could get away.

Domino focused on Cameo, but she also remained peripherally aware of Hayley Ward. For later.

As she sipped her wine and moved into the throng, stopping now and then to exchange pleasantries with someone, she watched Cameo do the same, working her way discreetly toward her.

Hayley was off to her right, chatting with an older man in a blue suit while taking notes. Once or twice, Hayley caught her looking and smiled.

Cameo brushed past her then and said in a voice only she could hear, "I'm on my way to see a friend." To her dismay, the blond operative walked straight to Hayley Ward.

Domino saw them shake hands, could almost hear Cameo introduce herself. She focused now solely on the two women. She hadn't recognized Hayley, and her instincts told her the woman didn't "have a problem" with her.

They made small talk, and now and then Hayley peered over Cameo's shoulder, as if to see if she was still there. When the growing crowd obscured her view of them, she moved closer, but off to one side, to watch them in profile. Cameo appeared to be engaging the redhead's interest, for now and then Hayley would laugh at some remark or nod and smile.

When dinner was announced, she waited until the two of them took seats at one of the large round tables, then claimed a seat opposite them. If Hayley had a problem with her, whatever that meant, she would know it soon enough.

The look on Hayley's face when she sat down was one of pleasant surprise, and Domino felt a small sense of satisfaction when the redhead turned from Cameo to concentrate her attention exclusively in her direction.

"Hi again," Hayley said, with a wry smile. "Glad you could join us. Did you take care of what you needed to?"

"Yes, for the moment," she said, smiling back. "I didn't mention it earlier, but you look familiar. Have we met before?"

"Highly doubtful," Hayley replied. "I'm certain I'd remember." All at once she seemed to remember the woman at her side. "Luka, this is Michelle." As the two operatives shook hands, Hayley added rather pointedly, "We just met."

Other guests began to fill in the seven other place settings at their table, but Hayley's attention remained on Domino. "So, what brings you here this evening?"

"It's a good cause, and I know a few people here," she replied. "Big affairs like this aren't usually my scene, but once in a while they take you by surprise, and you find yourself seated next to someone inspiring."

Hayley leaned forward with a pleased expression and, almost unconsciously, Domino did as well, wanting to bridge the distance across the table. "I'd agree with that assessment, for sure. So, you're an art restorer. What kind of medium do you work in?"

"It varies," Domino said. "I take on the occasional painting, but mostly I do murals in churches and cathedrals. I actually prefer those."

The waiters began serving, but the arrival of dinner did nothing to impede their discussion. Out of the corner of her eye, Domino noticed Pierce seated at the next table, positioned facing them. He seemed engaged in conversation with other guests, but he was watching them closely.

Not for the first time, she wondered what he was doing there. He rarely played a personal role in any assignment, but so much about this job was out of the ordinary, almost surreal. What was Cameo's objective with Hayley? And why had Pierce kept her in the dark about who they were to meet?

"Please tell me you're in Washington because you live here, and not merely for a restoration project," Hayley asked between the first and second courses.

"I do live here. I'm just back, actually, from a job in Malta."

"What paper do you work for?" Cameo inquired, breaking the spell and finally forcing Hayley to acknowledge her.

"The *Baltimore Dispatch*," she replied, more to Domino than the woman who had asked the question.

"What do you do there?" Domino asked.

"I'm a reporter."

Pierce's words came to mind. She wondered why a reporter might "have a problem with her." "That sounds interesting. What are you working on now?"

"Well, I'm currently covering this."

"That explains a lot." Domino kept her tone light and teasing.

"What do you mean?"

"All the questions you've been asking," she explained. "I hope they were all off the record. If not, then allow me to give you a worthwhile quote."

"Oh, I'm always receptive to what someone interesting has to say. Whatcha got?"

She thought a moment. "An artist's dream is to have inspiration fall in her lap." Domino could see in her peripheral vision that Cameo was staring at her, but she kept her attention on Hayley, delighting in the laugh her comment had produced.

"Does inspiration usually come to you that way?" Hayley asked with a crooked grin.

"No, that's quite exceptional," Domino replied. "Where do you find inspiration, Hayley?"

"Anywhere and everywhere," she said. "Usually when I least expect it. Take tonight, for example."

"What about tonight? Are you feeling particularly inspired?"

"Definitely." Hayley's grin widened, exposing those delightful dimples again.

Before she could ask anything further, Cameo tried to inject herself back into the conversation. "What will you write about the event tonight?"

"You mean aside from a certain artist's interesting quote…" Hayley never took her eyes off Domino. "The usual boring stuff. How much money was raised, a plug for the sponsors, a mention of the VIPs who attended. I really want meatier stories like investigative stuff, or politics, but those usually go to more senior reporters. Any I do, I have to enterprise myself."

"Are you working on anything of that sort right now?" Cameo asked.

That would've been Domino's question if a subtle signal from Pierce hadn't distracted her. He got up and headed toward the restrooms.

"Actually, yes. I may have a pretty big one in the works," Hayley replied. "But it's still too early to tell."

"Please excuse me for a moment." Domino got to her feet and followed Pierce. He was waiting for her out of Hayley's line of sight.

"She likes you. Use it." He said it in a low voice when she got within range, but he didn't outwardly acknowledge knowing her, and he continued toward the men's room.

Domino lingered in the women's room for another couple of minutes before she returned to the table. Pierce's instruction was to turn on the charm, get Hayley to like her. She'd been asked to do that many times before, had been trained for it, so she didn't question such instructions. But this particular assignment wasn't unpleasant at all.

As the waiters cleared away their dessert dishes, music began to play, the lights dimmed, and several couples started toward the dance floor. Cameo began to rise, clearly intending to ask Hayley to dance, but before she could, Pierce appeared behind her.

"Michelle. I thought that was you," he exclaimed as he put an arm around her waist. "I almost didn't recognize you, it's been so long. How's your father? Still spending every spare minute on the golf course?"

"Hey there, what are you doing here?" she replied, giving him a friendly peck on the cheek. "I'll tell Dad you asked after him, and yes, he's much worse since he retired."

"Favor me with a dance?" he asked. "I'll try not to step on your toes."

"You'd better keep that promise this time," she replied, turning briefly to Hayley and Domino. "If you ladies will excuse me."

They joined other couples, gay and straight, who were swinging to an up-tempo Michael Buble version of "Crazy Little Thing Called Love." Then Domino turned to Hayley. "Do you know what would make this night perfect?"

"Tell me."

"If you would dance with me."

"I'd love to make this night perfect for you," Hayley said. "Especially since it would do the same for me."

Domino rose and extended her hand, Hayley rounded the table to take it, and when they reached the dance floor, they fell into an easy swing step so comfortably in sync they seemed to have danced together many times before.

If Pierce and Cameo hadn't been so near, Domino might have had to force herself at times to remember she was here on business, for Hayley was engaging company. The dress she was barely wearing clung to her as she danced, outlining her hips and breasts, and from the provocative way she moved, her sexual interest in Domino was unmistakable.

Now and then she would drift close and whisper some amusing or racy observation about one of the other guests, her breath warm against Domino's neck, and each time she did, she also touched some part of her—her arm, her back, her waist, always with fingertips tracing a light but deliberate path—the first teasing touches of foreplay.

Domino smiled to herself at how easy she was finding this

assignment. It took no effort to charm Hayley Ward. When the songs changed, Domino didn't attempt to part company and end the flirtation. She simply fell into another kind of rhythm and they danced on.

The fifth song was a slow number, and as soon as it commenced, Hayley moved into her arms with an audible sigh, as though it was exactly the one she'd been waiting for. Domino was uncharacteristically content in the embrace, allowing herself a moment to forget why she was there. She could fully relish Hayley's arms around her neck, the feel of hands playing in her hair, the press of their bodies. Something about this whole situation was different. She was enjoying herself too much to care why Pierce had brought her here. "I might have to restate my earlier quote," she said softly, very close to Hayley's ear. "An artist's dream is to hold inspiration in her arms."

She had been well schooled in this kind of charming social repartee. But it felt less forced and artificial than usual. She encircled Hayley's waist, and a twinge shot through her groin when she touched the warm, soft skin exposed by the low scoop back of Hayley's dress. She was so immersed in the sensations, she barely registered Cameo's hand on her shoulder.

"Sorry to interrupt, ladies," Cameo said with a smile, as they parted slightly to acknowledge her. "I wanted to say I enjoyed meeting both of you, but I have to call it an evening."

Pierce deliberately but discreetly moved into Domino's line of sight behind Hayley, as she and Cameo exchanged polite good-byes. With an almost imperceptible nod and tilt of his head, he signaled that Domino had done well and should also make her exit.

Damn. Cameo left, and Domino allowed herself the rest of the song in Hayley's embrace. The night was ending much too soon, but at least she would soon learn what this was about.

The next song began, another slow one, but as much as she was enjoying this mating game, she knew Pierce would be waiting. She loosened her grip around Hayley's waist and led her off the dance floor. "I wish I could stay, Hayley, but I need to leave too. I have another appointment tonight, and I'm already a bit late."

Hayley's face registered her surprise and she stuck out her lower lip. "Now that's an awful shame. Sure you can't reschedule?" She planted a soft kiss on Domino's neck before whispering provocatively in her ear, "Come back to my place? I'll make it worth your while."

"I'd love to, and I'm sure you would." Domino gave her a naughty smile. "But it's out of my hands."

Hayley sighed, admitting defeat. "Then at least tell me you'll call me. I'd like to hear why you prefer churches and cathedrals."

"What's your number?" Domino had no idea whether she'd be able to comply with the request—that would depend on Pierce. But she hoped whatever the reason behind this evening's intrigue, she could reconnect with Hayley.

Hayley cocked her head and paused a beat, as though waiting for Domino to pull out a cell phone, or paper and pen. "Aren't you going to write it down?"

"It's not necessary." Domino smiled at her reassuringly, and Hayley recited her number.

Then, before she could go, Hayley took her hand, as though to make sure she had Domino's full attention. "Call me."

Domino nodded. "How could I not?"

Pierce was outside, waiting for her, far enough away no one would see or overhear them. They walked a few steps in silence,

"That went well," he said. "Miss Ward is obviously taken with you."

"Apparently," Domino replied. "What's going on? What was tonight about, and where's Cameo?"

"She's waiting in the car. Did Miss Ward mention anything of interest?"

"That depends on what you consider interesting. She said she's a journalist with crummy assignments."

"Anything else?" he pressed.

"She mentioned she prefers what she referred to as political and investigative stuff. That she does it on her own time."

"Is she investigating anything at the moment?"

"Didn't say." Domino felt impatient. "What's going on? Why all this interest in an insignificant reporter? Besides, you could have gotten all this from Cameo. This is her assignment, after all, and why are you even here tonight?"

"I recently received word on the missing tape," Pierce replied. "Whoever bribed the cop at the Miami PD had him send it to this particular insignificant reporter. I'm here to make sure this assignment goes to the right op."

"Hayley Ward has the tape?" A strange, sick feeling invaded her stomach. "I see."

"Yes. That much has been confirmed. But we don't know why they chose her."

"All this was about finding out if she would recognize me from that tape," she said.

"Correct."

"We apparently don't have to worry about that." Part of her was relieved Hayley hadn't recognized her. But another part knew there was more to come, something Pierce wasn't telling her. "What's going to happen to Miss Ward? How will Cameo proceed?" She knew better than to ask about another op's assignment, and she fully expected Pierce to tell her so. But she couldn't help herself.

"She won't. I've pulled her off this job." He took her by the arm and steered her toward the waiting limo, as though ending the debrief.

But when they reached the car, he faced her. "Miss Ward is your target, Domino."

The strange feeling in her stomach worsened. "Then why did you—"

"We'll discuss details tomorrow," he said, opening the door to prevent further inquiries. "I'll be staying at my residence here until further notice." He slipped into the seat beside Cameo, but Domino paused, staring back at the hotel.

CHAPTER SEVEN

Saturday

Hayley couldn't remember when she had been so unable to concentrate on a hot story or had enjoyed someone's company so thoroughly. She kept staring at the phone, willing it to ring and cursing herself for not asking for Luka's number or even her last name.

Of course *soon* didn't necessarily mean before ten the next morning, she told herself, especially since it was a Saturday, when most ordinary working folk slept in, or went to the market, or took their dogs to the park. And Luka had left her for another appointment...or was it a date?

Hayley freely admitted that impatience was one of her biggest flaws, though it kept her motivated when she was pursuing a story. Even when that story appeared to be a dead end, which the tape appeared to be, so far.

She had viewed it numerous times and still couldn't make out anything about the woman who had killed Guerrero and the others. She also hadn't been able to find any trace of this Elite Operatives Organization, and she continued to wonder who had sent her the tape. She absently stirred her coffee, frustrated that she had nothing useful.

The LexisNexis database of public records, court cases, and news stories had provided leads before, and she hoped it might do the same this time. She researched similar cases—other unsolved political murders and any involving professional assassins—sorting through the seemingly endless list of possibilities. So far, every call she made had wasted time and long-distance charges.

But the tedious chores would help keep her from going crazy as she waited for Luka to phone, so she returned to her list, and after two hours of scanning old Associated Press files, she found one that looked promising. An AP reporter based in Seattle had done a story on killers-for-hire more than a year earlier and might have some insights that could help her.

She glanced at the clock as she searched online for the man's home phone number. Only a little after seven on the West Coast, probably too early to call. Not everyone could survive on three or four hours' sleep like she did. She'd wait another hour, then try him on her land line. She wanted to keep her cell phone free, since she'd given that number to her intriguing dance partner.

❖

Domino left for Pierce's small ranch home in suburban Arlington when he summoned her the morning after the benefit. Because she was based in Washington, she'd been there a number of times.

"I don't think I need to tell you how unprofessional last night was," she said without preamble.

"Good morning," he said calmly, motioning for her to sit on the couch. He had forgone his usual suit for slacks and a polo shirt, but hadn't relaxed his paranoia for secrecy. All the blinds were drawn, as they always were in his office at school when he spoke to an operative.

"Why aren't you following protocol in this case?" She made no effort to disguise how unacceptable she found the situation.

"Remember who you're talking to," he said, more forcefully.

But she was determined. "I know damn well who I'm talking to. You sent me in there absolutely blind, when you knew she might recognize me. She's probably watched that tape a million times."

"I have my reasons, and I reassigned you on-site. You went in knowing everything you needed to know."

"I didn't know who to look out for, Monty. Now she knows my real name. I've been compromised, which makes this assignment way out of bounds. Perhaps you should do the remembering."

"I didn't intend for it to go like this," he said, with a friendlier tone. "But her apparent interest in you will help speed up this operation. You do realize the severity of this situation, don't you?"

"Of course I do. But severe or not, protocol is there for a reason. I should've been briefed. And I should have had a chance to objectify my target. Besides, we had a couple of dances, that's all. You're making more of it than it was."

"I can tell the difference between casual conversation and real interest. She's a potential threat, Domino, and that's all that matters. This is an assignment, an important one, so you'll do whatever it takes. Now, let's get down to business. This will be Operation Eclipse, and Miss Ward's code name will be Strike. We need you to get close, find out what she knows—who actually sent her the tape, and who she's shared this information with."

"Do we have any proof of her complicity?"

"It's hard to believe someone randomly chose her," Pierce said. "That's why you're to extract the information we need and find out who else is involved." He was watching closely for her reaction. "Because of your compromised situation, someone else will eliminate her, if necessary."

"When do I start?"

"As soon as possible." He pulled a file from his desk and tossed it in front of her, then sat back and folded his arms over his chest. "Strike's details. Find a way to contact her. I'm sure she won't object. Her number's in there—it's also in the phone book, if she wants to know where you got it."

"That won't be necessary," Domino said. "Ironically, my target gave me her number personally."

CHAPTER EIGHT

Saturday Evening

Domino stood before the large picture windows of her condo, all but oblivious to the lights of Washington and the smells of a barbecue wafting in on the breeze through the open balcony door. Her mind was entirely on Hayley. *Not Hayley*—Strike. *The target. Objectify her. You have to.*

But she found it more difficult than she imagined after having spent the evening before thoroughly engaged by Hayley and the last several hours memorizing her file.

She returned to the couch behind her and sank into the cushions. When she thought of Hayley, she didn't see the four-by-six photo from the file. She recalled the candlelit Hayley laughing across the table, or the Hayley on the dance floor looking at her with such flirtatious, open interest—not the flat and unsmiling version who had posed for a driver's license photo two years earlier, her dimples undetectable.

Domino had needed to get personal with a target before and had done so successfully. But this was different, not only because she'd gone in unprepared, but also because Hayley was somehow different. Perhaps her unpretentious approach to life had appealed to Domino, but her easy, untainted manner had certainly been contagious. Even if only briefly, she had realized what it must be like to be unguarded without facing possible repercussions. Hayley was different because she made Domino feel free.

She stared out into the night. *So damn free.*

The familiar whup whup whup of a distant helicopter, probably medevac or military, invaded her consciousness and grew louder as it neared. Then she saw it, its white and red lights passing almost directly overhead, and its sight and sound transported her to another place, three years earlier.

Domino ran through the rain forest of Gunung Leuser in northern Sumatra, trying to hide under the thick jungle canopy of trees, rifle strapped on her back, pursued from above and behind. Darting behind a massive kauri tree that stretched a hundred feet into the sky, she paused to catch her breath. The heat and humidity made her feel as though she was breathing water instead of air.

The sound of the pursuing helicopter neared, and the shooting resumed, coming closer. Her lungs protesting the too-short respite, she started running again toward Binjai, the nearest village, hoping for somewhere to hide.

They'd said the operation would be simple. Get into Indonesia and take down Eric Hudson, a man responsible for exploiting the poor and underprivileged. He promised them a new beginning and a better life in America. But after they boarded his ships, he sold the men to other countries as slaves and the women and children into prostitution. Those who didn't survive the trip found a more merciful end at the bottom of the Indian Ocean.

He had to be stopped, they said. It was a noble cause. But they didn't tell her how many were involved, how toppling Hudson would throw the entire Indonesian underworld into an uproar.

She had to get close, go in as a buyer, find out how many were involved, and ask for backup if necessary. And she got very close. She saw for herself how the poor people of the region were treated. Saw the buyers take women and children away, witnessed the hell their lives became.

The experience motivated her. She got close to Hudson and earned his trust. He shared information with her and introduced her to some of the other key players, Americans, Europeans, Asians—all sick, ruthless bastards.

When she had learned enough, she made the call and requested backup. They told her to start with Hudson, but to make it look accidental.

Getting to him was easy, for she was now a guest in his home, her balcony near his. One night she used the outside ledge to steal from her balcony onto his and crept into his room while he slept. Just enough insulin to make it look like a heart attack. That was the plan.

She injected him but had barely finished when his Indonesian sex slave surprised her. A fifteen-year-old girl, naked, walked in from the bathroom and screamed.

She put a hand on the girl's mouth. Show no mercy, they had taught her. Nothing could compromise an operation. Break her neck. But she couldn't. Not this child with huge brown eyes, already abused in so many ways.

She froze, uncertain, then heard footsteps—someone running toward the bedroom. The girl started to scream again, and Domino ran for the balcony, back to her own room. But she knew the girl would tell. Any minute they'd come to her door. She already had her gun, tucked into her jeans. So she dashed in long enough to retrieve her passports and vaulted over the balcony, one hand on the waist-high railing, and dropped thirty feet onto the patio one floor below.

She landed badly, on a bamboo chair, breaking two ribs then crashing onto the pavement on her hip.

The wind was knocked out of her, the pain so immense she wanted to scream but couldn't with no air in her lungs. Tears sprang to her eyes as she struggled to her knees, clutching her side and fighting to breathe.

Domino couldn't hear, see, or think beyond the pain. But her instinct for survival pulled her to her feet and sent her running into the jungle.

They hunted her all night, but she ran forward through the absolute black only the jungle canopy can create, falling again and again, sweat pouring off her. At times the pain was so intense she moved on her knees, pushing forward by lurches, fear driving her until she could rise to run again.

Occasionally she paused, for she had to be absolutely still to distinguish the sounds of her pursuers from the cacophony of bird calls and the constant shrieks and cries of the other creatures.

The T-shirt she fled in provided no protection against the undergrowth, so by the time dawn broke, cuts covered her arms, hands, face, neck, stomach. And the sweat that poured into them burned like acid.

In the morning, helicopters joined the search. One spotted her, and they opened fire like she was an animal. But she kept running, diving under cover when necessary, every labored breath an effort through the ache of her broken ribs, her leg stiff from the pain that radiated from her injured hip.

She surprised one of her pursuers and broke his neck, took his rifle. At least now she had more than just her gun.

Finally, she made it to Binjai. Hudson had taken children from the village, so they knew of him—feared and loathed him.

By then she was ready to collapse, filthy and bleeding. An old man with a five-year-old grandson agreed to help her when she told him who was chasing her.

He gave her meager food and water and hid her in a tiny shed already crowded with his cow, goats, and chickens. She lay hidden under hay and manure for two days without moving, always afraid they were outside. Every morning and evening, the old man would open the door to let the animals out and then back in again, but she had told him he wasn't to acknowledge her presence, and he complied.

On the third day, she emerged from her fetid sanctuary and, dressed in clothing she plucked from her benefactor's clothesline, made it to Medan disguised as a local, hitching occasional rides in local farmers' pickups.

In Medan, she knocked on the door of a home. In Dutch and in English, she said she'd had an accident, and they could see she was in trouble—dirty, hurt. They let her in and left her alone to call her husband at a nearby hotel to come get her.

When Pierce picked up his phone, she identified herself. "Book a room and wire money under ID B."

"Call me back in five minutes," he replied, "and I'll tell you when and where."

She informed her hosts her husband wasn't in their room but would be back—she needed to try again soon. When she did, Pierce gave her the name of the hotel where the arrangements had been made.

At last she could have a long, hot shower and a calm, safe moment to gather her thoughts. She took out her backup passport and studied the photo. This identity had short, very dark hair, so she called for a hairdresser to be sent up, and dinner, too, her first good meal in days. While she ate, her long blond hair was cut and dyed, and soon, except for the cuts and abrasions on her face and neck, she matched her passport photo perfectly.

Next came new clothes, which she also arranged to have delivered to her room. She was a different person now, still hyper-alert but more relaxed about appearing in public. She sought out the nearest public phone booth and called Pierce again.

"It's Domino."

"Target down," he responded. "Rest of operation has been compromised. Abort."

"Ticket ready?"

"Yes."

She hung up and headed to the airport. Nearly thirty-six hours later, when she landed in Colorado, she went straight to Pierce's office. She pleaded to be allowed to leave. Told him she couldn't do it anymore, she didn't want this life. She saw too much death, unfairness, cruelty, and corruption.

"I can't let you go," he had replied. "You see, Domino, this life doesn't come with options."

The sound of a car alarm under her window returned her to the present. She wondered if Hayley still had options. Pierce's instructions rang in her ears. *You are to extract the information we need and find out who else is involved…someone else will eliminate her, if necessary.*

She reached for her cell phone.

CHAPTER NINE

Hayley answered her cell before it could ring a second time and tried not to sound disappointed it was her sister Claudette instead of Luka. She was curled up on the couch in her sweats with a pint of Haagen Dazs rum raisin.

"Hey, Hay." It had been her sibling's standard greeting since childhood. "Whatcha doin'? Wanna catch a flick or something?" Unlike Hayley, Claudette had embraced the stay-at-home-mom lifestyle their father had long espoused, but every now and then, she required a girls' night out with her sister.

"Can't. Tonight is all work and no play, and I'm expecting a call." Hayley reached for the remote and paused her DVD copy of the assassination tape.

"Like that's anything new," Claudette griped good-naturedly. "Come on, take two hours and bring your cell. Don't make me come hurt you."

Hayley laughed. "Really, Claudi, not tonight. Soon, though, I promise."

But her sister wouldn't give up so easily. "You know what they say about all work and no play."

"If it's any consolation, this call I'm expecting would be all play, so no worries there."

"Oh? Do tell. Found someone interesting, have you?" Claudette pressed.

"As a matter of fact, very. An art restorer I met at that AIDS fundraiser last night. Bright, buff, and immensely cute." Hayley shut her eyes and recalled the feel of Luka's body pressed against hers on the dance floor.

"So why are you waiting for her to call and not calling her?"

"Uh...don't have her number?" Hayley confessed.

"What?" Claudette laughed loudly into her ear. "You let her get away without getting her number and your ace reporter skills can't track her down? Sounds like you're slipping."

"She'll call. Now let me go so the line is free, will ya? And I promise to do a movie some time next week."

"Yeah, yeah. Promises, promises." Claudette sighed for dramatic effect. "Good luck, Hay. Hope she does call. See you soon."

After her sister signed off, Hayley returned to her study of the assassination video. She was so intently focused on it when her cell phone rang again, she didn't answer for a full three rings.

"Hello, it's Hayley."

"Hi there. It's Luka."

Hayley's spirits brightened. "Luka who?" she deadpanned.

Laughter on the other end.

"No, really," Hayley said. "You never told me your last name."

"Madison. Do you still want to know?"

"You're referring to churches and cathedrals now. See how well I keep up? Of course I still want to know. I've been all anxious anticipation since last night." She spoke in a teasing way, though the statement was true.

Laughter answered her again. "A reporter doesn't sit around anxiously awaiting a stranger's call."

"That's where you're wrong," she said. "When you're a reporter, some of your best calls come from strangers."

"Are you busy? Am I interrupting anything?"

Hayley stared at the frozen image of the assassin, firing her second shot into Guerrero's head. "No, not at all. Actually, you're saving me from an aggravating blonde."

"Company?"

"No, only a difficult assignment." She clicked off the TV and returned her full attention to Luka. "Count yourself lucky you don't have to deal with 'em."

"Guess that's true. Art restorers don't get many of those. If you don't have a fear of heights, you're golden."

"So tell me. Why churches and cathedrals?"

"How about I tell you over dinner?"

The invitation sent a ripple of exhilaration through her. "Are you asking me out?"

"Only if you accept," Luka said.

"Dinner it is, then."

❖

Sunday

Senator Terrence Burrows took his morning *Washington Post* and coffee to a chaise lounge by the pool to watch the twins romp in the shallow end while his wife Diana cooked bacon and eggs.

It was still sixteen months until the presidential election, but the special section of the Sunday newspaper profiled all the major candidates and the status of their campaign coffers. Pundits predicted the eventual nominees would need to raise nearly half a billion dollars each, and Terrence had only a fraction of that, but he expected the numerous fundraising events on his calendar would keep him competitively in the running.

He hated that the EOO's shadow kept him from focusing entirely on his bid for the White House. He'd had the Guerrero tape sent to Hayley Ward five days ago, and he was spending far too much of his time wondering what she was doing with it.

Terrence pulled out his cell phone and dialed Jack's number. While he waited for an answer, he rose and went to stand nearer the house, where he could see the twins but not be overheard.

"Put a tail on Hayley Ward," he told Jack. "For now, at least, you can limit it to days and evenings. It's probably best not to have someone sitting outside her apartment overnight. I want to know where she goes, who she sees."

"I'll get right on it," Jack said.

Terrence worried that if the EOO found out what Hayley was up to, they might put someone on her themselves. "And use private detectives, Jack. Not anyone traceable back to you or me. Tell them she's a cheating spouse or something."

"No problem."

Diana appeared with his breakfast just as he disconnected and frowned when she saw the cell phone in his hand.

"I thought you were taking the day off," she complained, setting the plate down on a table beside the chaise lounge he'd vacated.

"I am." He kissed her on the cheek. "Just clearing the way to think of nothing but my family today."

❖

Leroy Deloatch finally returned Hayley's call on Sunday afternoon as she was deciding what to wear on her date with Luka. She'd narrowed it down to two possibilities—a low-cut green dress that highlighted her auburn hair, or a baby blue number with a scalloped hem that showed off her thighs.

The AP reporter apologized for not getting back to her sooner, explaining he'd been out of town on assignment. "What can I do for you?"

"I'm calling about a story you did a year ago on professional assassins," she said. "I wanted to ask whether you remember coming across anything about any women in that field."

"Okay, hang on. Let me call it up on my laptop." Hayley could vaguely hear the sounds of typing. Deloatch evidently had her on speakerphone. "Seems like there were at least a couple of cases." He typed rapidly. "Yeah, first one I found was fifteen years ago. A mob retaliation hit in Vegas was attributed to a tall, dark-haired woman. Young. Witness saw her flee the scene. She was never caught." He typed some more. "Eight years ago, the same woman may have made two hits back to back. The targets were both Yakuza members— Japanese mafia."

After even more typing, he said, "Three years ago, they got one on tape in Brooklyn, but it didn't give them anything 'cause it was shitty quality. A woman killed a state senator. Cops concluded she was a pro, but never got a line on her. And the last one I found happened just before I wrote the story…so that would put it about fourteen months ago. A woman was spotted running from a shooting in Belgium that had all the earmarks of a professional hit. The target there was a buyer in a major child-porn ring."

"Any way I can see the tape from the one in Brooklyn?"

"Dunno," Deloatch answered. "I can give you the name of the detective who worked the case. He's retired now. But something's not right about him, you know? Almost too determined, if you know what I mean. The obsessive, conspiracy-theory type. May have been why he left the force." She could hear the sound of papers being shuffled. "Here it is. Manny Vasquez. I don't know if the number I have for him is still any good, though." He read it off and she copied it.

"I'd also like whatever you have on the other cases involving women," Hayley said. "Do you mind faxing copies to me?"

"Nope. If you'll call me if whatever you're working on turns into anything. Give AP a bit of a lead in getting the story?"

"Got a deal." Hayley gave him her fax number.

When she signed off with Deloatch, she tried the number he had given her for the retired detective.

"Manny Vasquez?"

"Who wants to know?" He had the raspy baritone of a confirmed smoker.

"My name is Hayley Ward, Mr. Vasquez. I'm a reporter with the *Baltimore Dispatch*. Leroy Deloatch gave me your name in reference to a case involving a female assassin who killed a state senator three years or so ago."

"What about it?"

"Well, I'd appreciate any information you can give me on that case," she said.

"What do you want to know?"

"First off, is there any way I can get a copy of the tape of the hit?"

"Maybe. I'll scratch your back if you scratch mine," he replied.

From what Deloatch had told her, Hayley suspected the retired cop would be reluctant to share information unless he had some idea why she was seeking it, but she certainly couldn't tell him the particulars of what she was working on, or that she had the tape of the Guerrero hit. "You could say I've taken a personal interest in the subject. I'll be honest, Mr. Vasquez. I'm pretty new at this. You know how it is when you're trying to make a name for yourself. I'm looking for that breakthrough story."

"So, you're telling me you, Ms. inexperienced journalist, are checking out female professional assassins—a *muy* unusual and dangerous subject—just to get noticed? Do you have any idea what you're getting into? You're either really green or you know something you ain't giving up. Now, I don't know you...*pero* I been around the block enough to know you don't sound naïve. So let's take this again from the jump."

"I think I have a lead on a case similar to yours, and I want to see if they're connected," she offered.

The leather of his chair squeaked and she knew he had leaned forward. "Okay, go on," he said.

"I received an anonymous envelope in the mail. Whoever sent it wants me to do something with what was in it, but I don't know where to start. My first attempt has led me to you." It was all she dared tell him, and she hoped it was enough.

"So what was in it?"

"I'm afraid I can't share that with you," she said. "Not yet, anyway. But if there's a connection, I'll give you whatever I find out."

"No, no, no, Miss Ward. Tell me what you got or me and my tape are out of the picture. I got a lot of experience with this type of thing. Maybe I can help."

She was fairly certain if she told this cop—retired or not—that she had the missing Guerrero tape, she'd not only be off the story, but probably facing some kind of criminal charges. "What if we talk in person first and take it from there? I know you of all people understand you can't trust just anyone."

"*Si*, exactly. Why should I trust you?"

"You bring what you have and I'll bring my share," she proposed. "What do you have to lose?"

"*Mi tiempo?*"

"Trust me, Mr. Vasquez. What I have will definitely make up for your time."

She heard the flick of a lighter, then a long exhale before he answered. "*Muy bien.* Now the question is when. Can't tomorrow. Day after?"

"Sure, Tuesday's great. I can drive up after work. Eight o'clock okay?"

"Yeah, that works. There's a bar near my old precinct. The Three Sisters. I'll meet you there." He gave her the address.

"By the way," she added before signing off, "and I know you'll understand. If you tell anyone I've talked to you about this, I'll deny everything. This phone call never happened."

He chuckled. "You catch on quick, lady."

❖

Domino got the disquieting update from Pierce as she dressed for her date with Hayley.

"Strike's made a couple of noteworthy phone calls in connection with the tape," he said. "One to a reporter in Seattle and another to a retired police detective in Brooklyn."

She sat on the edge of the bed, waiting for the rest.

"The reporter's probably not an issue. But she's meeting the cop, Manuel Vasquez, Tuesday night," Pierce told her. "We know this guy. He did some digging of his own about us a while back but didn't get far. He's probably not a threat—but you need to monitor the situation closely."

"Understood."

She had never felt such mixed emotions heading into an assignment. Unfamiliar nervous anticipation about seeing Hayley again enveloped her, but the news that Hayley was avidly trying to solve the Guerrero murder and expose the Organization tempered her excitement. *Operation Eclipse*, she kept reminding herself. *Objectify her.*

After an unusually long time, she settled on a form-fitting black turtleneck, taupe low-cut trousers, and a black, double-breasted jacket. The restaurant she was taking Hayley to was quiet and upscale, with an ambience conducive to easy, unhurried conversation.

She had arranged to pick up Hayley so she could look around her apartment, not that she expected anything related to the tape or her newsgathering about the EOO to be sitting out in plain view. At precisely six, she rapped twice on her door.

"Hi." Hayley smiled, forcing Domino to admire her dimples. "The punctual type. I like that. Come on in. I'm almost ready." She was wearing an emerald green dress, well suited for her coloring and body type. Sexy but classic in its cut and drape, it allowed Domino a wonderful glimpse of her cleavage.

She was supposed to get close to Hayley Ward. Seduce her, if need be, to obtain the information she needed. Certainly not an unpleasant prospect. "You look great," she said as she stepped into the apartment. "I don't know what you need to finish."

"Uh-oh. A smooth talker, too. Pretty potent combination, and the same back at ya in the you-look-great department." She raised her eyebrows as she surveyed Domino approvingly.

"Thank you," Domino replied. She was well accomplished at gaining someone's interest, and she'd heard these lines before. But this time the compliment genuinely pleased her.

"Make yourself comfortable. I'll be ready in a minute." Hayley plucked a couple of newspapers off the couch to make a place for her to sit. "Can I get you a drink?"

"No, I'm good." Domino remained standing and took in the cozy clutter of mementos, pictures, clippings, and other personal effects. It was as different from her own spartan existence as possible, yet incredibly warm and inviting. "Nice. Very…you."

"Interesting observation," Hayley replied, looking at her curiously, "since we hardly know each other. Yet."

Domino shrugged. "I try to pay attention."

"Sorry I'm not ready, but time kind of got away from me today," Hayley called over her shoulder as she disappeared into the bedroom. "I know that sounds pretty bad coming from someone who works under a deadline."

As soon as she'd gone, Domino walked to the windows, surveying the view, checking for ways the second-floor apartment could be accessed from outside. The main entrance appeared to be the only way. The building had no external fire escapes or balconies.

Hayley's laptop was sitting on her desk, closed. Off. Domino put her hand on it—still warm. At least for the moment, it kept her attention on the job at hand. "Busy with business or pleasure?" she said, loud enough for Hayley to hear in the next room.

"Business. Always business, especially lately," Hayley answered. "Which is why I'm looking forward to a night of pleasure. Well, another night of pleasure. Because last night turned out to be more fun than work. Thanks to you."

"I had a nice time, too, Hayley. I can't stop thinking about how much you improved my evening." Domino scanned the assorted items on the desk. Her appointment book, closed. A couple of notebooks. Several newspaper and magazine clippings, none relevant. "Need any help?"

Hayley laughed. A nice laugh, with high, infectious overtones.

"Tempting. Very tempting. Maybe later I'll think of something I can get your help with." Hayley reappeared with a coat slung over her arm. "Shall we go?"

As soon as they were in the car, Hayley said, "So…we'll start with why cathedrals and churches." She settled into the passenger seat, but half turned to watch Domino as they headed toward the restaurant. "But I warn you, I *am* a reporter, so I want to know everything."

Domino knew she'd have to be on top of her game tonight and deceive Hayley about many things, but she could respond honestly to this question. "Because I think art should be there for everybody. You visit museums and galleries for the art. With churches and cathedrals, art is there for you. Nobody has to pay to get in, or pretend to know anything about it, or even like it. There are no pretentious bullshit comments on whoever's work. You can go there and just be. Whoever you are."

She had another reason too, but she couldn't enunciate it to Hayley. Bringing damaged things back to life and making them beautiful again gave her a rare sense of peace that contrasted so totally to the violent world she knew but couldn't change. On the job, another ten assholes endlessly sprang up for every one she dispatched. But restoring art truly gratified her.

"I've never thought about the art in churches that way," Hayley said. "Kind of art for the people, in other words."

"Exactly."

They arrived at the restaurant and sat facing each other at an intimate table for two overlooking the Baltimore skyline. For a time, they made small talk, extolling the view and comparing tastes in music, old movies and food as they studied the menu.

"Do you paint at all?" Hayley asked.

"Occasionally, but I prefer to sketch. Do you have any interest in art?" she asked after the waiter delivered their wine and appetizers.

"Well, I think a certain artist is pretty interesting." Hayley leaned toward her and grinned mischievously.

She smiled back. "I hope you're referring to someone contemporary."

"Oh, most definitely contemporary. Nothing beats the here and now, I always say," Hayley replied, all innuendo.

"You'd better be careful, then. Those artsy types can be tricky. Before you know it, they're asking you to pose for them."

"Hmm." Hayley cocked her head as though considering the possibilities. "I wonder what kind of poses this artist would have in mind."

"If I knew who you're referring to, perhaps I could help." She refilled Hayley's wine glass, then hers.

"Now, I know you're not that dense," Hayley teased. "You want everything spelled out, do you?"

"Preferably."

"Aw, and I was having so much fun with the roundabout approach. But okay. Spelled out, huh? I'm very attracted to you, Luka." Hayley was staring at her mouth in a way that made her feel as though someone had turned up the thermostat several degrees. "Is that clear enough, I hope?"

It was obvious that getting close to Hayley would not be a problem. However, she had to take it slow. She had to keep her interested until they found out everything they needed to know, and Hayley's file indicated she had a reputation for brief, casual affairs. "In that case, I'd pose you the way that best fits your personality. But I don't know enough about you…yet…to determine what kind of pose that would be. And since you're not dense, is it clear I'm very attracted to you?"

"Well, I'd say that's been pretty clear on both sides since last night, but of course it's nice to hear. I like the direct approach, Luka."

The waiter arrived with their meals. "Do busy journalists find time to play or is it a rarity?" Domino inquired.

"Oh, I like to play," Hayley said in her most suggestive manner. "Very much. And yes, I'm kept so busy it's rare for me, unfortunately. All the more reason for the direct approach, don't you think?"

Domino could see where this was going. "It's not in my nature to be that direct. I like to take my time…with everything."

The remark made Hayley smile. "That can be good. Some things, I agree, are best when you go slow."

"All good things are worth taking your time with. Make every moment last and count."

"Am I one of those good things?"

"I don't ask women—even if they're beautiful women like you—out to dinner unless I think so."

"Thank you for the compliment," Hayley replied with a pleased expression. "So do you think I can get you to take your time with me later?"

"I prefer to think of it as…eventually." Domino kept a flirtatious tone.

"Eventually?" Hayley's smile evaporated and became half frown, half pout. "Define 'eventually.'"

Domino looked into her eyes. "I like you, Hayley. As a matter of fact, I like you a lot. And I want to get to know you. Call me old-fashioned and you'd be right, but I'll be honest. You're the first woman I've ever felt compelled to want to see beyond one evening. I probably sound like an idiot, but I'm not. I'm merely trying to say that I want to take it slow because this feels different. Have I put you off? I truly hope I haven't."

"Actually, that's one of the sweetest things I've heard in a very long while," she replied. "I like you a lot, too, Luka. And I guess I can try slow. But let me tell you now, I'm not patient. When I want something, I go for it. Occupational hazard."

I can relate to occupational hazard, Domino thought wryly. It was time to steer the conversation in another direction. "I can see that about you. You seem very driven. Have you made any progress with this big story of yours?"

"Not enough. It's going to take some time. But it's an investigative piece, and they always do."

"Sounds like you have more patience than you give yourself credit for. By the way, have I mentioned you're a beautiful woman?"

"Yes, and flattery will get you everywhere," Hayley said. "So, where do you want to go? To my place for coffee and, *eventually,* dessert?"

Domino laughed. "You're relentless. Let's go." She signaled for the check.

All the way back to Hayley's apartment, she wondered how far she should take this hard-to-get approach. Hayley had been staring at her lips all evening, her intentions clear.

She had to set the tone for the rest of the night, arrange for further contact, string her along without crossing lines that might jeopardize her mission. Though she had been drilled in the art of social conversation—how to engage anyone's interest—she felt unprepared for this kind of intimate interaction. For the first time, she had to operate on a more personal level, answering as Luka Madison, not as some fictitious persona with any history she wanted to create. And the past that had been created for her as Luka wasn't one she wanted to discuss with a potential target.

"Come on in. Throw your jacket anywhere." Hayley headed toward the kitchen. "What do you take in your coffee?"

"Cream, please." Domino removed her jacket, folded it carefully, and set it neatly on the edge of Hayley's desk. Her nearby appointment book and her absence allowed Domino a quick perusal of a few pages of it. She knew, from Pierce's call, Hayley was supposed to meet Vasquez Tuesday evening. But she had written nothing in her calendar to indicate the event. Domino wasn't surprised, because she also knew a search of Hayley's place had turned up no sign of the assassination tape. She was being very careful.

Domino stepped back. Her jacket didn't look right. Not casual enough. Like she was still at the Organization. She picked it up and hung it carefully over the chair. Her orderly mind rebelled, but she knew it was still too perfect. Reluctantly, she picked it up again, threw it over the armrest of the couch, and forced herself to let it go. *What the hell.*

Hayley reappeared with two mugs of coffee. "So tell me all about yourself. Start with family. Do they live here? Any siblings?"

They settled onto the couch. Hayley kicked off her heels and put her feet up on the coffee table, atop a haphazard stack of magazines. Yet another difference between them, Domino noted. She took her boots off only when she went to sleep, because you never knew when you might have to run for the nearest exit. *They stay on.*

"I'm on my own. My mother gave me up for adoption when I was born, and I grew up in foster care. They told me she was young and I was born out of wedlock, but that was all." That's what Luka's bio said, anyway. Only the EOO knew she had really come from an orphanage in the Balkans when she was three. They never told her whether she had parents or siblings still alive.

"Did you ever try to track her down?" Hayley asked. "Nowadays, there are all sorts of ways to—"

"No," she said. "I have no interest in dredging up the past. She must have had her reasons."

"I don't know what I'd do without my family." Hayley certainly looked relaxed, but expertly reading the nuances of body language, Domino could tell she wasn't entirely so. She'd been touching her hair and chewing on her lower lip all evening. Domino was comforted that she wasn't the only one nervous and a bit self-conscious.

"We're your typical close-knit Scottish clan," Hayley continued. "Dad's overly domineering, not to mention that he has really antiquated ideas about what women should and can do. We're expected to appear at all birthdays, holidays, and other special events. But I wouldn't have it any other way. I can't imagine how difficult it must have been for you."

"It was rough. Still is at times, but I found a way to move on. Or so I tell myself. You're lucky to have such a close family."

"Yeah, I am. Even when I'm exasperated with one of them, or dreading yet another niece's pin-the-tail-on-the-donkey party when I'd rather be working. All I have to do is look around at some of my friends and co-workers." Hayley sipped her coffee.

"How do you reporters work, anyway? Do you pair up with anyone on your assignments, or do you work alone?"

"Depends," Hayley replied. "Mostly I work alone on stuff the paper assigns me—features and local events that are quick to turn around. A photographer may come along if the story has good picture potential. Now, on investigative pieces, that's different. Those can take days or even weeks. So a lot of times I'll use a colleague. Someone to bounce ideas off of, make phone calls. Use their resources. In journalism, there's a lot of 'it's who you know' that helps you get the story. You develop contacts in the police and fire departments, city hall, hospitals, snitches on the street. The longer you're on the job, the easier it is to track down what you need, because you have more sources to call upon or feed you information."

Like Manny Vasquez. Domino wondered who else Hayley had talked to. "What about this big story you're working on now? Getting help with that?"

"Some. Not enough. But things are looking up." Hayley extended her arm along the back of the couch to Domino's shoulder. The touch of her fingertips was light, but Domino was hyper-aware of it. "What about you? Are you working on something now?"

She shook her head. "I usually freelance, and I don't have anything lined up at the moment. I thought I'd take a time-out, and perhaps get to know you better, although I get the impression you're a very busy woman."

"Busy, yes. But I think I can find a break in my schedule now and then." Hayley continued to trail her fingertips very lightly along

Domino's shoulder as she talked, and though the touch delighted her, she had a hard time thinking.

"I hope you make time to see me because I...your hand on me is distracting...in a good way. I'd like to see you again soon." She glanced at her watch. "I should get going. When are you free for another dinner or whatever else?"

"Hmm. Well, I have an appointment Tuesday. But I'm free tomorrow night. Too soon?"

"Tomorrow's perfect."

"I get off at five, home shortly after. Pick me up around six?"

"Just leave everything to me." She reached for her jacket and got to her feet. Hayley saw her to the door.

At the threshold, Domino faced her. "I had a great..." Her voice trailed off when Hayley laid a hand on her chest, palm down, above her right breast. They were a foot apart.

"I hope I don't have to wait for *eventually* for a kiss," she said. "Has anyone ever told you, you have the most wonderful lips, Luka?"

Domino didn't get to reply before Hayley closed the distance and kissed her.

Their lips met, soft, sweet, and apparently altogether too briefly for Hayley, who let out a soft groan of disappointment when Domino withdrew.

"That's all I get?" She stuck out her lower lip in a pout, but her eyes were smiling. "Boy, you do move slow, don't you?"

"Like I said," Domino grinned at her as she reached for the door, "all good things are worth taking your time. See you tomorrow, Hayley. And thanks for a lovely evening."

"Tomorrow, Luka. And thank *you*. I had a great time, too."

She left, but she could feel Hayley watching her as she walked away, so she turned back for a last look and a wave. With her bare feet, slightly tousled hair, and dimples framing that pout of a smile, Hayley embodied the definition of sexy and irresistible. She had to will herself to continue toward her car.

CHAPTER TEN

Monday

Pierce summoned Domino to his Arlington home at nine the next morning. When she arrived, the blinds were already drawn and no lights were on in the living room. It was akin to meeting in a cave.

"Find out anything relevant yet?" he asked, pouring coffee for both of them from a carafe on his coffee table.

"At this point you know as much as I do. You heard most of it, didn't you?" She took a seat beside him on the couch.

"And what about what I didn't hear?"

"Nothing significant. I haven't found any evidence she's a threat, Monty. As far as I'm concerned, she's oblivious."

He pivoted to face her, his pale blue eyes like glacial ice. "She's no innocent. Stop kidding yourself. She's burning up the phone lines trying to find out about you, and about us, and she won't just stop and let it go." Pierce watched her reaction as if he wasn't aware Domino knew exactly why he was looking at her like that. "As you know, she's meeting Vasquez tomorrow. You'll be with Reno. He'll be inside the diner with them, you in the van outside."

"Why am I going? You said this guy's no threat."

"As far as we know he's not. But he's a fanatic, and who knows what he'll do if she's got information he wants. I don't want that tape passing from a reporter to someone even more unpredictable. If a situation arises, I want to be able to contain it immediately." He softened his tone. "And if you hear her digging for information about you firsthand, you won't think she's such a harmless innocent."

"What if Vasquez does get the tape?" Domino reached for her coffee and took a sip. "Who'll believe him? He lost his job because his own people think he's crazy. He's an unreliable alcoholic. Besides, if anyone could get anything off the tape, don't you think someone would have recognized me by now or come after me? Operatives have been taped before, and obviously those tapes alone haven't been enough evidence to harm us."

Pierce scowled. "But it is the first time someone aside from us has tried to retrieve a tape," he replied. "There's something different about this. What exactly I don't know, but I don't care whether you're visible on it or not. If you are, we can send you elsewhere, change your appearance." He was balanced on the edge of his seat, his posture anything but relaxed. "I do know this tape is important enough for someone to go to the trouble to steal it and send it to this woman, and therefore jeopardize our entire organization. *My* concern is who the hell *is* this son of a bitch who stole the tape and sent this note, and what the hell is he—or she—trying to accomplish? He's the threat, not Hayley Ward, and it's him I'm after. But if some innocent has to go down for the sake of the Organization, then so be it."

"This anonymous person has chosen Hayley because she's dispensable," Domino said. "He doesn't want to involve federal or local law enforcement to do his dirty work because he wants to be able to eliminate her once she's done her part. If we don't get her, he will."

"Why do you think he'd want to dispose of her?"

"He's obviously not playing by the rules or working within the law. If he was, why bother stealing the tape? The right people would already have it. He could simply feed them whatever information he has on the EOO. Whoever took it is trying to save his ass."

Pierce eyed her with admiration and nodded. She had just confirmed his own thoughts, and she knew it. "What are you saying?"

"Nothing you haven't already considered. It might be an inside job? That's why you didn't brief me before the benefit."

He nodded again and reached for his mug. "And while that remains a possibility, I want you to keep this to yourself."

"As with all things. I know. You don't have to remind me."

Pierce took a big sip of his coffee, then grimaced. "It would appear Miss Ward is genuinely attracted to you."

"Yes, it would appear so. Your point?"

"Keep in mind this is work and she's your target." He set the mug back noisily on the table as if to emphasize his remark. "As untraditional as this approach may be, you're a professional, and I expect you to act as such."

"That won't be a problem." Up to now, Domino had maintained direct eye contact with him. But as she said this, she looked away.

"You know what you have to do." Pierce got to his feet, dismissing her. "It's for the good of us all, Domino."

❖

When Hayley returned from lunch with a colleague, she found a single yellow rose on her desk, along with a note penned with a meticulous hand.

> *I want to share one of my favorite places with you this evening. Please meet me at the Anchorage Marina on Boston Street at six thirty. Look for slip D63. Bring a swimsuit— preferably a very brief bikini—and your appetite.*
>
> *Luka*

Hayley knew the marina near Fort McHenry. The bustling, lively place was near a myriad of romantic restaurants, and imagining what Luka might have planned for her there made it difficult to concentrate on work the rest of the afternoon. Promptly at five, she darted home and changed into shorts and a tank top because, though the sun was already lowering, the thermometer still read eighty degrees.

She had a difficult time choosing a swimsuit since she didn't know exactly where and under what circumstances she'd be wearing it. If they were alone, the white bikini might speed up Luka's *eventually*, but that scenario required her most provocative choice. She wouldn't wear it if they were going to be among a lot of other people.

Hoping she and Luka were on the same wavelength, she plucked the nearly transparent and very skimpy garment off its hanger and tucked it into her purse. With a smile still on her face, she set off toward Chesapeake Bay.

The vessel moored at slip D63 was a sleek sailboat, a thirty-foot Catalina C-30 sloop named *The Seawolf*. As Hayley admired its clean lines, Luka appeared from below, her finely toned body so enticing in a black bikini she could focus on nothing else. "Hey there, good lookin'."

"Hey. Hi." Luka leaned over the side of the boat and offered a hand.

Hayley carefully stepped over and into the cockpit, where she took in her surroundings with a pleased nod. The boat was probably fifteen years old or more, but didn't look it. Its chrome accents had all been polished until they shone, and the bimini shielding them from the sun was new. So were the plush cushions on the benches surrounding the navigation equipment. Peeking down into the main saloon, she could see the teak cabinets had also been well cared for. "Nice boat. Does it come with paddles?" she asked playfully.

"Oh, damn. I knew I forgot something," Luka replied.

"Looks like art restoration pays well."

"Let's just say I had to make a deal with the devil."

"I could use a few deals like that on my salary, too," Hayley said. "Maybe you could give me his number."

"Shall I show you where you can change?" Luka gestured below. "It's warm in the sun."

"Sure."

Luka led her down past the U-shaped galley and head, and stopped before the door to the forward cabin, which could sleep two in a bed shaped to fit the vee of the bow.

"Cozy. Very cozy." Hayley squeezed past her, delightfully aware of Luka's sharp intake of breath when their breasts brushed each other.

"Uh…can I…can I get you something to drink?"

When she pivoted back to face Luka, she caught Luka staring at her ass.

"Sure," Hayley replied, pleased to see Luka color slightly in embarrassment. "Whatcha got?"

"Beer, soda, wine?"

"Wine. White, if you have it."

As Hayley slipped into her bikini, she couldn't help but notice that everything seemed a little *too* perfect. The bed was made up with an almost military precision, the cover carefully tucked and stretched to eliminate any trace of wrinkle. The clothes in the open shelves on either side were meticulously folded and stacked according to type and color.

She didn't see many personal touches to give her any insight into Luka. A handful of seascape photographs she'd probably taken herself hung precisely above her pillows, and art supplies were tucked into a built-in niche by the door. She resisted the urge to glance through the sketchpad that lay on top, though the temptation was fierce.

But she did note a year-old ticket stub to a Formula One event in England sticking out of the sketchpad like a bookmark, and she wondered if it had any particular significance since Luka hadn't mentioned any interest in the sport.She finished changing and emerged to find Luka in the galley, pouring chardonnay into two wineglasses.

"Have you had the boat long?"

"Yes, it's…" Domino froze when she caught sight of Hayley's swimsuit.

Hayley smiled. "Well, you did specify a very brief bikini."

"I did. And you do it absolute justice," Domino said, unable to take her eyes off Hayley's body.

"Glad you think so." Hayley stepped closer and reached for one of the wineglasses, allowing her a very close-up view of the nearly transparent triangles of material that pretended to cover her breasts. "Have to say I'm enjoying that bikini of yours, as well. Very sexy."

Domino swallowed hard, her grip around the wineglass dangerously tight. The close proximity was about to break her. She made herself redirect her attention to the small cabin window behind Hayley.

"So, tell me. Where do you plan to take me?" Hayley's voice was mischievous. "Somewhere we can get wet, I hope?"

I don't know about you but I'm already there. "I thought we'd sail for a while and then stop to eat. I have dinner on board." She wanted to throw Hayley down on the deck right then and there.

"Sounds great. I'm sure we can find a way to work up an appetite."

They cast off, and Hayley settled onto one of the long benches in the cockpit as Domino raised the sails and maneuvered through the bay and out to sea, paralleling the coast. The sky was a brilliant blue, and once they were away from other boat traffic, she luxuriated in the wind against her face, the smell of the salt air, and most especially, the rare company.

She knew she had a job to do. And Pierce had been clear that she should use any means necessary to stay close to Hayley. But today, she realized, she was doing this for herself as well. She really genuinely liked Hayley and enjoyed being with her. That was one reason she'd brought her here, away from intrusive ears. She didn't know why, nor could she explain what at this point made her disregard her need to follow orders and, more importantly, her self-imposed rules.

The boat was and always had been more important to her than her own home. She had never felt attached to anything or anyone in her life except *The Seawolf*. It was the one place where she felt free yet anchored, as she chose. She was taking a chance bringing Hayley here, and she wasn't in the habit of doing so. But something deep within her kept answering the question of Hayley's presence onboard in the same way. A simple yet profound answer that confused her already complicated life. *It just feels right.*

She couldn't remember the last time she'd had such a carefree day. Though she often took to the boat when she needed to relax, memories of past events often haunted her time aboard, or the prospect of what was next preoccupied her.

Today was different. She felt *alive*. Even if only for today, even if just for this minute. She existed in the moment, with no past and no future. Like she could pretend the rest wasn't there, that nothing else mattered, that Hayley could be the object of her desire, not her objective.

She couldn't give in to those desires. Not yet. If this turned into a one-night stand before she found out what she needed, she might jeopardize the job. But as difficult as it was to maintain some distance between them, especially with Hayley in that damned delicious bikini, it was certainly worth it. For the first time in a long time, she didn't have to force herself to smile or pretend to enjoy herself. She didn't have to feign amusement at someone's witty remark or fake being aroused. She *was*, for *real*. And the feeling, although unfamiliar, exhilarated her.

"What are you smiling at?"

Domino turned her head toward the inquiry. Hayley lay stretched out to her left, all languid and lazy.

"You," she answered honestly. "Your ability to make me feel like this." She knew Hayley could probably never understand how rare it was for her to experience this kind of contentment. "How about you? What are you smiling at?"

Hayley shrugged. "What's not to smile at? Beautiful weather. Splendid setting. Great company. So, tell me…I make you feel like *this*?" She said the word provocatively, as though substituting something highly sexual for the term. "Care to explain what you mean by *this*?"

She stared toward the horizon and answered honestly, from her heart. "Like nothing else matters. Or ever has." She directed the assessment as much to herself as to Hayley, because her state of being was so unusual and surprising.

"That has to be one of the most incredibly romantic things anyone has ever said to me."

She gazed at Hayley, then away, unable to bear the sweet joy she saw on her face. She wished it could be so, that this beautiful day and their time alone together consisted only of romance, something she actually knew nothing of. But she was fooling herself, and Hayley's wistful answer had snapped her back to reality, reminding her that Hayley was her assignment. Her target. She didn't answer and kept her eyes on the horizon. She sensed Hayley studying her.

After a long while Hayley said, "You're not the easiest woman to figure out, Luka Madison. I didn't mean to make you uncomfortable."

She turned back to Hayley. One look at her and she was once again back in the moment. *Alive.* "You didn't." She brought *The Seawolf* close to shore, in a secluded alcove far from the crowds and pollution of the city. "Feel like a swim?"

"Sure." Hayley dove in as soon as she dropped the mainsail, then returned to the deck for another dive as she secured the anchor. "The water feels great."

Domino glanced at her as she took off her sunglasses, then immediately wished she hadn't. Hayley lingered, watching her, one foot on the edge. Getting her sheer bikini wet had enhanced its near-absolute transparency. And no way in hell could she keep from staring at those wonderful breasts, outlined in vivid clarity, the rosy areolas distinct and compelling.

"Coming?"

"How could I not?" The words were out before she registered what she was saying. As soon as she did, she started moving and had made it into the water before Hayley could respond.

But Domino saw the smile out of the corner of her eye.

They swam for a while, playful and flirtatious, Domino moving in for brief kisses and light caresses, then darting out of reach again to keep things from going too far. As the sun began to edge toward the horizon, they climbed back on the boat, where a close-up view of that irresistible bikini promptly confronted her again.

"Why don't you relax, and I'll start dinner." She tried not to show the effect their kisses and the sight of Hayley nearly naked were having on her. "Can I get you some more wine?"

"I'll be happy to help cook."

She waved her off and headed toward the galley. "Not necessary, but thanks. Leave it to me." She turned at the door and repeated, "Wine?"

"Yes, please."

She got Hayley settled comfortably back onto the cushions aft and set to work on the recipes she'd brought along. The fish was the only certain success. She rarely cooked, but she routinely cleaned her catch and made it palatable, a necessity when you spent a good amount of time on the water. She'd bought some flounder at the marina and knew she could do it justice.

Normally, though, she ate prepackaged potato salad or some other easy convenience. Food was seldom high on her priority list, but she wanted to make a good impression on Hayley, and her desire had nothing to do with her assignment.

She was determined to cook an elaborate meal for two for the first time in her life. After all, she had successfully navigated through unfamiliar terrain all over the world. How hard could it be to follow a recipe?

An hour later Hayley called down from the cockpit, "Sure I can't help?"

"Yes." Her answer came out louder and more panicky than she intended. "No...uh, it's all good. Thanks, though. Be right up."

Thank God she hadn't told Hayley what she'd planned to serve. She wouldn't have to explain that the wild-rice pilaf had turned into a gluey, overcooked mess while she tried to figure out what constituted "medium high" heat on her tiny galley burners, which was why they were having instant mashed potatoes instead. Or that the mediocre coleslaw she was serving was a last-minute substitute for the fancy salad spoiled by burning the pine nuts and dropping the goat cheese.

At least they would have plenty to eat, because she had seriously miscalculated portion control. She had cooked enough to feed Hayley and several members of her extended family.

In fact, the food wouldn't all fit on the small round table she'd put topside, so she placed the overflow on one of the benches.

"Are you expecting company?" Hayley asked with amusement as she set down the heaping pile of runny potatoes.

Domino was both relieved and disappointed to discover Hayley had put her shorts and tank top back on. Though the temperature was still mild, it was cooling off quickly as dusk neared, and there was a moderate breeze. She, too, had thrown on a T-shirt and shorts while waiting for the troublesome rice to cook. "I know it's quite a bit but…"

Hayley laughed. "Too much is better than not enough?"

Domino refilled their wine. "That, too. But I was going to say I'm no culinary princess."

At least the setting couldn't have been more perfect. The sun was very near the horizon and painted the western sky with brilliant, warm hues—from burgundy red to bright orange. And all of the colors were reflected perfectly in the placid water beneath.

She watched anxiously as Hayley dug into the food.

"This is great," Hayley enthused, after taking a bite of everything.

"Right." Domino laughed, for she had tasted everything while she was dishing it up and had debated whether to serve any of it. The Count Chocula cereal in the cupboard had begun to look like an appealing alternative.

"Hey, I mean it," Hayley replied, and Domino could tell she was serious. "After having to put up with my grandmother's cooking, I can easily say everything else tastes great."

"Not the domestic princess either?"

Hayley chuckled. "God, no. But you know what? I'd suffer through anything she cooked to have her back."

"I'm sorry, I didn't realize." Domino recalled the pertinent details she'd read in Hayley's file. Her maternal grandparents were both deceased, so she was talking about her grandmother Margaret, who had died of a heart attack at the age of 84.

"It's okay. It's been a year now, though it doesn't seem that long."

Hayley got a faraway look in her eyes, which grew moist with emotion. "Grammy was the one person I could turn to who never judged or pushed. And coming from a family whose members had militant beliefs and frequent arguments, it was a relief to hear an unbiased opinion. I didn't have to constantly defend my every thought and decision to her." Hayley gave a sad smile. "It wasn't easy to constantly have to prove you're as good as any guy and you weren't put on the planet to marry a comfortable existence and breed soldiers."

"Is your father in the military?" She knew the answer to this one, too, but she enjoyed hearing Hayley's take on her family. Even though her words conveyed her frustration with them, her tone and expression told Domino what a loving, caring clan it was.

"Dad *was*—four years. Brother *is*, he's a lifer—and my sister's married to a marine. All very stubborn men. For a while I did what Dad expected—went to nursing school, worked in a hospital. He saw nursing as respectable preparation for being a wife and mother. But I didn't want any of that."

"What did your mother say?"

"Oh, Mom is great, but she's so busy playing peacemaker she doesn't dare pick sides," Hayley said. "So she just stands on the sidelines, and when any conflicts arise, she pretends to remember she has something to do in the garden."

Hayley gestured absentmindedly with her hand, emulating her mother, and knocked her wineglass off the table.

Without thinking, without even looking, Domino caught it before it hit the deck. Then she placed it back on the table without comment or change of expression, as if she had done nothing special.

Hayley stared at her. "Jesus. How'd you do that?"

"Who knows? Luck." She shrugged it off. "I guess the missing never stops," she added, changing the subject.

The tactic worked. Hayley let the unintended display of her reflexes pass.

"No, it doesn't. But losing someone does make you stop and smell the roses. You realize what matters." Hayley's voice was wistful. "You know, before she died, I hadn't taken any real time off work for years. My career was everything. I even ended a perfectly healthy relationship just because it didn't fit in my professional master plan. But after the funeral, I realized drive is one thing—letting life slip through your fingers is another."

Hayley took a deep breath and let it out. "Not that I've made drastic changes in that department yet, but at least I'm aware of it."

"Making time to live is important," Domino replied. "But for whatever reason, always underrated. It's unfortunate how people need something drastic to happen before they realize that existing is not the same as living." She paused for a moment and looked down at the napkin she had been absently folding. Without looking up, she continued, "Everyone counts on there being a next year, or a next month, to take that vacation or make that phone call or visit someone who matters. But in reality you can't even count on there being a tomorrow."

Hayley studied her curiously. "You say that like you don't think there will be one."

She looked away. "I hope there will be. But I don't count on it. I try to live in the *now* because it's here. Living for tomorrow would be like living for something that may never come." Her words were out before she realized it. The slip scared and saddened her. Those weren't emotions she wanted Hayley to witness, but at the same time it had felt good to share them with someone.

Hayley took her hand, threading their fingers together. "You talk so little about yourself and continue to be such a mystery, I often try to fill in the gaps. You try so hard to hide what's there, but sometimes the sadness in your eyes gives you away. Hopefully some day you'll let me in. I won't push—I hate it when people do that—but I'd really like for you to open up to me. I'm a good listener, you know."

Domino looked over at Hayley, then down at their enjoined hands. So unfamiliar, yet comforting. "I can't tell you much, except I believe in enjoying every fleeting moment and, as far as tomorrow is concerned, I'd be content to sit here and wait for it with you."

Silence fell between them as they watched the last sliver of sun disappear beneath the horizon. Hayley broke it when darkness descended, and Domino rose to sail back home. "I hope we can share more times like these."

CHAPTER ELEVEN

Tuesday

For once, Hayley was glad her *Dispatch* assignment for the day was a light puff piece. She hadn't wanted anything to delay her meeting with Manny Vasquez, and she was too preoccupied with Luka to tackle anything taxing.

She put the top down on her red Ford Mustang for the long drive to Brooklyn, and the miles passed quickly. Most women, in her experience, talked easily about themselves. In fact, some could do little else. Luka, however, could always deflect the conversation away from herself and back to Hayley. By the end of the night, she'd confided all sorts of things she didn't normally volunteer but had learned very little about Luka.

And that was rare too, refreshingly so—that someone wanted to get to know her more than to get her into bed. She hadn't had anything more than a superficial relationship with a woman in what—three years? She missed real intimacy.

Her evening aboard *The Seawolf* had been one of the most relaxing and enjoyable dates she'd had in months. She wanted more chances to know Luka better.

She found The Three Sisters with little trouble, a seedy neighborhood joint that had seen its glory days three or four decades earlier. Now it was a convenient watering hole for undiscerning problem drinkers who didn't want to risk driving home after a bender.

The bar was dark and gloomy, but from the doorway she could make out fifteen or so tables with mismatched chairs, a long bar with several broken stools, and a jukebox currently playing an old country western tune. Heads of deer and other animals studded the walls, as did assorted beer and whiskey promotional posters so stained by tobacco smoke many were illegible. The entire place reeked of smoke and unwashed bodies, and she wondered what such a dive said about the guy she was meeting.

Because she was driving up to Brooklyn straight from work, intending to get a man to give her information, she had dressed that morning in a clingy purple dress that hugged her breasts and showed a little thigh. Not enough to make Vasquez think he'd get something he wouldn't, but enough to encourage his cooperation.

The dress was woefully out of place in The Three Sisters, but she'd have stuck out in anything that didn't scream *working girl*. The three other women among the fifteen or so patrons currently preoccupied with getting soused wore the kind of cheap jewelry, heavy makeup, and provocative trashy clothing that said hooker. The rest of the bar's clientele were mostly middle-aged men, with red noses and a look of despair, sitting alone, staring at their glasses or off into space.

A few, still sober, looked her way curiously, but most were more interested in the booze in their hands. When none immediately approached her, she went to the bar and perched on one of the barstools. The bartender, a tall biker type with a grizzled salt-and-pepper beard and beautiful blue eyes, wiped the counter in front of her with a rag that looked like it hadn't been washed in months. "What's your poison, babe?"

A bottle or can seemed less risky than something this man had been responsible for cleaning. "I'll have a Budweiser, please, and no glass."

He popped the top of a longneck and set it before her, and as she picked it up, a man entered.

She half turned to look at him, thinking for an instant it might be Vasquez, for he looked a bit out of place too. His pants were freshly pressed and he was too well groomed and clean shaven. She even caught a whiff of aftershave as he crossed to take a seat behind her, toward the front. But he only glanced at her as he passed and didn't speak.

She looked at her watch. A couple of minutes after eight. She'd had to leave work a little early and drive like hell to make the three-and-a-half hour drive and still arrive on time.

"Looks like you made it," came a voice from behind her. She smelled Manny Vasquez before she saw him. Dank and odiferous, like the setting.

She swiveled on her barstool. Vasquez looked as though he'd slept in his clothes for the past week. Well, except for the tie. She'd wager he put that on for her, since it was the only item not entirely wrinkled. He still wore a wedding ring, but was obviously living alone, with no wife to dress him, not only because of the creases everywhere but because nothing matched.

He had a receding hairline and a round face, bloated from drinking, and skin the color of caramel. The broken blood vessels in his nose and cheeks said he'd had the problem with booze for some time. Probably in his mid-forties, Hayley guessed, though his hard living had added ten years. She wondered whether his marriage had ended the same way his job had, probably from the alcohol, and she also wondered whether she'd made the trip in vain.

"Mr. Vasquez," she acknowledged.

"In the flesh." He looked her up and down with an appreciative leer. Vasquez might have a problem with booze, Hayley considered, but he was certainly still a red-blooded man, and his cop background was apparent from the way he surveyed the bar and its patrons after he had thoroughly checked her out. But he seemed much more nervous than a former detective should be.

He signaled the bartender. "Scotch. Double." When it arrived, he said to Hayley, "Let's go sit at a table."

"All right."

He chose one in the rear corner, where he could see the door and the rest of the bar. After taking a healthy swig of his Scotch, he set his glass noisily on the table in front of him. "Show me some ID, Miss Ward. *Por favor.*"

She extracted her Maryland driver's license and *Baltimore Dispatch* employee identification pass from her wallet, and he studied them and set them back in front of her.

"So what's this all about?" He continued his surveillance of the bar and its inebriated clientele, seeming to pay particular notice to the man who had come in right before him, seated several tables away near the jukebox, his face in profile.

"Is something wrong?"

His eyes narrowed as he kept half his attention on her, the other half on Mr. Clean. "Let's get to it, Miss Ward. What do you want?"

"Well, like I said on the phone, I'm looking into a case involving a female assassin." She was anxious and uneasy, and chose her words carefully. "I want to know if mine is connected to yours. Your tape might help me there. And of course, I'd like anything you found out while you were investigating the case."

"My case is officially *cerrado* and cold. Now, there is interest. Why you? Why now?" He focused his bloodshot brown eyes entirely in her direction, waiting for her answer.

"I think I told you that as well. I'm low on the totem pole at my job, and I'm hoping my story will be the big one. Get me better assignments."

"Why *this* story?"

"I got a good lead on it. An exclusive." Hayley wanted to be judicious in what she told him. Enough to get him to give her his tape and any information, but not enough to interfere with what she was doing or make her land in jail for withholding evidence. "But I've hit a dead end, and I'm hoping your tape will help break the impasse."

"What's in it for me?" He finished his double and signaled the bartender for another.

"How about a tip from an informant?" Hayley hadn't even tasted her beer.

"Okay, lady, you got my attention. But you don't get far in the Puerto Rican slums by taking someone at their word. Stop stalling. You said this would be worthwhile."

She plucked at the label on her bottle, considering how much to tell him. The bartender set Vasquez's second double Scotch in front of him, and he downed half of it.

"Do you know anything about a secret organization that trains assassins?" she asked.

Vasquez's attention, which had been on Mr. Clean, snapped back to her. "I believe something like that exists. Yeah."

"Do you have any proof?"

"Do you?"

"I'm being led to think so." Hayley finally took a sip of her beer, which was lukewarm.

"By who?" Vasquez pressed.

"An anonymous benefactor. Who's giving me very little to work with."

He seemed to consider her statement as he took another swig of his Scotch. "I'd hate to see you waste your time, Miss Ward."

"Hayley."

"Okay, Hayley. Call me Manny. In the past few years, I've also got tips...or was led to believe this killing school was real. But the point is, nobody steps up to the plate, which has turned me into a *pendejo*, a fucking idiot. It's cost me my job and my marriage. What makes you think you got the real thing and aren't being jacked around?"

"I don't know for sure...yet. But I believe my benefactor is a person of some significance."

"You have to have a reason, *nena*." Vasquez took out a crumpled pack of cigarettes and lit one. "What was in the envelope you got?"

"I can't tell you."

"Hayley, I get your need for secrecy better than anyone, *pero* you gotta give something up. You asking for my help and that ain't going to happen if you don't play it straight with me and spill it." He downed the rest of his second drink. "I already see the bottom of my glass and you still wasting my time." He signaled the bartender for another refill.

"Okay, okay. The envelope contained a note, among other things," she offered. "It said this school is called the Elite Operatives Organization. It's in Colorado, and its power extends to law enforcement, the media, and the government. And the note warned no one can be trusted, that this EOO can and will cover up its dirty work."

"Come on, girl, I know you didn't bring your booty here all the way from Baltimore to tell me you got a note from just anybody. You know how many of them notes I have, all the wackos who say conspiracy is everywhere? Oh yeah, they know where Jimmy Hoffa is buried and who killed Princess Di's ass." He leaned forward and used the gruff tone that had probably served him well interrogating witnesses. "I'm not playing. What else was in that envelope? Yeah, right, you're here because of some note."

"So maybe I have more than a note," she replied. "I can't talk exactly about what I have, but I can tell you this much. It was worth coming all the way here. I'm not on a wild goose chase. And before I got this envelope, I had absolutely no interest in this subject."

Vasquez was silent while he took another long look around the bar. "When did you get the envelope?"

"Recently."

"*Quando* recently? Last week? Last month?"

"In the last month," she answered.

He smiled, exposing teeth that looked like they hadn't been brushed since he'd last laundered his clothes. "The situation in Miami is pretty crazy right now. You hip to any of that?"

She met his eyes. This detective might be a drunk, but he was a sharp drunk, to put all of that together, and she figured he might have some useful information for her after all. "Possibly."

"You know anything about that missing surveillance tape?"

Hayley didn't answer immediately. While she considered what to tell Vasquez, she followed his gaze. He was watching Mr. Clean again, who was delicately holding his glass in a napkin, sipping his drink, oblivious to them.

Vasquez sat up, suddenly alert, which clued her in something was amiss. "Listen, since you got this envelope, have you felt threatened? Been followed or watched?"

"No. Why?" She could see nothing out of place in the bar and wondered if he was merely being paranoid or if there truly was something to worry about. "What's wrong?"

"Nothing." His tone was abrupt. Something had changed.

"So far, I've been doing all the talking," she said. "I still have no idea if you can help me. If you have anything to show me, I'm willing to put what I have on the table. But I need to know I'll get something in exchange. This is your chance to show them you haven't been crazy all this time and mine to come up with the story I've been waiting for." She waited for some acknowledgement from Vasquez, who seemed entirely preoccupied with Clean Guy now.

"Yeah, yeah. I get you. Go on."

"I'm in a very sensitive position, and honestly I'm glad you're no longer with the police," she continued, "because this could put me in a compromising position. Before I reveal what I have, I need to know that won't happen."

Vasquez turned to her. "*Vámanos*."

"Where to?"

"Where we're not being followed." He threw a few bills on the table, finished his drink with one swallow, and motioned her to precede him out the door.

CHAPTER TWELVE

Domino watched Hayley and Vasquez leave the bar and briefly converse in the parking lot outside. For a moment, she viewed them in a nonprofessional manner. Hayley definitely had a talent for picking clothes that suited her figure and personality. Her deep purple dress fit like a body glove, helping her exude an appealing, sensual self-confidence. And the ex-cop, Domino noted, seemed to enjoy the view as much as she did.

The two of them bypassed Hayley's red Ford Mustang and were headed toward Vasquez's battered station wagon when Reno's voice came over the transmitter from inside the bar. "Get pictures of the guy who's leaving. Blue shirt and tan pants."

She scrambled for a camera with a telephoto lens and snapped pictures of the man as he hesitated in the doorway and scanned the parking lot. When he watched Vasquez and Hayley leave in the station wagon, he pulled out a pad and paper, wrote something down, and hurried to a dark blue sedan. It peeled away in the same direction as the wagon, and Reno emerged from the bar and jogged to the van.

"Did you get all that?" he asked as she headed after them.

"Yes. Did Vasquez make you?"

"I'm pretty sure he didn't. I was sitting too close to know for sure, but I suspect he also wondered who the hell this guy in the sedan is. Vasquez may be a paranoid drunk but he's nobody's fool—seemed in a hurry to get out of there after he noticed the guy didn't want to leave prints." He retrieved the memory card from the camera and plugged it into a laptop computer that lay open on the console between them. "I'll put the office to work on his picture and plate number to see if we can ID him."

❖

Hayley noticed Vasquez kept one eye on the rearview mirror as they pulled away from the bar. "Where are we going?"

"My crib," he answered. "But I have to make sure we ain't being tailed. So we're taking the scenic route. In the meantime, just be quiet. Chill."

"Whatever you say," she replied, wondering again if he was being paranoid or smart.

They drove around for a half hour, with Vasquez making U-turns and cutting through alleys. At one point, he parked and watched the direction they had come from for five minutes. While they waited, he asked for her cell phone and checked it for a tracking device.

Finally they pulled up in front of a run-down apartment building. A sixty-something woman in a well-worn housedress watched them from an open first-floor window nearby. She was smoking a cigarette, her face in the shadows. She hailed Vasquez as he slammed out of the station wagon.

"Rent's late again, Manny. I need it today."

"I'll get it to you, Edna. You know I'm good for it." He headed toward one of several first-floor entrances to the apartment complex, just down from where he'd parked. Hayley followed.

"You know you're not supposed to have ladies over," the landlady called after them.

"She's my niece," Vasquez paused to reply. "I told you she was coming to visit—you musta forgot." He continued into the building and down a long hall, past several other doors. At the end, he followed another hallway to the left to apartment 117, where he pulled a heavy ring of keys from his pocket and fumbled for the right one. Hayley noticed his door held not the usual one or two locks, but a total of six, spaced from top to bottom.

"What was that all about back there?" she asked. "Your niece?"

"Old woman is senile as hell. Anything you tell her's gone in ten minutes."

Finding all the right keys took a couple of minutes. Once inside, Vasquez spent a few more locking up again and added a heavy metal bar across the door, fitted into custom hooks on either side. As he busied himself with the task, Hayley took in the filthy chaos that was his living room. No wonder he chose the Three Sisters bar. It was exactly like his home.

The half-dozen empty Scotch bottles scattered about and the dirty glasses everywhere confirmed that he was a serious and dedicated drinker. The overflowing ashtrays, soiled clothes, and old take-out containers spread throughout the room added to the stench.

The furniture was upholstered with repulsive floral prints from the 1970s, and she could make out random vomit stains among the sunflowers and daisies. *Oh yeah, that spruces it right up.* She kicked aside an old pizza box at her feet and sat on the floor. From there she could see something half underneath the couch that resembled a desiccated mouse corpse. *Oh, please. Tell me that's not what I think it is.* What would make a mouse drop dead in the middle of someone's living room?

"Want something to drink?" he asked.

"No," she replied, a little too quickly and a lot too loud. *Hell no.* The mere idea of drinking out of one of his glasses made her stomach churn. Why didn't she just drink out of the toilet? "I mean, no thanks." *Who lives like this?*

"Suit yourself. Don't mind if I do," he said, more to himself than to her, as he poured another Scotch into a glass that looked like something might be living in it.

"So what the hell is going on?" she asked, anxious to leave as soon as possible. "Why all the cloak-and-dagger in the bar and on the way here?"

He turned on a radio before he answered. "Have you noticed anything different in your house since you got your envelope?"

"Different? Different how?"

"Have things been moved around? Anything missing? Things like that?"

"No. Not that I've noticed, anyway," she replied. But in truth, she hadn't paid close attention. "Why?"

"Well, somebody likes you. That guy at the front of the bar, looked like he just stepped out of the shower? He was tailing your ass."

"Yeah, I know who you mean. I saw him, too. He came in right after me. But he didn't seem to be paying me any attention."

"Wouldn't." Vasquez sipped his Scotch. "But he was. He followed us for a while after we left the bar, but I lost him. Seen him before?"

"No. Never."

"Look, whatever you're being so mysterious about is enough reason for somebody to follow you. Now tell me what it is."

"Do you think I should be worried?"

"I'll know more when I see what you got."

She had to risk it. "I have a copy of the Miami tape. Not with me, of course."

"I knew it," Vasquez said. "In a safe place, right?"

"Yes. And I have a spare."

"What's on it?"

"Presumably a female assassin trained by the EOO. It's not great in terms of quality. You can't really make her out. It shows the four guys being killed—her accomplice, and Guerrero and his two men."

"I know a guy could clean it up, enhance her image." He was beginning to slur his words. "Sometimes you can pick up clues that way. Tattoos, birthmarks, shit like that."

"It sounds worth giving a shot." She berated herself that she hadn't thought of that. "So, what do you know about this organization?" Hayley hadn't pried much information out of Vasquez, but had volunteered a lot. She needed to get something in return, and soon. The way he was hitting the Scotch, he might pass out any time. But before he could answer, her cell phone rang.

"Go ahead." He waved vaguely in the direction of her ringing purse as he rose unsteadily to his feet. "I gotta get something to show you." He staggered toward his dented metal desk, which was covered with files, papers, and unrecognizable mummified food remains, and began to rifle through the drawers as she dug for her phone.

She smiled when she checked the display and saw who was calling. "Hi there, miss me already?"

"That transparent?" Luka replied. "Thought I'd see what you might be in the mood for tomorrow."

"Well...*you*. And I'm open to suggestions for the rest. Do you have something in mind?" she asked playfully, keeping an eye on Vasquez, who was mumbling to himself in Spanish. He gave up his search of the desk and tottered off toward what she assumed was his bedroom.

"Sounds like you're not alone. Sorry for interrupting."

"Hey, don't be sorry. I'm always happy to hear your voice. Besides, when I'm really tied up, I let it go to voicemail. But I *am* kind of on the clock and can't talk long. Actually, I'm in New York, following a lead on that story I'm working on. I won't get back till late."

"Making progress?"

"Things are looking better, I guess. Still kind of early to judge. So, what are you up to tonight?"

"Aside from sitting here alone missing you, not much else. Just listening to music and doing some things around the house. What do you want to do tomorrow? Shall we start with dinner again somewhere?"

"Sounds good to me."

"What do you like?" Luka asked. "Thai? Mexican? Steak?"

"All of the above and in no particular order. I'm not picky," she replied. "I'm more interested in the company than the cuisine."

"Perhaps we can take a drive after dinner. You can show me some of your favorite places around Baltimore?"

"Is that all you want me to show you?"

"I can't wait for the eventuality of you showing me more."

"And you call me relentless?" Hayley watched as Vasquez reemerged from the bedroom holding a VHS tape and a manila file folder. "I hate to cut this short but I gotta run. I'm happy you called, though, so keep calling. See you tomorrow?"

"You will definitely see me tomorrow. By the way, I know this place where they play classic movies seven days a week. Care to join me?"

"Sounds like fun. Count me in," she replied.

"Great. *Gone With The Wind* is playing next week. You name the night and I'm there. Guess I'll let you go. Reluctantly—but if I must, I must. Have a good evening, and I hope your lead pans out."

"Thanks, Luka. 'Night." She ended the call and slipped her phone into her purse. While she'd been occupied, Vasquez had slipped the videotape into his player and turned on the TV.

"Here's a taste of what I got." He hit the play button. "Victim was a state senator. Dennis Linden."

A dark-haired man in his mid-thirties, wearing a suit and tie, shook hands with supporters at an outdoor political rally. Red, white, and blue campaign signs bearing his name waved in the crowd. "Seemed like a regular guy, bright future in politics, but after he died, our investigation turned up evidence he was on the take, big-time. Nothing we could ever prove, and we never found out who he was working for, but large cash deposits had been made in bank accounts he had under a false name."

"This isn't a security camera," Hayley remarked. It looked like standard TV news-crew footage and was in color.

"No. That's coming." Just as Vasquez said the words, the tape changed to blurry black-and-white footage that looked similar to hers. "A surveillance camera outside a post office took this."

The view, from high up, showed a street with little traffic and few pedestrians. All of the faces were indistinguishable. "That's Linden," he said as a lone male figure appeared. A few steps behind him walked a woman, a head shorter, wearing a long dark coat, dark boots, and a dark hat with a brim that covered her face and hair. She had her hands in her coat pockets.

Hayley watched as the woman pulled a gun from her right pocket and shot the man in the back of the head. When he went down, she put another bullet into his head, slipped the gun back in her pocket, and continued walking. It all happened in seconds.

It was similar to the video Hayley had. The close range, second bullet to the head, the shooter's calm professionalism. But there was no way to tell if it was the same woman.

"How do you know this was a professional assassin?" she asked. "And not a jealous ex or something?"

"Had all the signs of a pro. Type of hit, weapon, ammo, cool attitude. And nothing in our investigation pointed to anything else. Again, nothing we could prove. But likely." He popped the tape from the machine. "This is my loony file. Letters and tips I got when I snagged the case. None of 'em went anywhere." He handed her the manila file, thick with printouts of e-mails and handwritten notes.

She leafed through them—several confessions, a few illiterate scrawls, some drawings, and numerous other missives.

"Just to give you an idea that notes in the mail claiming to know something are nothing new," he said.

"But they don't come with tapes stolen from major police departments." Hayley retrieved a copy of the note included with the Guerrero tape from her purse and handed it to Vasquez.

He took his time reading it. "Your informant's right about one thing. This EOO has a big reach. Some major players in its pocket." He took another swig of his Scotch. "Looks legit to me. And I think you're right. Got to be a powerful guy to get this tape away from Miami PD." He held up the note. "I'd like to keep this. Compare it against others I got."

"Nothing personal, but I'm not comfortable with that, Manny. For obvious reasons. I hesitated to even show it to you."

"How about if I promise not to make a copy and give it back to you in a couple days, after I've had a chance to check it out? No one else sees it, and I'll let you know anything I uncover. My word is my honor, Hayley."

She considered his offer for a minute. The note could really hurt her, but she had a gut instinct Manny was a straight-up guy, despite his drinking problem, and would keep his promise. "I'm going to trust you. Don't make me regret it, okay?"

He put his hand over his heart. "*Bueno*. Now tell me, what's your tape show?"

"For that, you've got to give me more," she said. "What do you have to trade? This, what you've shown me, doesn't help at all."

He scratched the stubble of beard on his cheek. "You trust me, I trust you. I got more. *Mucho mas*. Information about your EOO, for one thing. Maybe even an idea about who your mysterious informant might be."

"You know who sent me the tape?" Vasquez had her full attention now.

"Let's say I have a short list of suspects."

"Then why haven't you done anything with it?"

"Nothing I can do any more." He took another large swig of Scotch. "It was asking questions about these guys got me fired. No one will talk to me now, especially without a badge. I can't get near them. Shit, I think they'd shoot me on the spot."

"You think I'll have any better luck getting the answers?"

"You might. You're a hot woman—and you're a journalist. You can't do worse than me. What I don't get is why you? Why'd this guy send the tape to you?"

"I've asked myself that very question a million times, and I really have no idea. He makes it sound like he's doing me a favor, but I don't know anyone who owes me any favors. And he says he's been following my career. But it's not like I've done anything yet to warrant someone powerful thinking I can break a story like this."

"He was pretty smart concerning you, if you ask me," he said approvingly. "Here you are, after all. You found me."

"Yes. True. And you know something about this organization," she prompted.

"I interviewed a guy who did." He finished off his drink and poured himself another. Hayley wondered how he was still conscious. "Told me a big story. Hell of a story." He stared into his glass, as though remembering. "But he's dead now. Oh, yeah…they're good at covering their tracks. Real good." The bitterness in his voice suggested his personal woes had something to do with the EOO too.

"Tell me the story," she urged.

Vasquez settled back against the cushions of the couch with a groan. "Remember the Castellano case?"

"You mean the organized crime family?"

"That's the one. After Angelo Castellano got whacked, his guys started to panic and get sloppy. We arrested a shitload of them, and one was a guy called Frankie the Fox. We had him in custody, facing a lot of charges, and his lawyer was in and out of there for weeks, telling him his best bet was to give us names, locations, and anything else. Working a deal with prosecutors would get him twenty years with a good chance at parole if he cooperated. Otherwise he might get the chair. Frankie decided to take it, and I was the guy who questioned him." He lit a cigarette with slightly shaky hands.

"He told me he got involved in the Castellano family right after he spent six months working for a secret organization called the EOO. Said someone he knew put him in contact with them as a favor. This organization decided to give him a chance because of his military background and trained him—in spying, interrogation, torture, weapons. All stuff he hadn't learned in the army. They gave him a couple of assignments, but Frankie said it was boring, low-level stuff, and they cut him loose when he started asking for more responsibility. Afterwards, he worked alone for a few months as a for-hire thug and did a few hits for Castellano. Castellano liked his style and took him on full time."

Vasquez took a sip of his Scotch as Hayley waited impatiently for him to continue. "According to Frankie, a guy Frankie recognized as an EOO operative took out Castellano."

"He actually knew the assassin?"

"He recognized the style and methods, not the guy himself. Frankie said he could tell these things—they didn't call him the Fox for nothing. Claimed he knew the shit was going to hit the fan with his boss because some powerful guys owed him money. Men with influence. All with one thing in common. Gambling." He took another drag off his cigarette. "And guys like that, when they're scared, either run or come after you before you come after them."

"Your short list of suspects?" Hayley asked.

"You're a smart girl," he acknowledged.

"What else did he tell you about the Organization?"

"Said it was high security and remote. Mind boggling, the kind of training there. Turns out highly disciplined and resourceful ops, who do the kind of gigs the government can't, along with private jobs, too. The FBI uses 'em, and CIA." Ashes from his cigarette fell onto the couch but he didn't notice. "Said the organization's motto was Detect, Identify, Resolve."

"Did he say where it was?"

Vasquez took another drag off his cigarette, then stubbed it out in an already overflowing ashtray. "No. He was saving that, he said. His trump card, in case anything went wrong with the deal. But three weeks after I interviewed him, he was found dead in his cell. They said it was rat poison. I think the EOO discovered he was talking and got to him."

His voice took on that bitter tone again. "After Frankie died I started to ask around. Follow up on some of the names he'd given me. It didn't take long before my bosses took me off the case, said we didn't have enough evidence. I thought we had enough to go on, so I kept investigating on my own. They called me in a couple weeks later, asked me to resign. When I asked what for, they told me it was better to resign than get fired, because it would look bad on my record to get canned for being drunk and insubordinate. I knew then somebody big pulled the plug, and they were trying to cover up. I said this to my chief, asked him if someone had gotten to him—was he on the take—and he fired me."

"Who's on this short list, Manny?" Hayley pressed.

"For that, you owe me your tape," he said. "I'll give you my list and the tape of my interview with Frankie. There's a lot more on there about the EOO I think you'll be interested in."

"Okay, you got a deal."

"Late." He got up and stretched. "Want to sleep here tonight? You can have my bed, I'll take the couch."

She tried to mask her horror at the prospect. "Thanks, Manny, but I have to head home. Got to work in the morning. How about I come back tomorrow night and we trade what we have?"

"Works for me. I'll spend the day trying to match your note against letters I have, so I can brief you then about whatever I find."

"That'd be great."

"Same time?" he asked.

"Sure."

"Let's meet at the Three Sisters again, so I can make sure we're not followed back here." He fumbled in his pocket for his keys. "I'll drive you back to your car."

"Not necessary." She reached for her cell phone. "Better I call a cab."

"Whatever."

When the taxi arrived, Vasquez unlocked his fortress and let her out.

Hayley paused outside the door. "Manny, do you think I'm in danger?"

"Just be careful," he replied. "Watch your back."

She waited until she was in her Mustang and on the highway headed home before she dug her cell phone out and called Luka. "Hi, it's Hayley. Did I wake you?" The digital clock read eleven fifteen.

"Hardly. I'm a night owl, too. What's up?"

"This sucks but I'm going to have to reschedule our date," she said. "Looks like I'll be tied up tomorrow. Can we push our dinner back a day? Same time?"

"Of course. No problem."

"Oh, wonderful. *You're* wonderful for understanding. I am so much looking forward to seeing you again." She bit back the curse she wanted to holler at the tractor-trailer that cut her off, forcing her to brake suddenly.

"Me, too," came the response. "See you Thursday then?"

"Can't wait," she said. "'Night, Luka. Sweet dreams."

"Sure bet, since I'll be thinking of you."

Hayley smiled. She was really sorry to have to postpone seeing

Luka. "Like I said...smooth talker. I'm finding it hard to resist you, you know."

"Good, because it's mutual. 'Night, Hayley."

❖

Domino closed the cell phone, ending the call.

"That was close," Reno said. "She almost hit that truck."

"Too close," she agreed, wondering if Hayley's preoccupation with who she was talking to had diverted her attention. They were speeding down the freeway a few cars behind the Mustang. Though they'd lost Hayley during Vasquez's evasive maneuvers out of the bar, Domino had kept her talking on her cell phone just long enough for them to use GPS triangulation to trace her back to the ex-cop's apartment, where they'd picked her up again.

"Nothing on the guy from the bar yet," Reno relayed. He had the computer on his lap. "Car's a rental, nothing from the rental company either. And no match on his picture, but it's only been a couple of hours."

"Call Pierce and put him on speakerphone," she said.

"Strike's headed home," Reno relayed once their boss answered. "Don't have much on their meeting, because it adjourned to his place. But we had company in the bar. Someone else is interested in her. Trying to trace him now, so far unsuccessfully."

"Not an amateur, in other words," Pierce replied.

"No," Domino cut in. "But he didn't know in advance where he'd end up—he stuck out too much. And he lost her when they moved from the bar."

"Do we have to worry about Strike's new contact?" Pierce asked.

"Undetermined," she replied. "She broke our date for tomorrow to work. Could be related to their discussion."

"Okay," Pierce finally said. "Keep me posted if anything changes."

❖

Senator Terrence Burrows had barely turned in for the evening when his ringing cell phone broke the quiet. His wife Diana groaned and shifted restlessly on her side of their king-sized bed.

"Sorry, honey." He plucked the phone from the bedside table and flipped it open to silence the ringing but, seeing who it was, waited until he was down the hallway before he spoke. "Yes?"

"She went to Brooklyn tonight to meet an ex-cop," Jack informed him. "A detective named Manuel Vasquez—he left the force about three years ago. Still checking him out. They talked for a while in a bar, then left. Vasquez caught on they were being followed and lost my guy."

Terrence detoured to his den and poured himself a whiskey as he digested the information. Jack was patient with the long silence on the line.

"Anything else?" he said at last, sipping the whiskey.

"My man thought someone else may have been following them, in a van, but couldn't be sure."

"Okay, Jack. I'll give you a call back when I determine how to proceed."

Next he dialed an assistant chief in the New York Police Department whose private home number was on speed dial. "Hey, Calvin. It's Terrence. Sorry to call so late."

"Hey, man. What's up? Haven't seen you around in ages."

"No time for much fun these days," he replied. "Don't you ever pick up a newspaper or turn on the television?"

He heard laughter. "Yeah, seems like I read somewhere you got some big plans for next year."

"Listen, Cal. I'm calling about that matter I had you take care of for me. You know the one I mean."

"Hang on a minute." Terrence heard the chief tell his wife Florence not to wait up. Then he came back on the line. "Okay, Terrence. Go on."

"Any chance at all your guy took anything with him when he left? Files, copies of interviews, things of that sort?"

"Don't think so. But I can check. Need it tonight?"

"Yeah, Cal. It's important."

"Okay. I'll get back to you when I know something."

It took forty minutes, and the news wasn't good. Several pieces of evidence related to the Angelo Castellano murder investigation were missing, including witness-interview audiotapes and some of the case-file paperwork.

Terrence admitted to himself he'd made an error in judgment using Cal to eliminate Vasquez as a threat. Jack would make certain the ex-cop was silent for good.

One more phone call and then he could go back to bed.

CHAPTER THIRTEEN

Wednesday

Hayley hit the snooze button on her alarm clock for the fourth time, extricated herself from a tangle of sheets, and forced herself out of bed. Although she routinely functioned on only a few hours' sleep, last night had been particularly rough. She'd gotten back home a little before four, but had been too hyped up to sleep right away, her mind busily turning over what Vasquez had told her. So she'd walked around her apartment, trying to determine whether anything was missing or had been moved. It was useless. She was constantly losing her remote control, her keys, and assorted other items in the clutter.

A hot shower and three cups of coffee didn't do much to invigorate her. Two hours of sleep simply wasn't enough, and if she tried to do it all again tonight she'd be useless at work tomorrow. She probably wouldn't have to spend as long in Brooklyn this time, but Manny might get to talking again if he had a few drinks. And if what he had was of interest, she knew she'd stay as long as necessary to hear him out. Her best option, she decided, was to ask her editor Greg for a little personal time and move up the meeting.

She called Manny's place a little after eight as she was about to leave for work and was mildly surprised when his answering machine picked up. He couldn't be out and about already with all he'd drunk the night before. More likely he was passed out cold, sleeping it off. "Hi, Manny. It's Hayley. I checked around my place and everything seems fine. Nothing moved or missing as far as I can see. I'm calling because I'd like to come up a couple hours earlier than we planned tonight—at six, instead of eight—if that's okay. I hope that gives you enough time today to do what you can with what I left with you. And I'm really curious to see what you have to show me—it sounds promising. If my coming earlier doesn't work for you, let me know." She recited her cell-phone number. "See you tonight."

Though she'd rather not have the DVD copy of the assassination video with her at work, she didn't want to have to detour home first to retrieve it. Vasquez's paranoia and certainty she'd been followed to the bar made her nervous about having it in her possession, so she was on alert from the instant she left her apartment.

She was so on edge that when a colleague laid a hand on her shoulder as she scanned stories on her computer terminal, she nearly jumped out of her skin. "Christ, Amy. Don't do that."

"Jeez, Louise, what's got your titties in a wad this morning?" Amy Stockard was the only reporter at the *Dispatch* with less seniority than Hayley. "I was only going to ask if Greg had given you a story yet."

"No," she said. "Nothing's happening. He told me to check the regional wires to see if I could come up with anything worthwhile."

"Good luck," Amy said. "At least you might be the master of your own fate. I get to cover the planning-commission meeting. Whoopie."

"Oh, God. Take your No-Doz. Anything's better than that."

"I'm heading out now, but I should be back in a couple hours," Amy said. "Let me know if you're free for lunch later."

"You got it." Hayley returned to scanning the regional wires, filled with mostly minor stories, too insignificant for a half-hour TV newscast, but sometimes enough to warrant a few paragraphs in the paper on a slow news day. It was a little after nine thirty when she saw it cross the wires. Four paragraphs, delivered after a routine story on a new office complex opening in New Jersey.

> *Associated Press—New York*
> *An early morning automobile accident has claimed the lives of a former Brooklyn police detective and a couple from Queens.*
> *Witnesses reported a 1976 Ford station wagon driven by retired detective Manuel Vasquez, a 21-year veteran of the Brooklyn police force, crossed the center line of DeKalb Avenue shortly after one a.m. and hit a late-model Ford Caprice head-on.*

The Caprice was driven by a 23-year-old Queens man. He and his 25-year-old wife were pronounced dead at the scene. Identification of the couple is being withheld pending next of kin notification.

Vasquez died en route to the hospital. Officials say there is evidence alcohol was involved in the crash.

Hayley's stomach began to churn as the words sank in. *Dear God, no.* Manny had died about two hours after she left his apartment. It certainly looked like an accident, and he had downed enough alcohol that he should never have been behind the wheel.

But the timing…after all they had discussed, after his paranoia about her being followed. She couldn't help but wonder whether it was an accident at all. A chill ran up her back, and she glanced over her shoulder, suddenly fearful of being watched.

Though she'd spent only a few hours with him, she'd felt Manny was a good man at heart, a cop with integrity, with a true and sincere dedication to the pursuit of justice, whatever the cost. She thought back to his account of losing his job and wondered if he had been fired because of his drinking, as his chief claimed, or because someone was trying to silence him and cover up his investigation, as he asserted. She grieved that such a well-intentioned, honorable guy had ended up as he had—destroyed by alcohol, humiliated and haunted, his life cut short. Such a damn shame he'd never see justice in the case that had cost him so much.

She wished she could find that justice on his behalf, but now she didn't have a chance to get his short list of suspects—so far her most promising lead. Or the Frankie the Fox tape, which he claimed contained more information about the EOO. She should have pressed harder last night to get all the information he had. Maybe then she'd be able to get some of the answers he couldn't.

Then it hit her. *The note. Oh, my God. He has my note.* When she'd told him he could keep it, she'd watched him put it on top of his manila file of "loony" letters. It was probably still there, waiting for the cops to find when they looked through his apartment. *No. They think his death was an accident.* More likely, a relative would discover it, or the landlady, clearing out his stuff. Someone would, though.

And the note, together with the message on his answering machine, would incriminate her. The cops would arrest her and charge her with withholding evidence and who knew what else.

Her fear of winding up in jail overcame her sense of dread over recent events, at least for the time being. Her mind raced. She had to get the note out of there and erase the message. And she didn't have any time to waste. Manny had introduced her to the landlady as his niece, so she could use that. Talk her way into the apartment, get in and out fast while it was still daylight. It was a crowded building, so she should be safe enough. She told her boss she had a personal emergency and had to leave right away. Ten minutes later, she was speeding up the highway to Brooklyn.

❖

The Atlas Gym was old-school, designed for those serious about self-improvement. It had machines and weights and a locker room, plus a clientele who didn't give a damn about choosing the right exercise ensemble to make the opposite sex notice them.

"Easy, champ, we're not going for gold," Domino's sparring partner said, his voice a ragged whisper.

She released the pressure and removed her knee from his throat, then got to her feet and extended her hand to help him up.

"Fanatic much today?" he said playfully, punching her on the shoulder.

Domino smiled apologetically. "Sorry, didn't realize, I guess." It was out of character for her to get carried away like this. She was always very aware of the gym's rules and how far she should and could go.

She removed her headgear and started toward the press bench, pausing only to sip from her water bottle and swipe at her face with a hand towel. Her black sweatpants and tank top were already damp with sweat, but she planned to do another hour at least. Workouts were necessary in her life, and she enjoyed them, but today wasn't about enjoyment. Today was about trying to redirect her frustration. This assignment was getting to her, and she couldn't figure out why.

Twenty minutes pressing weights failed to diminish her rising turmoil. She needed some air. So she hit the showers, stashed her bag in one of the lockers, and changed into shorts and a T-shirt for a five-mile run. It was supposed to get well into the eighties again in the nation's capital, but at eight thirty a.m. under cloudy skies it was still comfortable, not that she wasn't used to workouts in every type of extreme weather.

The gym was in an office complex north of East Potomac Park, so her preferred course took her over the Fourteenth Street Bridge into Virginia and a paved jogging/bike trail along the river.

She heard a loud male voice coming from her right. A man was seated at the bow of a rowing scull, urging the women on board to row faster. It seemed as though they were keeping pace with her, while the man continued to count and urge, or was she keeping to their pace? She wasn't sure, but the loud, steady voice put her in a trance.

She closed her eyes for a few seconds, and when she opened them again she had been transported to a very different landscape.

"Faster, faster!"

She was fifteen, and this time the voice to her right was that of David Arthur, driving his jeep alongside herself and two classmates—a young man and her one and only friend, Mishael, also fifteen. They were in the Rio Grande National Forest. Her lungs hurt from running nonstop for more than two hours. The sandbags strapped around her ankles and the heavy rucksack, both wet after she'd swum across the river, made her feel as though she was dragging a lifeless body.

The male op to her far left fell, cursing. And again, the voice of Arthur. "Move on. Get up and move on."

She couldn't remember the last time she had felt more tired or more determined. Mishael was next to her and looked like she was about to lose her breakfast. She mumbled something about how easy it would be to kill Arthur with just one thumb.

Arthur drove the jeep in closer until he was at arm's length. "Do you feel the pain?" he shouted over the roaring engine.

"Yes, sir," Domino shouted back, never taking her eyes off the path.

"Do you want it to stop?"

"Yes, sir," she shouted again, knowing her agony was evident on her face.

"Then keep running," he yelled. "Keep going until you can't feel the pain. Until you can't feel anything. Until you don't want the pain to stop."

"Yes, sir, until I can't feel anything. No pain."

For most of the run, she went mindless, her feet pounding faster and faster, a steady pace on the asphalt. "Until I can't feel anything," she said out loud. She was halfway over the bridge when she suddenly slowed, then stopped. "Damn it," she spat to herself and kicked the cola can at her feet.

Running was all she had known—from others, from herself—until she couldn't feel anything. Why wasn't it working now, why was Hayley making her feel as though she didn't have to, and why did it hurt to lie to her? She didn't have the answers to all these whys, but she did decide to walk the rest of the way to the gym.

Her cell phone rang as she neared the entrance. It was Pierce, relaying information provided by the operative monitoring the listening devices in Hayley's apartment.

"Strike just called her new friend in Brooklyn," he said. "She left a message on his answering machine."

"I'm listening."

"She apparently gave him something, and he told her he'd give her something in return tonight…something that 'sounded promising.' She's heading up to meet him at six. Get up there now, pick up Reno en route. Send him into the guy's apartment, and see if you can recover what he got from her and whatever she was going to get from him."

"On my way." She retrieved another change of clothes from the trunk of her car before she returned to the locker room.

An hour out of Brooklyn, Reno began to complain he felt ill. Probably, he said, from the seafood buffet he'd overindulged in the night before. By the time they reached their turnoff, he was heaving violently into a plastic bag in the back of the van. So weak he could barely sit up, he couldn't possibly go into Vasquez's apartment.

Domino waited for an elderly woman who was putting out trash to get around the corner of the building before she exited the van and went inside. No one else was around, and no one saw her. The evening before, she'd scoped out the complex and had seen the bars on the two back windows in Vasquez's place. Going in through his front door was her only option.

She grimaced when she saw all the locks, though they really didn't surprise her. She'd been briefed the guy was the paranoid type. But it would likely take a minute or two to get in, and several other apartments led off his hallway. She could be discovered at any minute. First she knocked, loud enough so he would hear, but not enough to alert any of his neighbors. When there was no response, she set to work on the locks and was inside three minutes later.

Though she'd been in all kinds of unsanitary places during her career, she'd never experienced anything this bad in a first-world country. Aside from the filth and mess, the stench was so bad she had to breathe through her mouth. She searched the place and quickly found Hayley's note, stuffed inside a manila folder lying on Vasquez's couch. Though she spent several minutes scanning the contents of a couple dozen more manila file folders crammed into the desk drawers, she didn't discover anything else of interest in his living room.

Voices at the door made her duck into the bedroom as the deadbolt—the one lock on the door she'd bothered to set—sprang open. It was the only one on the inside that didn't require a key.

Her curiosity turned to alarm when she recognized one of the voices as Hayley's. "Thanks, Edna. I really appreciate this."

She heard Hayley enter the apartment, then the door close again. Domino squeezed behind the bedroom door, where she was well hidden but able to glimpse some of the living room through the crack at the hinge. Hayley passed by her narrow field of vision, then she shuffled some papers and cursed. Domino knew if Hayley had entered the apartment without Manny being there, she was apt to continue looking for the note until she found it. Silently, she slipped off her small backpack, reached inside for her ski mask, and put it on. She *had* to prevent Hayley from seeing her.

She heard Hayley play back the message she'd left on Manny's answering machine, then delete it with a beep. Shortly after, she opened the squeaky drawers of Vasquez's desk and shuffled more papers. After a couple of minutes, Domino sensed Hayley's approach and saw her cross her thin field of vision, headed toward the bedroom.

Pressing tighter against the wall, her backpack now at her feet, she braced for a confrontation. When Hayley entered the bedroom, Domino smelled the familiar jasmine of her perfume as she passed. Then she held her breath, every nerve ending alert, her heart racing.

She was more anxious, more tense than usual in such situations, and she wondered briefly whether her growing attraction to Hayley made the difference.

More drawers opened and closed, presumably in the dresser near the bed and the two nightstands she'd glimpsed earlier.

Hayley mumbled to herself, "No shit," and shuffled more papers. Domino risked a quick glance. Hayley was only a few feet from her, facing away and bent over the bed, reading papers spread across the mattress. "Jesus. Oh, Manny." Her voice was enthusiastic, and as Domino watched, Hayley picked up a large envelope and tore it open.

She crept from her hiding place, but Hayley seemed to sense her and began to turn in her direction just as she reached her. To keep her facing forward, she embraced her in a half nelson to control her arms. Under ordinary circumstances, she would have immediately knocked her victim out, but something prevented her. Instead, she pushed Hayley's head forward, which threw her off balance, and put her face-down on the bed.

She started to struggle, but Domino pinned her with her weight, pulled her gun, and pressed it hard against Hayley's back, near the middle, next to her spine. She didn't cock it. Then she spoke, one word only, in a tone lower than her own voice, hoping Hayley wouldn't recognize it. "No."

Hayley froze, face buried in the mattress.

Her labored breathing sounded loud to Domino, and she could smell her fear. She hated having to do this, but she didn't have a choice. Keeping the gun against Hayley with one hand, she used the other to scoop up the envelope Hayley had just opened and the other papers scattered on the bed. Then she backed away, slowly, praying Hayley would be smart enough to remain where she was. She had to risk speaking again. Low. Gruff. Threatening. "Don't move."

Backing away, she retrieved the backpack on her way to the living room, then paused beside Vasquez's couch to search Hayley's purse for the assassination tape. What she found instead was a DVD marked *Madonna HBO Special 2003*. The smart move almost made her smile. No wonder they hadn't found it in the toss of her apartment. She stuck it in her backpack and glanced once more at the bedroom door, relieved Hayley didn't attempt to look at her, or follow.

As she opened the door to the hallway, she stripped off her mask, grateful that none of Vasquez's windows overlooked the parking lot so Hayley couldn't see her leave. Her heart boomed in her chest. No one was about. No one saw her leave. Her relief quickly turned to anger when she realized what had almost happened. The possibility of having to hurt Hayley if she'd tried to run made her stomach turn. She walked back to the parked van, curious to find out what the hell Reno had been up to and why he hadn't warned her. He was laid out flat on his back, cold sweat pouring off him.

She called Pierce with an update and asked whether they should stick around to follow Hayley or return to Washington. He told her to stay put and see where Strike went next, so she donned a red wig and sunglasses and moved the van farther from Hayley's Mustang. While she waited for Hayley to emerge from the apartment, she put the DVD into the laptop and watched the surveillance tape without emotion, studying it for signs it could be used to identify her.

Had she gotten it all, everything Manny had and everything Hayley had left? Pierce wasn't pleased by the day's events, but she hadn't been willing to hurt Hayley. The objectivity that normally characterized her assignments was simply impossible with Operation Eclipse.

CHAPTER FOURTEEN

Hayley didn't move for at least five minutes, her face buried in a noxious, stained tangle of sheets Manny had probably never changed. It took that long for her heart to stop thumping, and she was too afraid the intruder who'd subdued her would return. She knew, from the bare glimpse she'd had of the figure in black, from the voice, and most especially, from the feeling of the breasts against her back as she was thrown onto the bed, the intruder was female. And very strong. From the EOO?

The possibility this was the same woman from the tape, here to erase her tracks, almost made her lose her breakfast. That could be why she hadn't found her note in Manny's file. The intruder must have it. Hayley ran to her purse. The DVD copy of the tape was also missing, so they now knew she had the original. Her fear turned into panic and for an instant she couldn't breathe.

The intruder had also taken all the papers she'd been looking at—copies of the case files of the Dennis Linden assassination. Included in the file were Manny's handwritten notes and a business card for a Timmy Koster, Video Specialist. She prayed he was listed in the phone book. It was all she had to go on, now.

Manny's death most probably wasn't an accident. And this secret organization did exist, determined and able to cover up its lethal missions.

Maybe the intruder didn't have time to search all of Manny's belongings, if that was what she was here to do. His short list, the Frankie the Fox tape, and whatever else he'd planned to show her could still be here somewhere. But it was unlikely. The masked woman would have knocked her out, or worse, if she had reasons to look further. Miraculously she was still alive, but she wondered why they'd let her live. A cold shudder of fear skittered up her back. It was time to get the hell out of here.

All the way back to Baltimore, she kept glancing in the rearview mirror.

❖

The first day of July had dawned overcast, but by late afternoon the skies were blue and cloudless, and a steady breeze made the summer heat comfortable, so it seemed everyone was outdoors. But at Monty Pierce's Arlington home, every window was closed and every curtain drawn.

Pierce leaned back into the cushions of his leather couch and studied Domino, sitting in a matching armchair to his right. On his TV screen, the assassination DVD was frozen on Domino's image. "It's reassuring there's nothing to worry about on the tape, but I still wish we had the original." The note that had been sent to Hayley and the rest of the items Domino had retrieved from Vasquez's apartment lay on the coffee table in front of him. "This can't be everything. There's nothing 'promising' in this case file. That's old news."

"If anything else was there, it was well hidden," she replied. "My search was obviously interrupted, but I got through his desk."

"Why the hell did she go up there early, and why was she searching his apartment, that's what I want to know," Pierce mused aloud. "Her message indicated he'd promised to give her whatever he has tonight." He raked a hand through his thinning blond hair and scowled. "I need to put someone on this guy, find out what the hell's going on. Now Strike's confirmed this note she received has validity, which will make her even more determined. If she'd recognized you, we'd have had to take care of her, and she's our best hope of finding out who's behind all this."

"I'm not happy about this either," Domino said. "I was taking a risk going up there to begin with, and I shouldn't have been in that apartment. You need to bring in another op to work with Reno. If I continue with this assignment, I need to stay exclusively with Strike— eyes only. Today could have blown my cover."

"Agreed. We'll put you on twenty-four-hour surveillance. I'll arrange a place with a good vantage point and move you in there tomorrow. And you need to put a tracker on her car." Pierce picked up his phone and ordered the Organization's logistics office to immediately secure a home, office, or apartment with a good view of Hayley Ward's place. It was to be outfitted with the usual equipment and readied for immediate occupancy. He also ordered an operative be sent to Brooklyn to tail Manny Vasquez.

The prospect of watching Hayley day and night through high-powered lenses sent a warm and very unprofessional sensation through Domino's body. She'd been on such details before and knew the types of images she would likely see—the subject emerging from a shower or undressing before bed. Or entertaining someone in their bedroom; she'd certainly seen that often enough.

She had no idea what she might observe Hayley doing. Their file on her, and Hayley's own admissions, indicated she was inclined toward brief sexual encounters. One-night stands, mostly. Whether they happened in her apartment or elsewhere wasn't known. The prospect of this eventuality should have left her cold, but it didn't.

It had little or no relevance to the mission. In actuality, it would be better if Hayley did continue her pattern of casual affairs, because they would keep her too preoccupied to dig for further evidence of the EOO. But Domino realized to her surprise that she rather hoped Hayley *had* stopped seeing other people.

❖

Hayley was so shaken by her experience at Manny's apartment she considered calling her sister to come over to keep her company, but didn't want to expose anyone else—certainly no one close to her—to any type of danger. So instead she went from room to room, checking twice to make sure all the doors and windows were locked and looking again for evidence someone had been in her apartment while she wasn't there. She inwardly cursed herself for being so messy. Trying to find anything out of place was almost impossible when things were always scattered everywhere like a strong breeze had blown through.

Once she felt relatively secure, she settled onto her sofa with a martini and considered her next move. The knowledge that the EOO probably had her note and the DVD of the surveillance tape unnerved her. But she reasoned it probably wouldn't do any good to drop her investigation. It wouldn't make her any safer in the long run. She'd just have to be especially careful from now on. Manny's words—*watch your back*—rang in her head. Maybe it was time to start thinking about going to the police.

She was tempted to at least contact Manny's former precinct anonymously, to suggest his death hadn't been an accident. Possible evidence from the car crash might help solve this mystery and bring those responsible to justice. Although…the Organization wouldn't leave that kind of evidence behind, would they? And tipping off the police might only involve her further, make her look even guiltier.

She'd been at Manny's apartment. His landlady, and people at the bar, had seen them together. Could the police find her from that? If they did, she'd have to tell them about the assassination tape. Explain why she hadn't come forward earlier. Now that the EOO had what they wanted, maybe they would leave her alone. If they'd wanted to kill her, they could have.

For the time being, she would do nothing but be especially cautious, she decided. Or…maybe it was time to think about getting a gun.

❖

Thursday

Domino took in the sparsely furnished studio apartment across the street from Hayley's apartment complex. She had an excellent view of Hayley's living room and bedroom windows from one floor above. With her right hand she absently worked the ever-present domino she carried with her, playing the black bone over her knuckles and back again.

They'd set her up with the basic essentials. Against one wall, a thin camping mattress with sleeping bag, though she didn't expect to use those much. A box of latex gloves. Audio/video equipment and a listening device tuned in to the bugs in Hayley's apartment and the trace on her home phone. Two sets of high-powered, digital-zoom binoculars, one with night vision. Portable radar equipment, to monitor the tracking device she'd just attached to the undercarriage of Hayley's Mustang. A makeup kit, wigs, and other items she might need for a disguise. And in a metallic case, a British-made L96A1 sniper rifle, which had a range of 1100 meters.

She brought a minimum of personal items in case she had to flee quickly. It was one of the first things she was taught: you never leave your stuff behind. And she would be back and forth to her own place often enough, accessing the apartment from a convenient rear entrance, while Hayley was sleeping and working.

Domino saw movement in Hayley's apartment with its open curtains and reached for the binoculars. Hayley, dressed in a burgundy business suit, crossed from her living room to her bedroom. Reaching down, she pulled off a matching pump, then disappeared, presumably into the bathroom. Domino let the binoculars fall to her side and started to lean forward to rest her forehead on the window when she stopped herself. The grease she would have left there would have been as good as a fingerprint. She stepped back and almost knocked the audio equipment over. Exasperated, she ran her hand through her hair. This carelessness was very unlike her. And this whole damn operation was very unlike any of her previous.

Working for the Organization, for a better world, had always been a noble cause, But she had doubts about this assignment and was in no position to express them.

All orders always included *by any means necessary.* And if that meant seducing, sleeping with, lying, and faking it all, so be it. She had no virtues or identity of her own to have to stay true to.

But it all felt wrong. Hayley was innocent. She didn't doubt that, no matter what Pierce might make her out to be. Someone with ulterior motives had picked Hayley. They should be the one paying, not her.

Domino looked at her watch. Fifteen minutes until time to meet Hayley. She walked into the apartment's tiny bathroom to check her appearance, rested her hands on the sink, and stared down at it. Would she be able to cope with having to sit back and watch someone take Hayley out? And what upset her most—the fact she was an innocent or that it was Hayley? Not being able to give herself an objective answer troubled her.

She'd had her share of women. Beautiful, eager women who wanted more than she could give. Was Hayley so tempting because she was forbidden fruit? She'd be fooling herself if she accepted that excuse. There was more to this attraction, and it was something unfamiliar.

Hayley didn't push or probe, she didn't demand. She just wanted her, no questions asked, and she was willing to wait for her body and mind. She had accepted her silence and evasive answers and was content to be in her presence.

But although Hayley was accepting the person she thought was Luka, in many ways she was accepting Domino, the woman who couldn't always give answers or explain.

Domino, surprised, raised her head to look at herself in the mirror. What she had seen in Hayley's eyes on the boat as they sat in silence and watched the sun go down wasn't just about getting through the night. It was about hope for a tomorrow. Now she knew what that unfamiliar feeling was.

❖

Hayley had been jumpy all day at work. Remembering her encounter with the intruder in Manny's apartment, she was still perplexed about why the woman hadn't killed her or knocked her out. She'd done only the minimum necessary to subdue her.

A bit paranoid being out in public now, she was always scanning her surroundings, trying to pick out someone too interested in her, or a car she saw more than once. She briefly considered canceling her date or asking to stay in, because she worried Luka might distract her so much she wouldn't be as alert to danger as she should be. Or that if she *was*, she would be lousy company. But she was too eager to see Luka to postpone again. She was very compelling, and inexplicably Hayley felt safer when near Luka's calm strength.

A nice dinner somewhere quiet and then back here would make her forget her worries for a while. If anything could do it, looking at Luka could. The image of her in her black bikini came vividly to mind.

She'd always been attracted to women with lean, athletic figures, and Luka certainly epitomized the buff type, with her flat stomach, tight ass, and lightly muscled arms and thighs. Hayley laid several dresses and skirts on the bed, considering what to wear. She wanted to turn the heat up on Luka's *eventually*, so she selected a low-cut, dark gray blouse and short black leather skirt to go with the lacy and provocative red bra and panties she hoped might later draw an appreciative comment.

❖

Domino glanced at her watch as she stood before the window. Another five minutes. When she looked back up, she saw movement in the window again and picked up the binoculars. She didn't expect to see anything significant; she knew Hayley was getting ready for their date. She just wanted to look at her. Though she might tell herself over and over it was only a job, she couldn't help it.

She gripped the binoculars tightly when Hayley passed by wearing only a red lacy bra and panties and turned away to face her closet. Then she noticed something on Hayley's back, zoomed in, and focused. Guilt replaced arousal as she realized she was staring at the bruise her gun had made when she had pressed it against Hayley's back to keep her from moving.

She had been trained to ignore remorse and guilt, and for good reason. They clouded your judgment and made you hesitate unnecessarily. The reality of who she was and what she had been assigned to do reminded her of the dangerous foolishness of such emotions.

CHAPTER FIFTEEN

Domino still had the image of Hayley clad in only her red bra and panties in her mind a few minutes later when Hayley opened the door for their date.

And the current view wasn't much less provocative. Hayley's blouse exposed a good bit of her breasts, and her short leather skirt revealed a lot of thigh. Try as she might to act unaffected, Domino found it hard to look her politely in the eye. She could only stare at the creamy skin of her chest and imagine her mouth there.

Hayley smiled. "I guess that means I look okay?"

"I'm going to have to work on my transparency."

"I'd miss it if you did. I love how it makes me feel."

But Domino sensed immediately that although Hayley was trying to act normal, she was on edge, looking past her, over her shoulder and into the corridor. A pang of guilt dampened her pleasure at the sexy view. The feel of Hayley's body beneath her on Vasquez's bed flooded her senses. "Everything okay?"

"Yeah, sure," Hayley replied lightly. "Come on in." She stepped aside to admit Domino.

"How about we combine dinner with a film, since you like old movies. There's a place where we can do both." She entered the apartment and tried to keep from staring at Hayley's chest.

"That sounds great." Hayley seemed relieved. "I was looking forward to a quiet evening. Far from crowds and busy restaurants."

"Are you sure you're all right?"

"Oh, I'll be fine. It's just been a rough couple of days and it's all kind of catching up with me, that's all." She reached for her purse.

"Would you prefer we did this some other time?"

"No," she was quick to respond. She looped an arm through Domino's and leaned against her. "I'm happy for the distraction, especially when it comes in such enticing packaging."

"And I'm more than happy to provide that for you. If you want to talk about it, I've been known to be a great listener."

"Thanks, Luka. I'll keep that in mind."

Domino almost immediately realized they were being followed. Hayley's eyes were frequently on her side mirror as well, and she wondered whether she had also picked up on the plain dark sedan pacing them from several cars back.

Suddenly she swung into the drive of an auto insurance place with the right kind of driveway and no other places to stop nearby. She knew the sedan would have to pass by and drive around the block to pick them up again.

"Sorry, I just remembered," she said, retrieving her cell phone from her pocket. "I meant to call a neighbor of mine earlier. Forgive me for a moment."

"Sure."

"Hi, Ben, it's me. On my way out this morning, I saw a car hit yours and break the taillight. I got the license-plate number—it's AND 492." She paused to listen. "No problem. Good luck." She ended the call and pulled back out into traffic. As she expected, the sedan quickly reappeared behind them.

It was still following them when they reached the Bistro, a quaint old movie house with a refurbished art-deco interior. "Would you go in and find us a table?" Domino asked once she had paid for their tickets. "I forgot something. Be right in."

She waited for Hayley to get inside before she returned to the lot. The sedan was just parking. She watched it surreptitiously through the dark windows of a parked SUV. The driver was nondescript, in his thirties, average height and weight, dressed in jeans and a dark polo shirt. He looked around as he got out of the car and headed toward the theater. Domino slipped inside ahead of him, unseen.

The Bistro had replaced half of its original stadium seats with low tables and comfortable cushioned couches and chairs, and Hayley had chosen a small table in the back corner with a deep padded loveseat barely large enough to accommodate both of them. Domino couldn't have chosen a better vantage point herself.

The driver of the sedan entered and took one of the only remaining tables, twenty-five feet away, also toward the back. He sat facing the screen, but with his body slightly angled so he could glance their way on occasion without drawing too much attention to himself. It was still several minutes before showtime. The theater lights hadn't yet dimmed.

"So they only show foreign films, and dinner is always themed to the movie?" Hayley studied the menu as a waiter delivered plates laden with egg rolls and Mongolian beef to the next table. Tonight's offering was Chinese because the featured film was *Crouching Tiger, Hidden Dragon.*

"That's right." Domino tried to keep one eye on the mystery patron without alerting Hayley, who seemed oblivious to their unwelcome company. "It's a limited menu, but always good, because some nearby restaurant caters it. Next week it's Italian and *La Dolce Vita.*

They both selected the Moo Goo Gai Pan, one of four main courses offered, and Domino noticed the driver of the sedan ordered as well. He had to, to sit close to them, because only dinner patrons could occupy one of the tables.

Her cell phone vibrated in her pocket as their food arrived. She retrieved it and flipped it open to find a text message. BEAGLE. EOO-speak for private detective.

She considered the ramifications of this latest development and began to understand Pierce's paranoia. This wasn't the same guy who had followed Hayley from the bar in Brooklyn. Someone had definitely taken an interest in her and was hiring people to keep an eye on her much of the time. Was it the person who'd sent her the tape? Whoever it was, they would certainly take an interest in who she was *with* and wonder if their relationship was personal or professional. She had to make sure it appeared purely personal, that they were clearly out on a date.

"Not very hungry?" Hayley had her chopsticks halfway to her mouth and was looking back at her from the table. The lights dimmed, and the screen brightened, airing advertisements while soft music continued in the background.

Domino was slumped against the cushions. With the light provided by the screen, her peripheral view alerted her that the sedan driver was watching them. She sat up and placed her hand on Hayley's back, caressing it lightly through the thin silk. "It's hard to concentrate on food with you looking like you do."

Hayley's face registered delighted puzzlement at the unexpected directness. Domino didn't want the stranger to see the obvious surprise, so she cupped Hayley's cheek and kissed her neck.

Her body, however, would not respond, as though it knew she was doing this in the line of duty—for *his* benefit, not hers. The soft skin at the base of Hayley's neck was exquisite, and as she let her lips caress and suck, Hayley's heartbeat pounded beneath her tongue, quickening at her touch. A twist of arousal began, low in her belly, and coiled tighter when Hayley moaned.

She realized suddenly she had unfastened two of Hayley's buttons, opening her shirt to expose the edge of each nipple. Hayley shifted, as if getting more comfortable, and Domino snapped out of it. She had to stop before she couldn't, but Hayley's perfume was hazing her mind. She craved to put her mouth back where it had been, but finally forced herself to pull away.

Hayley was breathing hard and took a moment to open her eyes. She looked at Domino in a smoky, seductive way that said she was well excited. "I think I need more distraction." She leaned slowly forward, her intention to kiss her completely clear.

Domino *could* not have, *would* not have resisted if she hadn't noticed the stranger get to his feet and start toward the lobby. She pulled back with a rueful smile. "Please excuse me, Hayley. I need to use the ladies' room."

"Now?"

"Be back in a minute."

"I'm counting."

Only a handful of people clustered around the concession stand, and a late-arriving couple were entering the theater. She glimpsed the stranger ducking into a stairwell leading to the restrooms and followed, catching up to him outside the men's room. "I couldn't help but notice you've been enjoying the view. But of the wrong show. You got a problem?"

"I don't know wha—"

She grabbed him firmly by the balls. "What're you up to?"

The private detective tried to pull away, but she had a good grip and wasn't letting go. "You've been watching us more than the screen. Do you usually follow women into the movies? Maybe I should call security and have them take over."

"It's not like that," the man protested, then wheezed in pain. "You're really hurting me." He tried to pull away again, but stopped when she applied a bit more pressure.

"I can hurt you a lot more if you don't tell me what the hell you want before I start screaming for security and let them know you jumped me here."

"No! No security," he said quickly. "I'm only doing my job."

"What's your job, asshole?" she snarled. "Staring at lesbians and jacking off in the toilet?" She stuck her free hand into her back pocket for her cell phone and flipped it open.

"Look, some guy hired me to keep an eye on his girlfriend, the redhead. Thought she was cheating on him. Asked me to watch her, see who she was meeting and let him know the nature of the relationship," he said. "That's it. That's all I know."

"Who was this guy?"

"I can't say," the man declared. "I can't—"

Domino squeezed his balls harder. Tears sprang to his eyes as he tried again to get away, but she had her forearm against his throat now. "Guess the self-defense course paid off." She held him with no effort. "She never told me she had a boyfriend, so you see, I'm kind of interested myself now. What'll it be? His name? Or security?"

The private detective coughed against the pressure on his windpipe. "Okay. Okay. He said his name was Joe Poliza. That's all I know. He calls me once a day, every day, for an update."

"How long have you been watching her?"

"Couple of days," he rasped.

"Did you take pictures of her too, perv?"

"No," he said. But his pupils dilated. A sign of deceit.

She tightened her grip around his throat, and he made a choking sound.

"No. I swear, no pics yet," he said. "I was going to get some tonight, of the two of you, but it's been too damn dark so far."

Luka removed her hand from his balls and reached into the pocket of his jacket. She found a small digital camera, and without even looking to see whether there was anything on it she dropped it and stomped it with her boot heel. "Get the hell out of this theater, and tell your Joe Poliza the lady apparently prefers to be with me."

He glared at her but nodded when she stepped back, then headed for the exit.

When she returned to her table, Hayley was waiting for her with an expectant and very confused expression. She'd missed a good bit of the movie. "You left so fast and were gone so long I started to worry. Something I said?"

Domino smiled. "No, not at all. There was a long line. Have you noticed how most women take forever in the restroom?"

"You really had to go right *then*, at that particular moment?"

"Let's say I couldn't take the heat. I had to get away before we gave a show here."

"I'm fine with leaving, you know." Hayley put one hand on her thigh and shifted her weight as she edged closer. But as she resettled, she flinched.

"Are you okay?" Domino asked.

"I'm fine," Hayley replied. "It's nothing. My purse has sharp edges, and it hit a tender spot on my back."

"You look like you're in pain."

"I backed up into the door handle. No big deal." The lie came only after a slight hesitation, which told Domino volumes. Hayley wasn't entirely comfortable deceiving her, but she was determined to keep her secrets.

"So?" Hayley repeated. "Do you want to leave? Back to my place, for a bit more private distraction?" The way Hayley was looking at her made Domino's stomach clench. She inhaled a whiff of Hayley's perfume, only now she could swear it bore the subtle undertones of something else—the musky scent of arousal. Glancing down, she saw that Hayley's skirt was hiked up so high it would take nothing at all to reach between her legs. They were slightly open. Inviting. Beckoning to her, like the dark and endless pupils in Hayley's hazel eyes.

She feared adjourning to Hayley's apartment, not at all certain she could withstand the temptation to sleep with her. Not with the look in her eyes. *I want you*, the look said, in a fiery way. An ageless, primitive way. And that was the way she knew best.

But she had to get information out of Hayley, which meant alone time, where Hayley felt safe. And usually nowhere felt safer than home. "Let's go."

❖

Though Monty Pierce wanted to remain close to Operation Eclipse, other ongoing missions had necessitated that he return to the EOO's Colorado headquarters. He'd taken the red-eye the night before and was badly sleep deprived, about to nod off in his office chair when his cell phone rang. Automatically, he drew the blinds before answering.

He listened as details of Domino's call about the license plate were relayed to him. "It came back as a private detective's?" he repeated. "All right. Let me know when they get back to Strike's apartment."

He had barely disconnected when his cell rang again. The display identified the caller as the operative he'd assigned to Manny Vasquez. The man had been positioned outside Manny's apartment building for more than twenty-four hours, but an hour earlier had still seen no sign of the detective. Pierce had told him to start calling the morgue and area hospitals. "Yes?"

"Vasquez is dead," the caller relayed. "Car accident, his fault, looks like he was drunk. Happened about ninety minutes after Strike left his place."

Pierce replaced the phone in its cradle without replying. *Dead?* He stared, unseeing, at the closed blinds, and found it hard to believe Vasquez's death was a coincidence, drunk or no drunk. Vasquez must have had something of consequence. And that's what Hayley was there looking for the next morning. She must have known he was dead. But how? And did she find what she was looking for after Domino left? Where was it now?

Once again, the question of who was behind it all worried him. Did the same person who had sent Hayley the tape hire her tails? And had he also had Manuel Vasquez killed?

Pierce had a call made to Domino's cell phone. The operative he chose to dial the number spoke only one word when the phone was answered—Domino—then disconnected. Domino's callback would come to his secure line.

Things were heating up. He knew he'd likely be spending a lot of sleepless nights soon.

CHAPTER SIXTEEN

Domino's cell phone vibrated against her hip while they were still a few miles from Hayley's apartment. "Sorry, I have a voicemail." She flipped it open, listened, then returned it to her pocket. She'd have to find a way to call Pierce back without Hayley overhearing.

"I have to make a quick stop at this gas station, hope you don't mind." She turned toward Hayley as she unbuckled her seat belt. "Can I get you anything?"

Hayley slowly shook her head and gave her a half smile that revealed only a hint of her dimples. "Just your rapid return." Her attention was focused primarily on Domino, and she had the same sort of smoldering sensuality about her Domino had found so compelling back at the theater. But Hayley seemed to be aware of danger nearby too. Every now and then, she would follow some bit of movement in her environment. She looked like a rabbit, ready to bolt.

Domino found a quiet corner inside the station and called Pierce. He briefed her on Manny Vasquez's death, and her already heightened sense of danger surrounding Hayley shot into overdrive. Had her mysterious benefactor turned lethal? That didn't make sense. If he wanted to bring down the Organization, why silence someone who might help Hayley do so? She wondered again what the ex-cop had told her the night he died and what "promising" stuff he had that Hayley was so anxious to see.

His death explained Hayley's unexpectedly early arrival on the scene while she had been searching Vasquez's apartment. Hayley had somehow known he was dead and had decided to get the note and erase her message from his machine, to make sure police didn't connect her to him. Had she found what Vasquez planned to show her? She had remained inside a good five minutes, which would have given her enough time.

Domino had to find out what Hayley knew and what evidence she had, one way or another, because apparently the only other person who might have been able to tell her anything was dead. But the idea of sleeping with Hayley merely to get information increasingly bothered her, and the prospect of silencing her once they got what they needed bothered her even more.

As each day passed, she became more convinced that Hayley was only a pawn, swept up in someone's effort to bring down the EOO.

She returned to the car and slipped into the driver's seat. Hayley smiled at her so enticingly, and her skirt length left so little to the imagination, Domino had to grip the steering wheel hard to keep her hands from exploring the warm softness so invitingly within reach.

And Hayley was clearly not going to make it easy on her. She apparently didn't believe restraint had much merit, because as soon as Domino started the car, Hayley touched her softly muscled thigh and began to stroke it lightly but purposefully.

The slow, old-fashioned approach wasn't going to work much longer.

❖

"Run that by me again, Jack?" Terrence hated to hear about snags in his plans. The political power he had amassed guaranteed he rarely heard any kind of pessimism these days, at least directly. Problems or obstructions were quietly taken care of without his intervention, or his aides presented the unwelcome news with enough positive spin to mitigate the sting. But this particular matter was requiring a lot of his personal attention. Way too much.

"The dick was made," Jack said. "Your reporter was out with some jealous girlfriend who thought our tail was leering at them or something."

"Jealous girlfriend?" Hayley Ward was a damn attractive young redhead. That, combined with her clear ambition and drive, had made her stand out when she'd interviewed him for some college newspaper. He pictured her naked, writhing beneath some equally attractive woman, and the image almost made him smile. Almost. But this dalliance was keeping her from the task he'd assigned her.

"Yeah, we checked the other woman out," Jack continued. "An art restorer from Washington. Guy we hired said she was strong as hell. Subdued him with stuff she claimed she learned in a self-defense class, but he was skeptical. Claims she went all GI Jane on his ass."

"All right, Jack. Keep an eye on our Miss Ward." He disconnected.

❖

"Coffee or a nightcap?" Hayley inquired once they were back in her apartment, Luka seated on the couch watching her, Hayley leaning against the kitchen doorway, arms folded. They stared at each other a long time, the question hanging in the air.

Flirting with women—and men, in the line of duty—had become a practiced skill Hayley rarely gave a second thought. Her looks and practiced way of putting people at ease had always made it relatively simple for her to get the story she needed, or the body she wanted into bed. But something about Luka made her feel…nervous, almost giddy nervous…in a way she hadn't felt since she was in her teens.

So far, Luka struck her as someone very different from any woman she'd ever met. How was it possible someone so intelligent and attractive had never had a serious relationship? What was it she'd said? *I think you're the first woman I've ever felt compelled to take it slow with, to want to see beyond one evening.*

Some reporter she was. Time and again, Luka had managed to deflect any personal questions. After a handful of dates, she knew virtually nothing about Luka except she had grown up in foster care.

And she carried herself in an unusual way, as though extraordinarily self-confident. Luka also seemed to be more aware of her environment than anyone she'd ever met. She always appeared, even when relaxed and reclining, to be…*poised.* For what, exactly, Hayley wasn't sure. Just *ready*, somehow, for something to happen at any moment.

But though her eyes seemed to be everywhere, taking everything in, when they got in close proximity, and only then, Luka seemed to find it hard to maintain direct eye contact with her.

And Luka seemed to be guarded not only in her personal revelations, but also in her expressions. Very well practiced in not letting anything that was happening within, whether emotional or intellectual, show on her face. Her eyes were often blank, and Hayley was a bit frustrated by her inability to tell what Luka was thinking. Someone else might not notice these things, but her job had taught her to read between the lines, to know when whoever she was interviewing was saying one thing but feeling another. Still, her failure at being able to read Luka hadn't stopped a real spark of attraction from developing.

Though Luka was still a virtual stranger, for some unknown reason, being around her made Hayley feel safe. She had an aura of rock-solid reliability, was the type to be calm in a crisis. Those were immensely appealing qualities, as were her humor and charm.

And she certainly could wear anything and make it look sexy. Hayley practically licked her lips as she admired Luka. Her low-cut jeans hugged her body, as did her tailored long-sleeve shirt, a deep eggplant purple. Her black leather boots were well worn but polished, as was her belt. Luka wore no jewelry or perfume. And she had no piercings or tattoos, not even pierced ears.

But she needed none of that. Luka was beautiful from any and every angle just as she was—the kind of woman who looked stunning when she rolled out of bed in the morning.

Part of Hayley was ready to pounce, remembering the way Luka's mouth on her neck had excited her. That part was ripe for some hot and heavy, sweaty and nonstop sex.

But the other part was quite enjoying the anticipation, this *eventually* taking-it-slow thing. While she was eager to feel their bodies move together, she was also interested in getting to know the woman beneath the unreadable façade and feeling the chemistry build between them. *Jesus, those kisses.*

"Just water, please." Domino's insides were twisted. Her body wanted Hayley. Here before her was a beautiful, sexy woman, one who appealed to her more than any she could remember. All night she had been simmering with arousal. It didn't matter that Pierce was listening. It didn't even matter right then that it would be a lie. She tried to tell herself it was part of the job—she had fucked for work before and that's all it was now. She was so excited the pain in her groin was a dull, steady throb that ached to be relieved.

And the way Hayley was looking at her nearly broke her. All that kept her from acting on her arousal was her ignorance of how Hayley might react if she did. If Hayley ended their affair as soon as they slept together, she would fail in her mission. Pierce would send someone else after Hayley to find out what she knew, and probably in much less pleasant ways.

Hayley removed her heels, one at a time, resting one hand against the door frame as she did. Domino thought her extremely provocative. "Why don't you take your shoes off and kick back on the couch. I'll be right over to join you," she said, before she disappeared into the kitchen.

"You seemed very excited on the phone about your story," Domino called. "I guess the lead worked out."

Hayley reappeared with a glass of water in one hand and an amber liquid in ice in the other. Domino could see the change in her face at the reference to Vasquez. She handed the water to her and set the other down, then walked over to stand before the window, looking out.

"Are you all right?" Domino asked.

"I'm not sure. The story…my lead was an ex-cop," she replied. "A good source. I had only started, really, getting information from him when I met with him the other night, but before I had a chance to see him again, he was killed in a car accident."

"I'm sorry to hear that. You seem upset about it. Did you know him well?"

"No. But he seemed like a nice guy. What's bothering me is I'm not sure his death was an accident." Hayley drew the curtains shut and went to sit near her on the couch.

"Sounds hectic. What makes you think it was deliberate?"

Hayley pursed her lips. "Well, this story, is…how can I put it? Potentially a huge, explosive kind of story that could have serious repercussions for powerful people. And I believe the criminal types involved got wind we were talking about it and silenced him." When Hayley took a sip of her drink, her hand trembled.

"Does that mean you're in danger? Have you talked to the police?" Domino asked, as the siren of a police car in the distance grew louder. Hayley hurried to the window and looked out anxiously as the siren reached its peak then began to die away.

"I can't go to the police with this because…it's just too complicated. And I don't know for sure if I'm in danger, but I guess I could be," she said, returning to the couch. "He told me to be careful. And…and I had a kind of fright about it earlier. Nothing real serious," she lied, then took a healthy swig of her drink and gave Domino a forced half smile. "You helped take my mind off it for a while tonight, but I'm still a bit jumpy. It's hard to get it completely out of my mind."

"What kind of fright?"

Hayley leaned her head back and closed her eyes. "I don't want to discuss it any more, Luka. It…it was a pretty terrifying experience and it's still fresh. If I think about it too much I'll never be able to get to sleep."

"I'll let it go for now but I'm here to listen if you need that. Sometimes it helps. And if you decide to go to the police, I'd be more than happy to go with you." She rubbed the back of Hayley's neck, and Hayley sighed, relaxing into the caress.

"You know what would help?" she asked some time later, without opening her eyes. Domino thought she had fallen asleep.

"Name it."

"Could you spend the night with me?" She roused herself to look over with half-lidded eyes. "I could use the company right about now. I don't think I'm up to being alone tonight. I know you don't want to rush things, and I promise to behave. I'll even let you have the bed to yourself, if that's what you want."

Despite her light tone, Domino could sense, almost smell Hayley's fear, a skill she was very practiced at. Usually she welcomed the knowledge her targets were afraid. But that was certainly not the case now. She knew Hayley was remembering being pinned to Vasquez's bed, a gun to her back. "Of course I'll stay with you. I hate to see you this worried."

"I'm not worried, just…jumpy," Hayley said. "I think your presence will help me relax. It's soothing to be with you. You make me feel safe—you always have."

The irony wasn't lost on Domino. "Why don't you get me a pillow and blanket," she replied, "because I insist on taking the couch, and don't bother with arguments. Then get yourself into bed. It's getting late, and I know you have to work tomorrow."

"But I really—"

"Couch or nothing," she insisted.

Hayley smiled at her, and Domino saw relief replace some of the anxiety in her eyes. "Be right back."

CHAPTER SEVENTEEN

Luka's solid presence in her apartment helped Hayley relax, and she actually dozed for a while. But her sleep was restless, and at two a.m., she was wide awake and thinking about the nearest and best distraction from her worries—the sexy woman asleep in the next room. The memory of how Luka's mouth had felt on her neck at the theater warmed her from within.

Suddenly, she heard talking...no, not talking...Luka was shouting something, but she couldn't make out what it was. She leapt to her feet and hurried into the living room.

Luka was sprawled on the couch, caught in a nightmare. Her rantings were indistinguishable, but she was clearly upset. As Hayley approached to wake her, she noticed Luka was still fully dressed—even down to the boots on her feet. She had eschewed the offered sheets, pillow, and blanket, which were folded in a neat pile on the coffee table.

Who sleeps with their boots on? Why couldn't Luka relax entirely? Was it customary, or was she different under a stranger's roof, with the threat of danger near?

Stooping to sit on the edge of the couch, she intended to wake Luka, but the instant her body settled onto the cushion beside Luka, she came awake—wide, *wide* awake. An instant later Hayley was suddenly on her feet again, propelled there by Luka's blur of motion and her elbow suspended in mid-air—seemingly forever, though actually only a second—hanging there half an inch from Hayley's throat.

Hayley didn't have time to feel frightened. But then she slowly began to wonder what sort of secrets Luka was hiding behind her guarded expressions, lightning reflexes, and ability to skillfully avoid personal questions.

Domino stood in the dark, her eyes adjusting and her mind still fuzzy, panting because of what she had almost done. "Damn it, Hayley.

I almost k…hurt you," she said shakily, as she slumped onto the couch. She tried to calm her pounding heart.

"That was unbelievable." Hayley shook her head. "I've never seen anybody wake up that fast. Or react and move so fast, like a soldier in a foxhole. God, Luka! Don't you ever unwind? What *is* it with you?"

"I guess our earlier conversation got to me," she replied vaguely, looking up at Hayley. It was the best she could do. Then, in the scant moonlight from the window, she realized Hayley was wearing only skimpy briefs and a short tank top that hugged her breasts. The view did nothing to help calm her racing pulse.

In the long silence that followed, she could hear Hayley's loud, accelerated breathing and see the rapid rise and fall of her chest, and she knew Hayley could see hers. They couldn't hide their acute mutual arousal.

Somehow she was on her feet and Hayley was in her arms.

Her hands tightened around Hayley's waist as Hayley's entwined her hair. As their bodies pressed together, she found Hayley's neck, the skin soft and warm, and at the base of her throat, her pulse was pounding so fast Domino could feel it beneath her mouth.

Her mouth trailed up and along Hayley's dimpled cheek toward those wonderful lips, and when Hayley groaned, the urge to kiss her tightened into a fist in her belly.

The kiss began as a wisp of an idea, a glancing whisper of lips, the final delicious delay of anticipation. Then, when they met again, it was still the lightest, sweetest kiss she had ever experienced. Hayley's full lips were exquisitely soft and her tongue maddeningly light as it teased her own lips with slow, light caresses.

The fist inside coiled tighter, and the rising passion engulfed her. She deepened the kiss, unleashed some of the coil, her mouth claiming Hayley's with a sudden flare of heat. Hayley kissed her back with equal ardor, their tongues stroking deep, making clear the mutual depth of their attraction.

She lost herself in the kiss for several minutes, the mission forgotten.

Hayley's body began to move against hers, and she was powerless to resist. She thrust a muscled thigh between Hayley's legs and felt her answering moan of pleasure as a vibration in her mouth. The rocking of their bodies together increased in intensity and pressure, and Hayley's nails raked the length of her back, descending rapidly to urge their pelvises tighter together.

Her resistance evaporated as Hayley began to roughly massage her ass—she'd always been particularly sensitive there, and the sensation sent her arousal into overdrive. She got wetter as she pressed her thigh more firmly against Hayley's center.

Hayley took her tongue into her mouth and sucked hard, and her clit responded—rock hard in an instant and ready to blow. *Christ.* She slipped her hands beneath Hayley's tank top, reveling in the softness of her skin. Hayley moaned into her mouth, and the encouragement was too much. She stripped off the tank top and simply stood there, mesmerized by the sight of those wonderful breasts and erect nipples.

"I need you to touch me, Luka," Hayley whispered, as she took Domino's hand and placed it against her breast.

Beyond thought, she explored Hayley's breasts with both hands, caressing, dancing lightly over the nipples and delighting in Hayley's answering moans and sighs. Then she took one of those incredible nipples into her mouth.

Hayley pushed against her and raked her nails down her back again, beneath her shirt. She kissed her way up Hayley's body and back to her mouth, and they clung to each other, furious with need.

Hayley pulled away to unbutton her shirt, quick and urgent, continuing to the button of her pants. Then the zipper was down, and Hayley was inside her jeans, cupping her over her thong, and she was so ready she thought she might come instantly.

"You're driving me crazy," she told Hayley, before roughly sucking the skin at the base of her neck, bruising her.

"I want you so much." Hayley's voice was breathy, anxious. "I know you want to take this slow, but this isn't just about sex, you know."

The words cut through the fog of arousal that had enveloped her. No, it wasn't all about sex. Hayley had feelings for her, and she had feelings for Hayley. Amazingly, for her, it wasn't about the job. How had this happened? She was angry she'd let herself fall, and feel, and forget that she was supposed to remain detached. Guilt poured through her and over her, crushing desire. She couldn't do this to Hayley. Or herself.

She pushed Hayley away, almost roughly. "We have to stop."

Hayley fought the urge to slap Luka silly. *Fucking tease is what you are.* But she could see how Luka was struggling. She clearly wanted this as much as Hayley did, but something wouldn't let her, and the conflict was eating her up inside. It was the first time she could read something in Luka's expression, and she almost hurt for her, for the pain there. "Okay. Although it's everything but okay," she said, her throat tight with frustration. "I only came in to ask if you were comfortable. Good night, Luka."

Hayley remained where she was for a few more seconds, hoping something would break Luka's inertia and allow her to give in to what was between them. But when Luka didn't move, she strode into the bedroom and shut the door, wishing like hell she knew what haunted Luka in her sleep and kept her from acting on her desires.

It had been more years than she could remember since she had cared so much what made someone tick.

Domino remained rooted where she was long after Hayley had closed the door between them. Her body was on fire and she couldn't focus. She'd been trained to operate according to her mind, never her heart, and she had never had a problem doing so. Sex for her was always without emotion. Either a quick and anonymous encounter in some dark place to satisfy a need, or part of a job, as this was supposed to be.

She felt totally inadequate, ill-equipped to deal with this overwhelming guilt and her less-than-honorable intentions toward such a woman. She had no right to take, when she had nothing to give.

Standing before the window, she stared out into the night. Her need to crawl in bed with Hayley was strong, and she wondered whether she could escape her nightmares there.

She watched as the sun came up and cast a warm glow on the building across the street, and gradually she began to realize how difficult it would be on the outside again looking in, watching Hayley on this very spot. How would she cope with constantly seeing what she could never have and, even worse, with what she had never even known she needed?

CHAPTER EIGHTEEN

Friday

Hayley roused herself with difficulty after hitting the snooze button on her alarm for the fourth time, coming fully awake only when she remembered the feel of Luka's body, and mouth, the night before. She couldn't have stopped what was happening between them, but Luka apparently had reason to pull away. What could it be? The question had kept her tossing and turning half the night, and she hoped today Luka might be more ready to volunteer what was holding her back.

She threw on a robe and went into the living room, only to find it vacant, the pillow and blankets she'd left for Luka still in a neat pile, unused. On top of them was a note.

Sorry about last night. Had an early appointment and didn't want to wake you. I'll call you later.
Luka

Hayley crumpled it and tossed it into a wastebasket en route to the shower. Talk about poor timing. Here she was, on the precipice of what could be the biggest story of her life, when she should totally focus on the job, and what was keeping her up at night was some mysterious near-stranger whose kisses left her breathless.

As she showered and dressed for work, she forced herself to replay her conversations with Manny Vasquez, to see whether she might have missed anything that could help in her search for more information about the EOO.

All she had to go on was the name Timmy Koster—the tape specialist whose business card she'd glimpsed in his apartment, and she wasn't optimistic that would lead anywhere. She'd looked at the

Guerrero tape so many times she was convinced there were few clues there. The assassin's face was too well obscured throughout, and she didn't think any technical enhancement could do much to change that.

Still, it was all she had for now, so during her break at the office she searched online phone databases, focusing on the New York area. She discovered nothing relevant in the business directories, but she came up with five possibilities in the white pages: two Timothy Kosters and three T. Kosters. She found the one she was looking for on the third call.

"Hello, my name is Hayley Ward and I'm trying to track down a Timmy Koster who's a videotape specialist. Do I have the right number?"

"Who did you say you were?" the man on the other end replied.

"Hayley Ward, Mr. Koster. Manny Vasquez gave me your name." *Or he was about to. Before he was killed.*

A few seconds of silence elapsed before the man spoke again. "Manny, eh? Are you a cop?"

"No, I'm a reporter. Following up on a case similar to one you helped him with." She glanced around to make sure no one could overhear her. "I have a black-and-white security tape Manny said you might be able to enhance." She realized she would be taking a hell of a risk letting this man see the video. The content was self-evident, and Koster was known to work with law enforcement. Who was to say he wouldn't immediately turn her over to the authorities? She had to trust that if Manny had suggested using him, he would be discreet.

"I'd have to see it first to tell you if I can give you anything. What's on the tape? And when do you need it?"

"The tape shows a crime in progress," she replied vaguely. "And I need it as soon as possible."

"I can work on it tonight, but a rush job isn't cheap. I get one-fifty an hour to enhance video. Two hundred if you want the audio done too."

"You can enhance audio, too?" She pictured the inaudible exchange between the assassin and her dying co-conspirator. "Amplify it enough to hear a whispered conversation, maybe?"

"Entirely possible, but like I said, I can't promise anything before I see the tape."

Hayley wasn't looking forward to driving to New York and back again. And the cost of gas plus Koster's fee added up to a nice chunk of change if it yielded nothing of value. But possibly something could come of it. She wished her mysterious benefactor would send her another clue or two. She was rapidly approaching a dead end. "Okay, Mr. Koster, you've got a deal. I can drive up after work and be there any time after eight, if that's all right. Where would you like me to meet you, and when?"

After they'd made arrangements, she dialed her brother's cell phone. "Hey, Ted. I need the envelope I asked you to put in your safe. Any way you can drop it by my office?" Since the intruder in Manny's apartment had taken her DVD copy of the tape, she needed to make another to give to Koster. That was one benefit of working in a newsroom. Though the *Dispatch* was a print entity, it was well equipped with the latest audio/video equipment.

Koster estimated it would take him an hour or so to enhance the tape. That would give her enough time to run by Manny's apartment again and maybe find out whether the police or relatives had been by to go through his belongings. The fact she hadn't found the Frankie the Fox interview tape he'd promised her, or his "short list" of suspects, haunted her. So did the trauma of her encounter with the intruder, but she told herself surely no one would be in the apartment this long after Manny's death.

I should have stayed and looked around some more. She was fairly certain she'd interrupted the intruder, since she'd gotten to the file in Manny's bedroom first. And it would have been risky for her assailant to return to search further, not knowing whether Hayley might contact the police.

The evidence could still be there. Fear and shock had driven her from the apartment, but with time, that fear had begun to dissipate, replaced by curiosity. Yes, it might be worth another visit. She was certain the landlady would let her in again.

❖

Domino flipped the bone absently between her fingers as she waited, enjoying the ivory's smoothness against her skin. She relied on her old friend whenever she had a problem to resolve or job scenario to figure out.

I can't do this any more. She'd come too close to sleeping with Hayley. Pierce would have to assign someone else. Being close to Hayley was driving her crazy, her instinct to protect her completely at odds with her assignment. Usually she had no problem carrying out her orders, because her targets more than deserved whatever justice the EOO or she personally might require. But Hayley certainly did not. Each day, Domino felt more unable to objectify her.

She knew, however, that even if she were able to convince Pierce to take her off the case, Hayley would be in even more danger. She had to stay with her and pray to hell she could keep her from getting hurt.

As much as she would like for them to have something together, as much as Hayley had touched her as no woman had before, Domino knew they could never have a future. Their entire relationship was built on a lie, and Hayley would never want to be close if she knew the truth, only more determined to expose her and the Organization.

Domino had been so many people in her life—from cleaning lady to CEO, from waitress to woman of influence—that she scarcely knew who the real person was beneath the chameleon exterior the EOO had created. Her existence resembled a life sentence, one from which she had no appeal and no escape. She had long ago accepted her fate, but Hayley made her question everything.

Maybe she couldn't do much about her own future, but she would do her damndest to make sure Hayley had one.

She slipped the bone in her trousers pocket when Hayley unexpectedly emerged from the side door of the *Dispatch* building, more than a half hour before she was scheduled to get off work. Her sense of alarm increased when Hayley detoured from her usual route home to the highway for New York instead. But Domino did not immediately call it in to Pierce, as was expected.

Instead, she followed at a discreet distance, hoping Hayley wasn't pursuing something that would make her conscience battle even more.

❖

When she got to New York, Hayley lingered at Timmy Koster's long enough to ascertain Manny had planned to recommend him because he was used to keeping secrets. Once she was relatively certain that the police would not be waiting for her upon her return, she handed him the DVD and headed to Manny's apartment building. She hoped his senile landlady would remember her this time around.

The landlady cracked her door but kept the chain on. She was wearing faded pink pajamas beneath a red robe and matching slippers. Behind her, the television loudly blared a repeat of *The Golden Girls.*

"Hi there. Edna, right? Sorry to be stopping by so late." She tried to defuse the woman's suspicious expression with her best hundred-megawatt smile, but she knew her charms had infinitely more predictable effect on men. "Do you remember me? Manny Vasquez's niece?"

Recognition dawned on the woman's face, and her frown faded. "Oh, yes. I remember you. If you've come to get his things, I need the back rent he owed before I can give 'em to you."

Fat chance of that happening. "I won't have time to do that tonight, but I did stop by to see how much he owed," she lied. "I'm trying to get his affairs in order."

"He gave me a one-month deposit in advance," the landlady said, removing the chain from her door. "And I need his things out of there so I can rent the place, so I'll waive the last couple of weeks. You can have everything for the seven-fifty he owed for last month."

"That sounds fair," she answered, but she didn't intend to drain her bank account. She thought fast. "Can you let me into his apartment again? I have power of attorney to settle his accounts, but I need to find his checkbook and insurance papers."

"I can do that." Edna fished in her robe for a bulky ring of keys. "Oh, and you need to clean out the stuff he kept in storage, too. There isn't much—just a couple of boxes."

Hayley was instantly alert. Sounded exactly like the sort of place a paranoid guy like Manny might want to keep something he didn't want anyone to readily locate. "Storage?"

"Yes, dear, everybody's got a secure space in the basement. Most of the tenants jam theirs full of all sorts of shit, but Manny's was always nearly empty." She picked at a piece of lettuce embedded between her teeth. "Funny, though, he wouldn't give the space to anybody else. And I seen him go down there a lot to check on those boxes, like he was afraid someone would take 'em or something. Why he didn't keep 'em in his apartment, with all those damn locks of his, is beyond me."

Hayley fished in her wallet for a twenty-dollar bill. "Do you mind if I take that stuff with me now?" She offered the money to Edna. "I bet one of the boxes has the insurance papers I'm looking for."

The landlady took the bill. "Fine by me, if it'll get things settled quicker." She led Hayley down a steep stairwell to a basement that ran the length of the building. Fenced-in cubicles held lawn furniture and ski equipment, golf clubs and other overflow possessions. As Edna had said, Manny's held only two medium-sized cardboard boxes, both taped shut.

Ignoring a tug from her conscience, Hayley stripped the tape off the first box and looked inside. It was full of old case files. Most were duplicates, she realized, since the labels were in Manny's handwriting and the contents were mostly Xeroxed copies of original police documents. But some looked like originals.

The second box held videotapes, cassettes, and personal items—letters, police cap, passport. It would take some time to go through it all, but a shiver of anticipation tore through her at the prospect.

She carried the boxes out to the Mustang and locked them in the trunk before she headed back to Koster's to see what he'd come up with.

❖

Domino considered breaking into the Mustang to see what was in the boxes Hayley had retrieved from Manuel Vasquez's building, but decided the risk was too high. While Manny had lived in a run-down apartment complex, with a dark parking lot and tenants who lived in fear behind shuttered windows and double-locked doors, Hayley's other New York stop was a decidedly more upscale and secure apartment "community," which featured surveillance cameras, outdoor lighting, and a roving security guard in a golf cart. Tenants at this complex felt safe enough for barbecues on the patio and long walks on the grounds with their dogs, so the place was busy with people during the entire half hour Hayley spent inside.

But the biggest risk was the blue Chevy Malibu that had been following Hayley since they left Baltimore.

It was reasonable to surmise it was another private detective or similar flunky, hired by the mysterious "Joe Polizo" to watch Hayley.

And if Domino's encounter with the last one in the movie theater had been any indication, this one probably wouldn't know much about the guy who'd hired him, either.

Bad enough she'd had to demonstrate some of her abilities on the other private detective. It wouldn't do to have this one, or another flunky, report back that Hayley's new girlfriend was now following her and taking items from her car. No, she'd have to wait for a better opportunity once they got back to Baltimore.

Domino was well aware she had veered from EOO protocol in not reporting in as soon as Hayley had taken the expressway to New York. And she'd compounded that digression by not calling Pierce with the news Hayley had returned to Manny's apartment for something and that she was being followed yet again. But she knew to update the Organization with this evening's activities would only make Hayley seem even more of a risk. Pierce might order her silenced immediately. And she couldn't have that.

She wasn't sure when her loyalty had started to turn. But she was now putting Hayley's safety ahead of her commitment to the Organization. During her hours standing at the window in Hayley's apartment the night before, she'd accepted that she was incapable of seeing her harmed and would do whatever she could to protect her.

Domino had no idea what Hayley was doing here or who she was seeing. The surveillance team monitoring Hayley's home phone that day hadn't sent her a report today, so evidently Hayley hadn't discussed her plans for this evening, and Pierce didn't know about them. And Domino couldn't easily find out which of the dozens of tenants Hayley was visiting, since all the apartment entrances were located off interior hallways.

So she was forced to wait and wonder. But she caught sight of Hayley's face in her binoculars as she exited the building and passed near one of the bright parking lot lights, and her heart sank. Hayley looked happy. Excited. This couldn't be good.

❖

Hayley drove back to Baltimore in a much more ebullient mood than she'd experienced on the trip up. She'd been worried about Koster's discretion and hadn't expected him to find anything significant. But he'd proved reliable and obviously very good at what he did.

He'd been able to enlarge and enhance the image of the assassin frame by frame, until he found something on her chest, the left side, just above her low-cut dress—a tattoo or birthmark, he thought, that she'd tried to conceal with makeup, not entirely successfully.

And the enhancement of the audio had been productive as well. She'd been able to listen in on the conversation between the assassin and her accomplice, and that had given her a name—Domino.

It was something. And the impromptu trip to Manny's apartment had also yielded unexpected results. She was so anxious to delve into the contents of the boxes in her trunk, she had trouble not speeding all the way home.

The digital clock on her dashboard read ten thirty. Her mind drifted to Luka, as it did with ever-increasing frequency. The note she'd left promised she would call "later," but there had been no word from her, unless a message was waiting on her answering machine at home. It was probably just as well, she told herself, since she'd be wrapped up in going through Manny's case files for the foreseeable future.

Still, it was the first time in years any woman had made her think about and want anything beyond the next big story. The memory of their fevered kisses the previous night made her ache for more. And she couldn't stop wondering what made Luka struggle so with what they both so obviously wanted.

❖

Senator Terrence Burrows was already in a foul mood when the call came. He'd been on a winning streak for the first ninety minutes of the evening's high-stakes poker game, but he hadn't had a decent hand since and was down nearly six thousand dollars.

When his cell phone rang, he was inclined to ignore it, then thought perhaps a few minutes away from the table might do something to shake his turn of bad luck. He stepped outside onto the terrace for privacy and a cigar.

Tonight's game was in a private home in a posh section of DC, and though it had all the usual expected accoutrements for its wealthy and powerful players—the finest liquors and upscale call girls—the host had asked that pipes and cigars be taken outside.

"Yes, Jack," he answered, after taking a long pull off one of the spicy Cuban Robustos he'd gotten from his favorite lobbyist earlier in the week.

"Your girl has been back to New York tonight," Jack reported. "Took a couple of boxes out of the ex-cop's place and stopped at another apartment building there for about a half hour."

Terrence's blood pressure escalated and he squeezed his cigar so tight it almost snapped in two. "What else do we know?"

"She talked to an old woman at the cop's place—probably the manager. Couldn't tell who she was seeing at the other," Jack relayed. "And our guy was sure that someone else was following her. Too dark to make out anything about the driver, or get the plate, without getting made."

This time the cigar did break in half, and Terrence dropped it at his feet. He started to pace and curse at himself for having screwed up. The journalist had managed to find one of the few people in the world who might have been able to tie him to those bastards. But was she smart enough to have figured out where he kept the tapes and files he had taken? He continued to pace and curse while he grabbed a fresh cigar from his pocket.

He had instructed Jack to make sure the men hired to take care of Vasquez also searched his apartment for audiotapes and case files related to the Castellano assassination, but neither turned up in a thorough search of the place—which was underway even before the ex-cop was officially pronounced dead in the ambulance. *What was she taking out of there, then? Could those fuckers have missed it?*

Also very worrisome was the confirmation that someone else was keeping tabs on Hayley. He was certain it was the Organization, which could only mean she was getting close to something.

This whole affair had been a stupid gamble. It was looking more and more like he should bag the bad idea. Cut his losses and try some other way to get the EOO off his back.

CHAPTER NINETEEN

It was a warm night, so Hayley changed into briefs and a cropped T-shirt and made herself an ice-cold martini as soon as she got back to her apartment. She jammed the enhanced DVD Koster had made for her into her player to study it again and set the boxes she'd taken from Manny's storage space on the coffee table. But before she started what was certain to be a long night's work, she carried her martini to the open window to let the evening breeze blow the perspiration from her heated body. The scent of hyacinth was in the air. As she stood there, looking out, it started to rain.

She closed her eyes and stretched, arching her back, and allowed herself to remember the evening before, how Luka's kisses had inflamed and aroused her. The woman certainly had wonderful lips. Soft, yielding. But why hadn't she called? Tamping down her disappointment, Hayley settled onto the couch with her martini and reached for her remote.

Who are you, Domino? She watched the blond assassin coolly dispatch her second shot into Guerrero's head, then share a tender exchange with her fallen accomplice. How could an organization turn a seemingly compassionate young woman into a cold-blooded killer?

As a reporter, she had certainly seen numerous accounts of females being used as purveyors of violence and death. But most were women who were also victims—coerced in the name of religious or nationalistic fervor into sacrificing themselves in a suicide bombing.

That was certainly not the case this time.

She paused the DVD when it reached the part where Koster had been able to isolate and enlarge the woman's image to faintly show the ill-concealed tattoo, or birthmark, or whatever it was, above her left breast. Her only distinguishing characteristic, and it wasn't much to go on.

Hayley took a long swig of her martini and opened the first of Manny's boxes. She carefully removed his personal items and set them aside. What remained was a handful of videotapes and at least a dozen audiotapes. Her heart started beating faster when she found the cassette labeled "Frankie the Fox, Part 1." Sorting through the others, she was relieved to find one bearing the words "Frankie the Fox, Part 2."

She stuck the first tape in a portable boom box and set it to play, then leafed through the numerous case files in the other box until she came to one labeled "Castellano, Angelo."

Manny's voice came on. It sounded somehow more professional than she remembered. Sharper. More alert. Without the slight slur and frequent pauses his drinking had caused.

The first part of the tape was pure police procedural, with Manny stating for the record the time, date, and place of the interview, and eliciting the witness's name. Next came a recitation of Frankie's duties within the Castellano family. As she listened, she began to go through the case file.

What stood out was a plain piece of yellow notebook paper—a handwritten list of names and phone numbers—about a dozen in all. Beside a few were cryptic notations in Manny's nearly illegible scrawl. She recognized only two of the names. One was the CEO of a Fortune 500 company based in New York, and the other owned a major-league baseball team. Manny's description of his "short list of suspects" sprang to mind. *Men with influence. All with one thing in common. Gambling.*

But she knew it might not be that at all. It could as easily be a list of Manny's sources. All cops had them, just like reporters. Powerful contacts used for information or favors. Or the list might be something else entirely.

She folded the paper and stuck it in her purse. As soon as she got to work in the morning, she'd start making phone calls.

❖

When Domino first reached the surveillance apartment, she turned up the speakers transmitting audio from the bugs in Hayley's apartment. She kept the room dark. Then she picked up the high-powered digital zoom and focused on Hayley's living-room window, only to get a magnified image of Hayley's ass, clad in skin-tight, pink satin briefs, as she bent over one of the boxes she'd taken from Manny's apartment. The image was so unexpected Domino dropped the device, fumbling for it as it clattered noisily to the floor. "Damn!"

By the time she brought it to her eyes again, Hayley had turned around and was headed to the window with a martini glass in her hand, and now all she could focus on was the faded slogan emblazoned across Hayley's T-shirt, which was so damn tight it showed every inch of those beautiful breasts. *Newspaper Reporters Do It Daily,* it said, and Domino felt a warm rush of arousal in her groin.

The Organization had certainly prepared her for a multitude of situations, but never quite like this. She knew she should have been looking for clues to the contents of the boxes, should be formulating some plan to protect Hayley and keep her from getting in any deeper.

But watching her there at the window, with a sexy half smile on her face as she stretched, made Domino's stomach twist in the most exquisite torture. All she wanted was to hold her. Kiss her. Touch her everywhere, in every way. She wanted her so much her entire body hurt.

It started to rain, light enough that it didn't obscure her view, but it apparently chased Hayley back inside, for she abandoned the window and sat on the couch. She reached for a remote, then became engrossed in her television, but no audio was coming from the transmitters in her apartment except the occasional clink of her glass on the coffee table or other incidental noises.

After a few minutes, Hayley opened one of the boxes from Manuel Vasquez's apartment and pulled out a number of video and audiotapes. Domino stiffened and gripped the scope tighter.

Hayley picked up a tape and disappeared briefly.

About the time she reappeared, to sit back on the couch, a man's voice—Hispanic—came over her speakers.

From the initial minutes of the recording, Domino ascertained it was Vasquez, interviewing a jailhouse witness named Frankie the Fox about the murder of Angelo Castellano. It meant nothing to her, and she almost relaxed.

But twenty minutes or so into the tape, all of that changed.

"Let's get to the hit," Vasquez said. "How far away were you standing when the shooting started?"

"When he fired the first time, I was probably thirty yards from them," Frankie replied. "Angie was just going down."

"Did you get a good look at the shooter?"

"No, man. I wasn't really watching him, you know? It all happened too fast. I mean, it took me a second or two to even realize what was happening, and by then, he was just…gone. Like a ghost or something. I couldn't move, and I was looking at Angie—at his *head*. Shit, man. It was all over the wall." Frankie continued after several seconds. "Besides, it doesn't mean crap if I did or not 'cause they're always masquerading as someone else. But I can tell you straight off the bat he was EOO."

"How are you so sure?" Vasquez asked.

"The way he did the job. I know their moves and shit. I mean, fuck—I was one of 'em for a while. The way he pulled it off was standard EOO procedure. All cool and calm, like it was any day's work. No distractions or hesitations. He was there with a purpose, and once he finished the job, he casually walked away like he knew where the nearest escape route was. Know what I mean? Real organized shit. No moblike macho bullshit. Just calculated, perfection kinda thing." Domino heard a snort of bitter frustration. "I could'a been one of 'em, you know? But the fucks never gave me a chance."

"I want to hear more about this EOO. You've told me it stands for Elite Operatives Organization," Vasquez said. "Did you ever get to see the inside workings of this place?"

"You asking if I ever been there?" Frankie said. "Yeah, I was there. A couple of times."

"So you know where it is?"

"Sure as fuck I do."

What followed was only static. Domino watched through the zoom scope as Hayley ejected that tape from her player and rifled through the others on her coffee table.

The next words she heard over her speaker, Hayley's barely audible "Part two, where are you? We're just getting to the good stuff," got Domino moving. She grabbed her jacket and bolted out the door.

She had only the short distance to Hayley's to figure out what she was going to do. Detect. Identify. Resolve. How could she explain why she was showing up after midnight without any warning?

She had to stop Hayley from listening to any more. And she had to figure out a way to look at all that material herself, without Hayley knowing about it and before she had a chance to hide it somewhere. Because it sounded as though there might be something very damaging to the EOO on those tapes.

The more Hayley learned, the more determined Pierce would be to silence her. All Hayley needed to do was make one call about this, and the Organization would know from the tap on her phone what she was up to.

And Domino would have to start explaining why she hadn't been reporting in as expected all night, why she wasn't keeping to protocol.

She was one of the EOO's most resourceful operatives. A plan came to her as she knocked on Hayley's door, the one obvious solution that would satisfy everything she needed to accomplish.

CHAPTER TWENTY

L uka?" Hayley looked surprised but pleased. She hadn't bothered to throw on any additional clothes before she opened the door.

Domino couldn't help herself. She let her gaze travel up and down the length of Hayley's body, drinking in all the exposed skin. The zoom scope was good, but up close and personal was definitely better. From this distance, the rigid bumps of Hayley's nipples through the thin shirt were readily, beckoningly apparent. "I…I had to see you." It was the truth. But she felt so fucking torn about what she was about to do, she felt like she was dying inside.

"*Had* to…did you?" Hayley repeated, her smile growing as she let her in.

She took a few steps into the room and quickly assessed that Hayley had shut off the audio tape, but Manny's boxes were still on the coffee table and a handful of files lay open on one side of the couch.

And there, frozen on Hayley's wide screen plasma TV, was Domino, caught from above, in the bottom of the frame as she was about to leave the garage. The top of her head, all blond wig, her features indistinguishable from that angle. At the upper part of the picture, four men lay dead or dying.

She turned to Hayley, showing nothing of what churned inside her. Looking into Hayley's eyes, she could almost see her mind turning over questions about why she was here, why she hadn't called, what had changed since her abrupt departure that morning. And she had no adequate answers, so she did the only thing she could.

She closed the distance and pressed Hayley up against the nearest wall, finally allowing the fierce attraction that had been tugging them together to have its way. "Yes. No. Needed to," she said, her voice husky with arousal, and her heart soared at the instant dilation of Hayley's pupils as their bodies came together.

She roughly cupped Hayley's ass as Hayley's arms encircled her neck, and then they were kissing, the exchange heated and furious with need. Domino's control slipped away, and she was lost.

Hayley's hands caressed her back, nails digging in. Hayley's breath hitched in excitement when their lips parted, and their bodies started to move as one, rocking pelvis to pelvis, breast to breast. For several blissful moments, she was only Luka, her sensations unmarred by thoughts of duty or guilt.

But Hayley slowed their frenzied coupling to look in her eyes, and when she spoke, her voice had a sweet, open vulnerability that made Domino's heart clench. "I want you, Luka. I…I'm falling for you."

Domino came undone. *Don't!* she wanted to scream. Frustration and despair roiled up in her, like a sudden storm at sea, and she lashed out, her fist impacting the sheetrock wall behind Hayley's shoulder and leaving an impression.

Hayley didn't flinch, but confusion washed over her face.

"Don't say that." Domino's words came out sounding almost angry, and she averted her eyes and fought back tears, not from the pain in her hand, but from her ache of longing, brought dangerously and uncontrollably close to the surface for the first time in her life. "You can't fall for me. You can't fall for a lie."

"A lie?" Hayley gently cupped her face, ensuring she couldn't look away this time. "What's going on with you, Luka?" she asked when their eyes met. "What hurts so much?"

She couldn't answer these questions without further deceit. And she wanted no more lies between them tonight. Those already there would haunt her enough.

"No more talking, Hayley." To stem her inner tide of torment, she reached for the light switch next to Hayley's shoulder. Darkness, that's where she could see the best, focus the best, distance herself, and make whoever she was with anonymous. There she didn't have to fear what someone else might see in her eyes.

She told herself Hayley wanted only sex, and she knew how to cope with that. Hayley tried to kiss her again, and instead she lifted Hayley's T-shirt to kiss and lick her stomach, stroke her back, hips, thighs firmly and purposefully.

Pure sex wasn't the comfortable and mindless retreat from emotion she hoped it would be, that it always had been. She didn't really want this with Hayley, and Hayley didn't deserve it. But she couldn't surrender to the unfamiliar. And it was still exciting beyond belief to touch that sweet, soft skin.

Her hands left Hayley's ass and moved up to cup her supple breasts. Her heart was thudding hard in her chest. Soon she would feel the wetness she knew was there and held her breath in anticipation. Still on her knees, she started to remove Hayley's panties.

"Stop." The near-whisper didn't immediately register in Domino's haze of lust and arousal. She didn't react; her head moved lower.

"Luka, please stop." A little louder, but still gentle. More plea than command.

This time she froze.

"Not here," Hayley said in that same slow, breathy voice. "Not like this."

She rose and stood silent before Hayley, who stripped off her jacket and threw it toward the couch. Then Hayley took her hand and wordlessly led her to the bedroom.

The lighting in the cozy room was romantically subdued; two small lamps shone on nightstands cluttered with books and clippings.

Almost automatically, as they crossed the threshold, Domino switched off the light. Hayley turned it back on. "No, Luka. I want to see you. I want you to see me. I want us both to remember everything about this night." She smiled and squeezed her hand. "All good things are worth taking your time. Make every moment last and count—isn't that what you said?"

She smiled back. "I see you've been taking notes."

"Occupational hazard," Hayley replied, leading her to the bed. She pulled back the covers, then faced her.

Domino stood transfixed, uncertain and unsure. She wanted to turn the lights off again. When she didn't move, Hayley slowly stripped off her T-shirt, then stepped out of her briefs and stood before her, naked.

Domino held her breath. *Such beauty.* Sculpted by the master, perfectly proportioned, Hayley had smooth skin unmarred by blemish or birthmark, each curve and valley begging to be touched. They had been so frenzied the night before, she was happy for the chance to study Hayley's body leisurely.

Her breasts were round and high, her rosy aureoles in stark contrast to the ivory porcelain that surrounded them. Her thin waist curved nicely into full hips, and the hair at the apex of her thighs was a perfect reddish blond triangle.

Domino remained rooted, unable to meet Hayley's eyes, trying to keep from shaking. Hayley caressed the side of her face.

"Look at me."

She slowly turned until their eyes met. "Do you have any idea how much I want you?" Her voice was thick with need.

"As much as I want you," Hayley replied.

"Show me."

"I intend to." Hayley loosened her belt slowly, drawing it out provocatively and tossing it aside.

Domino reached for the buttons on her own tailored black shirt, but Hayley stopped her hands. "No. Let me. I want to enjoy every second of showing you."

Every nerve ending in her body poised in anticipation. Her heart pounded in her ears. Deafening.

Hayley took a few seconds with each button, working top to bottom, pausing as she freed each one to kiss the skin beneath. When she finished she pulled Domino's shirt from her jeans and slipped it off her shoulders, pausing when she spotted the two-inch scar above her left breast. A flicker of concern crossed her face, and her fingers trailed gently over the thin white line, then she kissed that, too, before she straightened to toss the shirt on a chair.

Then Hayley strolled around her, leaving kisses along her arms, back, shoulder blades. She unfastened her black silk bra and kissed her way around the other side, until they faced each other again and Domino was naked from the waist up.

"Beautiful," she whispered. "God, Luka. You're beautiful." She admired her breasts before trailing her fingers lightly down Domino's inner thighs as she stooped to help her out of her boots.

When she rose again, her fingers followed the same tortuous path, moving upward atop the inside seam of her jeans, but dug in more firmly this time and crossed over her sex as they inched toward the button at her fly.

The feel of Hayley's fingers on her abdomen as she unfastened the clasp and slowly unzipped her jeans made her tremble. Not from nerves, but from wanting to take control and wrap Hayley in her arms.

She didn't associate the words *slow* and *deliberate* with her past sexual experiences. But as eager as she was to touch Hayley, as hungry and heated as her body felt, she was as determined as Hayley to make it last. It wasn't only their first time together, but her first real experience with true intimacy. And probably also her last.

Hayley slid the jeans slowly down over her hips, taking her black thong with them as she slipped them off and tossed them atop the shirt.

She reached for Hayley then, and as they came together, their bodies melded along the full length in an almost liquid way, every centimeter of flesh joining. Hayley's face pressed against her throat, and she closed her eyes and arched her neck when Hayley's soft nips and kisses punctuated the wisps of warm breath against her skin.

Hayley moaned in satisfaction, a long, sustained sound from the back of her throat, and Domino experienced the vibration as an internal caress. "So good," Hayley sighed as she ran her hands over Domino's thighs and cupped her ass. The muscles there clenched when Hayley's nails raked them, urging their pelvises tighter together. "So good. God, Luka, you excite me so much. So damn much."

The jasmine of Hayley's perfume, mixed with the clean undertones of citrus from her shampoo, filled her nostrils, overloading the last of her heightened senses. All her life she had been taught to view each situation from a purely rational perspective, but now her surrender to this onslaught of sensation made her suddenly weak.

As though she could sense this—or perhaps it was because she felt the same—Hayley separated from her long enough to pull them both onto the bed, Hayley on her back, with Domino's body covering hers, and they kissed—taking their time, building their excitement with teasing strokes, deep tongue thrusts, and nips and sucks at swollen lips.

She pushed one muscled thigh firmly between Hayley's legs, and then they were moving together. Torturously slow at first, so they could appreciate each brush of breast against breast and gyration of groin against groin. But when Hayley's nails raked across her ass again and started digging half-moons into the flesh, keeping the rhythm of each thrust of her hips, she quickened the pace until the pounding of their bodies against each other matched their rapid, loud exhalations.

Hayley's wetness coated her thigh, and her clit hardened. A guttural, animal sound escaped her, and she anchored one hand around one of the brass bedposts, the other around Hayley's ass, so her frenzied pumping could benefit them both.

"Luka, you're going to make me come." Hayley's voice was strained, and the declaration produced even more slick moisture along Domino's thigh. "Inside. *Please.* I need you inside me."

Domino's clit got harder still, the sweet pain there almost unbearable.

She slipped the hand she had on Hayley's ass between their bodies as she slowed the thrust of her hips. And then she found the warm and welcoming folds of Hayley's sex. Her clit was so swollen and sensitive she cried out when Domino skimmed her thumb over it, and she was so open and wet that when Hayley's hips rose, demanding more, she easily pushed three fingers inside.

The driving rhythm of their bodies resumed, her hand matching each move, stroking Hayley deep as her thumb thrummed over her clit.

Hayley bit her shoulder as she roared to climax, tightening in spasms around her hand, and Domino's heart was thumping so hard against the walls of her chest she could have sworn Hayley could feel it too.

"Oh, yes, oh, yes, yesssss!" Hayley's hips rocked madly, rising high off the bed as she came, and then she slumped back against the pillows, clutching Domino as she fought to regain her breath.

She was on fire, more aroused than she could remember, her physical excitement enhanced by her growing feelings for Hayley and by Hayley's responsiveness to her touch.

"I want so much to make you feel what you make me feel." After Hayley whispered breathily, she tongued Domino's ear and suckled her earlobe.

And then Hayley was moving beneath her, no—*writhing* beneath her—and the pressure for release built into a hard knot at the base of her abdomen.

"Hayley...*please.*" She spoke eight languages and had used them to become so many people in so many situations, she could never remember them all. But she could find no words to tell Hayley she was ready to burst from the longing for her touch.

"Soon."

Hayley's hands moved purposefully from her ass to her waist, guiding her, urging her up until she was on her knees, straddling Hayley, looking down on those beautiful breasts, the nipples rigid as stones.

Hayley's hands roamed her body, caressing every inch of her— up her sides, then raking down her back to roughly massage her ass, then over her thighs and up, lightly skimming the flat plane of her stomach to finally find her breasts, lingering there to cup and caress, pinching her sensitive nipples lightly until she felt the sensation in her clit.

She gritted her teeth, fighting the urge to touch herself, the need to come so overwhelming her hands shook. "Hayley."

As if sensing her desperation, Hayley took her wrists and guided her hands to the cool brass bedposts. As she gripped them, Hayley's voice beckoned, "Look at me, Luka."

It was easier than she expected. She looked down into Hayley's eyes, the pupils so huge and black with arousal the irises had disappeared.

"I want to make you come so hard," Hayley said, guiding her by the waist again, pulling her forward until she was on her knees over Hayley's face.

Hayley's hands wrapped around her thighs, and she pulled Domino's clit to her mouth, teasing her with quick strokes of her tongue.

She groaned and gripped the bedposts tighter and pushed down into Hayley's mouth, but Hayley only skimmed her tongue even lighter along the length of her sex, making her harder still, but no closer to release.

The ecstasy was so excruciating that she wanted it to continue as much as she needed it to end.

Hayley worked her as she hadn't believed possible, bringing her to the precipice again and again with rapid strokes of her tongue and sucking her to the limit of her endurance, only to back off just enough to keep her there without plunging over. Soon she was dripping with sweat, every muscle tensed, every nerve ending singing out for satisfaction. She was breathing harder than she did after running a mile.

She was an inch away from begging, crying for mercy, when Hayley took her clit into her mouth and shattered her, left her weak and gasping and unable to support her own weight in the trembling aftermath of her orgasm.

She collapsed onto the bed, Hayley's body became her blanket, and they lay there, wrapped in a tangle of arms and legs, until her breathing returned to normal.

Only then did she become aware Hayley had fallen asleep.

Luka wanted to lie there forever, locked in the circle of her embrace.

But Domino had work to do.

CHAPTER TWENTY-ONE

When Domino crept back into the living room, she immediately saw her image from the assassination tape frozen on Hayley's TV screen. She played the DVD and felt a cold chill down her back when she got to the place where it had been enhanced. The area of enlargement showed a small shadow where makeup had failed to completely conceal her scar, the result of a knife thrust during a training exercise at the school. *Damn.* Had Hayley made the connection when she'd seen her scar while undressing her? Surely she wouldn't have made love to her the way she did if that were the case.

But how long would it be before she did make the connection? And then what? She couldn't afford those thoughts right now, she had work to do. She played the DVD again and left it paused at the same spot.

As she perused the Castellano case file, which lay scattered on the couch and coffee table, she listened to the second Frankie the Fox tape through the iPod earphones she found in Hayley's purse, but kept one ear free so she could hear any sound from the bedroom. Hayley had apparently just started to listen to the tape. It was in the cassette deck, paused only a few seconds into the interview.

Ten minutes in, Frankie got to the really damaging stuff. The rough location of the school. Descriptions of a few of the people he knew, information about some of the training. Damn amateur, they probably owed someone a favor when they took him in. No wonder his stay was short-lived.

She knew that all the senior operatives—members of the Elite Tactical Force—and most of the regular ops had been adopted as infants by the EOO, as she had been, and brought up fully within the system. You could immediately single them out by their presidential surnames.

It was rare the Organization used someone like this man, who was obviously lacking in so many of what they considered essential skills: strong self-discipline, keen intellect, resourcefulness, ingenuity.

She could not allow Hayley to listen to the tape. The Castellano case file was less worrisome. Nothing potentially damaging to the Organization there, at least not obviously so. And nothing in the rest of Manny's case files, or on the rest of the tapes, though she wasn't able to read and listen to everything in the box as thoroughly as she would have liked.

Domino left everything exactly as she'd found it and slipped back into bed beside Hayley about an hour before dawn. She couldn't sleep. Listening to Hayley's soft breathing and admiring the soft swell of her breasts, illuminated by the moonlight streaming in through the window, she was too caught up in planning how she could keep her out of trouble.

❖

Saturday, the Fourth of July
6:30 a.m.

Hayley groaned and slapped blindly at the alarm clock. Workaholic that she was, she didn't ordinarily mind pulling a holiday shift. It came with the job. News stopped for no one. But when she'd volunteered to sub for a colleague today, she'd had no idea she'd be waking up next to Luka.

"Hey. Good morning."

The vision that greeted her when she opened her eyes and stretched was of a smiling Luka, propped on one elbow on her side, watching her. The sheet was pulled up, leaving the toned muscles of her shoulders and arms exposed, but hiding those magnificent, firm breasts and flat stomach she had so enjoyed exploring with her hands and mouth just hours earlier.

The memory of their coupling sent a quick rush of arousal through her, and she unconsciously pressed her thighs together to feel the vestiges of the wetness Luka's touch had produced. The faint scent of sex hung in the air.

Luka's unexpected arrival had turned her inside out, made her forget entirely about the evening of work she'd planned. It had been the most wonderfully satisfying evening she'd had in years, both sexually and emotionally. Their growing connection had compelled her to confess her growing feelings for Luka.

At the time, she had been too turned on and caught up in the moment to dwell on Luka's response to her declaration—hitting the wall, her face a study in torment. Now Luka's words echoed in her mind, demanding further consideration. *Don't say that. You can't fall for me. You can't fall for a lie.*

"And a good morning it is," she replied, smiling back at Luka. "I really wish I didn't have to go to work today." She wanted to find out more about this lie that haunted Luka. And she *really* wanted to linger here in bed and have some more of what they'd had last night. But she didn't have time for either.

"Impossible for reporters to just take the day off?" Luka frowned playfully in disappointment.

She softly caressed Luka's hip. "Believe me, I would if I could." She knew she should continue going through Manny's box after work. But the thought of more intimacy with Luka and the opportunity to get to talk to her about what was happening between them was too compelling. "Tonight?"

"Definitely." Luka moved nearer until their bodies were close. She pressed her lips against Hayley's forehead as she enfolded her in a warm embrace. "What time?"

"How about here at six? We can have some dinner and make some fireworks of our own." She sighed and closed her eyes, relishing the feel of their bodies wrapped together. Luka's thigh slipped between hers, and she pushed her hips forward in response. "Mmm." She squeezed Luka tighter to her. "You can get me started again way too easily. I better hit the shower, or I'll be late."

"Whatever you say." Luka kissed her wetly on the cheek, making no move to loosen her embrace.

"Here I go." But instead of pulling away, she turned her head to meet Luka's mouth with her own, and they kissed, slow and languid and long. At some point, Luka moved on top of her and their bodies began to rock against each other, and she would have been very, very late to work if it hadn't have been for the shrill interruption of her cell phone.

"I could kill whoever invented those things." She rolled away from Luka reluctantly and hurried into the living room to retrieve it, horrified to see they had already kissed away her breakfast and early morning news-program time. She'd be lucky to take a shower.

And it wasn't a good day to be late. Her colleague Amy was calling from the office, to tell her about an impromptu staff meeting that would begin in less than an hour.

She darted into the bathroom after she hung up, long enough to turn the shower on to warm up. Then she returned to the bedroom to find Luka dressing. She had her shirt on, but her bottom half was still wonderfully, distractingly naked. "Sorry I have to hurry like this but I have to get to a meeting."

"No problem. Should I be sorry for making you late?" The smile on Luka's face said it was a rhetorical question and that she wasn't about to apologize.

Hayley smiled back mischievously. "Yes, and you should think of a way to make it up to me…later. Now get yourself some coffee, I'll be right out."

It took her five minutes to shower and fifteen more to get dressed and do her hair and makeup. Luka had fixed her a cup of coffee, but she only had time to take a couple of swigs from her mug as she threw Manny's tapes and case files into one of the boxes. She also included the DVD of the enhanced assassination tape.

Manny's personal belongings went into the other box. She'd see those were returned to his apartment so his family would get them. But she would keep the tapes and files with her. If the EOO could search his apartment, they wouldn't hesitate to break into hers, either. Until she could go through everything, she wouldn't let the evidence box out of her sight.

"I called a cab while you were in the shower," Luka said as she gathered up her things. "I'll wait outside for it. I had a friend drop me off last night."

Something—jealousy? doubt?—twisted in Hayley's gut and made her wonder exactly what kind of friend Luka had been with. And what had propelled Luka to her door so late at night, suddenly ready to consummate their sexual attraction when she had been so intent on taking things slow? Some kind of lie was standing between them. Was Luka with someone else?

"You're not going to take a taxi all the way to DC, are you? I mean, I'd drive you, but—"

Luka cut her off as they both headed for the door. "It's fine. I'll take the cab to the train station and be home in no time. See you at six."

She shifted the box to one hip so she could kiss Luka good-bye. "You'd better be prepared to see all of me at six."

"I'll be counting the minutes."

As she pulled out of the lot, she waved at Luka, patiently seated on the stairs leading into her apartment building. Maybe Luka would begin to open up to her tonight. She hoped so, because she had a growing certainty that what was happening between them could grow into something very special if she did.

Today she was supposed to cover the myriad acts performing at the Inner Harbor Amphitheater, which kicked off Baltimore's Fourth of July events. And that didn't start until eleven. So, after the morning staff meeting let out, she spent the next ninety minutes calling the numbers listed on the yellow notebook paper she'd found in the Castellano case file. She had no idea whether it was indeed the "short list" of suspects Manny had promised her, a list of his powerful sources, or something else entirely, but it was certainly worth checking into.

The calls hadn't yielded much. Of course, she was only making somewhat general inquiries at this point. She couldn't very well refer to the tape, or ask if the person she was talking to had a gambling problem.

Nearly all of those she reached claimed to have no knowledge whatsoever of the Angelo Castellano case or an organization called the EOO, and couldn't recall speaking to a Detective Manuel Vasquez about any murder case.

The eighth name on the list was a David Rabinowitz, and the number had a Washington, DC exchange. She didn't recognize the name, but it was unusual enough that she Googled *David Rabinowitz Washington* while she waited. A Web site for Political Perspectives, a team of independent political advisors, came up. A David Rabinowitz was one of them.

His online bio indicated he had eighteen years' experience behind the scenes in politics, having served as speechwriter or press secretary to a dozen members of Congress before starting his own advisory group. Most of the names of his former bosses were familiar, because many were still in office and she'd interviewed a few of them.

"Mr. Rabinowitz?" she inquired when he came on the line. "Sorry to interrupt your holiday. This is Hayley Ward. I'm a reporter." She didn't want to give the name of her paper, because she didn't want anyone at the *Dispatch* to get wind of what she was up to. But she knew her status as a journalist might keep anyone from hanging up on her.

"This is David Rabinowitz. What did you say your name was?"

"Hayley Ward, Mr. Rabinowitz. I'm a freelance reporter, doing a story about organized crime in New York and an organization called the EOO. I ran across your name in connection with the Angelo Castellano case. He's the mob boss who was killed three years ago in Brooklyn?"

"Freelance, you say?" he asked after a long silence. "Who are you doing this story for?"

That was interesting. He hadn't started the conversation with *I don't know what you're talking about*, like most of the others had. "I'm not sure where this story will appear yet, Mr. Rabinowitz. Though I'll keep you informed when it does. Did you talk to a Detective Manuel Vasquez about the Castellano case?"

"I know nothing about this case of yours, or any Detective Vasquez. I'm sorry, Miss Ward, but I have to take another call. Good luck with your story."

"Wait, please! Don't hang up." She didn't hear a dial tone, so he was still on the line. "Here's my cell phone number. Please call me if you think of anything or know of anyone who might be able to help me." She gave him the number.

"Good-bye, Miss Ward," he said and disconnected.

It was very much like the other calls she'd made, but different enough that she put a star by his name before she continued to the next.

❖

When Hayley left for work, Domino waited on the steps of her building for a few minutes to make sure she didn't double back before she returned to the surveillance apartment across the street. She was certain Hayley was driving straight to her office and relatively sure she would keep the box of evidence with her until she had a chance to go through it.

Trying to retrieve it from Hayley's car at work was risky—or worse yet, from inside the *Baltimore Dispatch* building itself, right under Hayley's nose—but it was the best way to get it without casting suspicion upon herself, so she walked over to her surveillance apartment, pulled out her makeup kit, and started transforming herself.

An hour later, wearing worn-out jeans and a sweatshirt, she was unrecognizable, with a black wig, brown eyes, and much darker complexion. She put on yellow plastic cleaning gloves and emptied wastebaskets in the *Dispatch* newsroom into a large rolling cart she'd found in one of the janitorial closets, happy it was a holiday with few people around. At one point, she got close enough to Hayley's desk to see the box beneath it. Now she needed her opportunity.

She waited. She watched. She cleaned. And a little after ten a.m., when Hayley stepped away from her desk and headed toward the break room, she was very, very quick.

❖

Hayley was halfway through her coffee before she realized the box she had shoved beneath her desk was gone.

Oh, my God. The shock hit her like a blast of icy air. She stood up and searched the newsroom for an unfamiliar face. There were none.

"Hey, Phil," she called out to the weekend assignment editor, who was proofing copy on his computer fifteen feet away. "Did you see anyone near my desk?"

He looked at her above the bifocals pinching his nose. "Huh? Sorry?"

"Did you see anyone around here in the last couple of minutes? I had a box under my desk." She held up her hands to roughly measure the dimensions. "It's gone."

Creases of concern knitted his forehead. "Gone? You mean stolen?" Now he looked around as well and reflexively patted his back pocket to reassure himself his wallet was still there. "No, Hayley, sorry. What was in it?"

"Never mind," she said quickly, trying to head off any further explanations. But she knew despite her best efforts her voice betrayed her growing panic. Somehow, someway, the EOO had gotten in here in the scant two minutes she was down the hall in the break room and had made off with Manny's box.

How the hell did they know I have it? That what was in it was worth the risk?

She couldn't finish her workday. The theft of the box had ripped any remaining sense of safety from her. She kept looking around, almost expecting someone to come back for the list or to catch some unscrupulous colleague keeping tabs on her. *No. Impossible.* But the anonymous note had said the EOO had contacts in the media. Was it so far-fetched and paranoid to think someone at the *Dispatch* might be involved in all of this? Was that how she had been selected to receive the tape in the first place?

All she knew for certain was she was being watched...closely. And for the first time, they had invaded her turf, violated one of the few places where she had felt absolutely secure. To chance coming into the *Dispatch* offices in broad daylight surely meant they would do anything, go anywhere, to keep their secrets from being discovered.

What would they do next? She reached for the phone on her desk and took it apart, looking for something that didn't belong. What did a bug look like anyway? She wasn't sure she'd know one if she saw it. She should have asked Manny about them when he was checking out her cell phone. She found nothing, which reassured her a little, meaning they might not know about all of the phone calls she'd made that morning. She fished in her pocket for the list of names. At least she still had that. Thank God she hadn't left it lying on her desk.

She regretted most the loss of the second Frankie the Fox tape. Although Manny had told her Frankie hadn't disclosed the location of the Organization, it sure sounded like he had something concrete to offer about it. After all, they had gone to the trouble to steal it from her. That had to be a measure of its significance.

Nowhere is safe. Nowhere. Certainly not my apartment. I can't stay there. She told the supervisor on duty she had a personal emergency and needed to leave, then headed toward her car. Her gut instinct told her not to go home at all. But she'd left in such a hurry that morning, she'd taken nothing but her purse, Manny's box, and the clothes on her back. *I'll leave now, while they think I'm still at work, and make a quick stop there.* She'd pack a bag, grab her checkbook, laptop, a few clothes. Quick in and out. Should be safe. She tried to reassure herself, but she wondered whether she would ever feel safe again.

❖

Senator Terrence Burrows stretched out on the couch in his den, sipping coffee in his bathrobe while he pored over the latest popularity polls in the race for the presidency. He'd slept in until nine, which was virtually unheard of, but he would be up very late with his guests that evening, and he had to be on top of his game.

The *Washington Post* poll had him as the favorite candidate, but not by much, only three points ahead of the blond, blue-eyed former-war-hero junior senator from Maine—which was within the margin of error. But he was throwing a backyard barbecue today for some of his wealthier supporters and expected to receive some hefty donations to his campaign war chest. A few more national ads, and he was confident he'd pull ahead of the pack.

His cell phone rang, and when he checked the display he was surprised to see his former political advisor was calling. He hadn't talked to David Rabinowitz in more than six months. "Hi, Dave. Been a while. Is something up?"

"I just got a phone call I thought you should know about," Rabinowitz replied. "She identified herself as a freelance reporter—Hayley Ward—and wouldn't say who she was working for. Claimed to be investigating a story about organized crime in New York and said she came across my name in connection with the Angelo Castellano case. She also mentioned something about an organization called the EOO."

Terrence sat up. "What did you say?"

"The truth. That I didn't know anything about it," Rabinowitz replied. "But I thought you should know. She also asked if I'd spoken to a Detective Manuel Vasquez, and she left me her telephone number in case I knew anyone who might help her."

"I see. What's that number?" Terrence walked to his desk and copied it. "All right, Dave. Thanks for the call. Let me know if she contacts you again." He had let none of his inner turmoil show in his voice, but as soon as he disconnected, he started to pace. This whole thing had gotten out of control. How the hell did Hayley Ward get Dave's name? He could see all he had worked for going down the toilet before his eyes. All he had wanted to do was get the EOO off his back. *Fuckers. Damn fuckers.* But he might have just dug his own grave. Now, not only might his association with them be made known, but everything else as well—his gambling problems, the lies, the diversion of campaign funds to cover his debts. And the Castellano murder. He thought that nightmare was over. It was more than his career he was talking about, now. This could send him to prison for years. He had to stop this while he still could.

Terrence heard the twins pass the closed door to the den, laughing. *Too much at stake.* He had to get rid of Hayley Ward. It seemed his best option. She already knew too much, and she was getting closer all the time to his dangerous secrets.

The loathsome voice of his father, long dead but still influential, reverberated through him unexpectedly. *"You never did think before you acted. That's what makes you weak, Terrence."*

Terrence could see he was on the way to proving the asshole right. *No. Not going to happen.* He admitted to himself he might be thinking irrationally at the moment, so he'd do nothing until he calmed down and considered all his options. Think things through. No knee-jerk reactions.

Noise from outside drew him to the window. The caterers had arrived. As he watched them set up for the party, he mulled over a number of possibilities. Maybe he could take care of both of his problems without getting his own hands dirty.

First, he had to make sure the EOO knew it was Hayley Ward who was trying to expose the Organization. But he couldn't make them suspect that he had sent her the tape. They'd want her so bad he could use her as a bargaining chip to get out from under them for good. It sounded like a workable plan.

He called Montgomery Pierce as soon as he was safely ensconced in his den. "What the hell's going on?" he asked in his most outraged tone. "Some reporter named Hayley Ward has been sniffing around, bothering me. Asking an associate about that matter you took care of for me. The one you were *supposed* to have taken care of *permanently*," he emphasized. "*And* she asked whether he'd ever heard of an organization called the EOO."

"Where did she get her information?" Pierce asked.

"How the hell do I know?" he shouted. "That's why I'm calling you. How did she get my name?"

"Calm down, Terrence. We're working on this problem." Pierce seemed to be less cocky than usual. "But it may be more complicated than we thought. It appears as though we're having internal difficulties. We may need your help."

"You can't keep using me like this," he argued. "I can't keep taking these risks. What's it going to take to cut me loose?"

"We don't have the kind of agreement that expires. We'll never cut you loose. Now do you want to save your precious career or not?" Pierce sounded angry. "I'll get back to you." The line went dead.

Terrence slammed the phone down. *Fuckers.* Pierce had bought his outraged-victim act. At least they wouldn't suspect him. But he'd have to take care of Hayley Ward personally. And the EOO too, if he was ever going to get out from under them. He dialed Jack's number.

"I want your men to detain our reporter friend. As soon as possible. Don't harm her. Just keep her in seclusion until I give you further instructions. Let me know as soon as you have her."

CHAPTER TWENTY-TWO

10:30 a.m.

Domino wasn't surprised to see Hayley emerge from the *Dispatch* offices and hurry to her Mustang not long after the box had disappeared from beneath her desk. The look on her face—anxious, distressed—made a pang of guilt tear through Domino. But she was trying to protect Hayley, she told herself.

She still wore her disguise, and she'd added sunglasses, though any passersby in the *Baltimore Dispatch* parking lot would have had trouble seeing her at all in the back of the panel van. Manny's box was at her feet. She'd just started going through its contents again more thoroughly when she spotted Hayley leaving work early. What was she up to?

She moved forward into the driver's seat and followed Hayley to her apartment, staying well back in traffic to avoid detection because she knew Hayley would now be on high alert. A short distance from Hayley's apartment, the Mustang pulled over unexpectedly and parked, then, after a couple of minutes, continued.

Once they got there, Domino decided to remain in the van for a while rather than return to the surveillance apartment across the street, to make sure Hayley wasn't planning to go out again soon. In her increasingly paranoid state, anything was possible.

Keeping one eye on the Mustang, she returned to the back of the van and stripped off the wig and the rest of her disguise, then got into her own clothes, staying out of sight and wishing like hell she knew what Hayley was planning.

❖

Hayley checked the rearview mirror often during the ride home from work. But traffic was far too heavy for her to determine whether anyone was following her.

Now she knew why Manny had all those locks on his door. Not that they'd kept them from getting to him. If they could sneak into the *Dispatch* offices in the middle of the day, they could certainly get into her apartment while she slept. She wasn't safe there any more.

They might already be there. Waiting for her. The thought gave her pause—she pulled the car to the curb with shaking hands with three blocks left to go. She had to make this very quick, leave the door open, maybe, so the neighbors could hear. Before she drove the final distance, she made a mental checklist of what she needed to pack.

Where to go? She didn't want to involve her family or friends and endanger them, too. Better to find a nice quiet motel somewhere, she decided. Pack a bag, maybe have her landlord keep an eye on her place, give her a call if someone came around.

She parked in front of her building but didn't get out immediately. She studied the cars in the lot, and the people coming and going, for signs of anything unusual.

Finally she got out and approached her apartment with leaden steps, taking deep breaths to calm her racing heart. She gently tried the knob to reassure herself it was still locked, then put her ear to the door, half-expecting to hear voices inside. Nothing.

When she reached into her purse for her house key, she brushed her cell phone. *Hey. That's not a bad idea.* It wouldn't hurt to have someone on the phone with her who could call 911 if she encountered a problem. She dialed her sister's number and waited for her to answer before she put the key in the lock to click it open.

"Hey, Claudi, how's it going?" It took an effort to sound nonchalant.

"Hey, Hay. What's up?"

"Oh, nothing much," Hayley replied, as she gingerly pushed open the door and listened for sound from within. "Just called to say hello."

"The boys have been asking when you're going to come over for a rematch at Scrabble," she said, as Hayley began to quickly reconnoiter her few rooms to reassure herself she was alone.

"Soon, I promise," she told Claudette, cradling the phone between ear and shoulder so she could throw a few clothes into a bag. "It's been crazy lately with work, but I'll get there as soon as I have some time off."

"Yeah, yeah. I've heard that more than a time or two," her sister replied, more with humor than reproach. "And Dad's started complaining to *me*, by the way, about how you haven't been over for dinner once in the last month."

"What else is new? I'll call Mom soon, I promise." Hayley took her bag into the bathroom and threw in a few essentials, then carried it to the living room and set it on the coffee table. "Say, Claudi, I'm going to be in and out a lot the next few days. If you need me, call my cell."

"You work too hard, Hayley. You need to get a life. Speaking of... did you ever get a call back from that art restorer?"

Luka. She'd forgotten all about her date tonight. She made a mental note to call her and cancel, once she reached the motel. "Sure did, and as a matter of fact, she's turned out to be somebody special." She gathered up her cell-phone charger, checkbook, and a few other essentials and stuffed them into her bag. "You'll get the full story the next time I see you, I promise. Don't have time now."

Out of the corner of her eye, she spotted a piece of paper half tucked under one of the couch cushions. It was an evidence receipt that had evidently fallen out of one of Manny's case files while she had been looking at it the night before. Nothing significant to the Castellano case, or the EOO, but it prompted her to search the couch thoroughly to see if she'd missed anything else when she'd packed up Manny's things in such a hurry that morning.

When her hand found the cool, smooth rectangle and dug it out from behind the cushion, her blood ran cold.

A domino.

She dropped it like it was on fire. *Stop it. It can't be. You're letting your paranoia run away with you.* It didn't mean anything, didn't prove anybody was here. It was only a toy that one of her nephews or nieces had left here ages ago. They were always forgetting game pieces and little army men.

"Hay? Did you hear what I said?" The blood pounding in her ears distorted her sister's voice. "Want to bring this new woman in your life over for dinner sometime?"

"Gotta go. Call you back." Hayley snatched her bag and bolted for her car.

❖

10:45 a.m.

Hayley ran out of the building like the devil himself was after her and peeled out of the lot so fast that Domino, surprised, had to hustle back into the driver's seat to keep behind her.

On a busy one-way street halfway to the expressway, Hayley braked without warning, causing a cacophony of horns, and pulled to the right curb in front of an ATM. Domino heard another blare of horns as a sedan with tinted windows in the left lane abruptly stopped to park on the opposite curb.

Damn. Hayley evidently had a tail again. Domino wondered if it was yet another beagle. There was nowhere for her to park except beyond both vehicles. As she passed, she watched Hayley jump out and head toward the ATM. No one left the sedan and she couldn't see inside the reflective windows.

Domino parked at the right curb in the next block and kept both cars in sight through her side-view mirror.

Hayley returned to her Mustang and pulled back into traffic. The sedan followed suit, following five cars behind in the same lane. Domino managed to slip between them, two cars behind Hayley, and a block farther on she saw her opportunity.

The blinking pedestrian light at the crosswalk in the intersection ahead told her the light was about to change, so she slowed. Horns blared behind her, but she ignored them. The sedan tried for the other lane to get around, but the cars there were bumper to bumper as well and wouldn't let it in. Hayley made it through the intersection, and Domino stopped as the signal turned yellow, blocking the sedan.

When the light turned green again, she kept to a crawl, trying to give Hayley as much time as possible to put some distance between them. By the time the sedan managed to pass her, she knew they had lost Hayley, because the tracking device on the Mustang told her Hayley was now two miles away on the expressway, heading south.

She picked up Hayley again a few minutes later and followed her to a two-story motel in the countryside, a half hour outside Baltimore. After registering at the office, Hayley let herself into a ground-floor room on one end and closed all the curtains.

It was all Domino could do not to get out of the van and knock on the door. She wanted to comfort Hayley and find out what exactly had happened during her brief time in her apartment. Certainly the theft of the box had rattled her—but something else had obviously transpired there to panic her.

She stared at the closed curtains for a long time, willing them to open, wishing she had the equipment to monitor what was going on inside. *What are you up to, Hayley?*

To pass the time, she resumed her meticulous examination of the contents of Manny's box. Once she was satisfied nothing else there could endanger the Organization, she thought about Hayley and the night before.

The look in Hayley's eyes. The complete purity of her surrender. The shiver she'd known at the slightest touch of Hayley's hand. And the way she had let Hayley look at her. Let her really see, not fearing Hayley would reject her for what might be there, because once again Hayley had made her feel like nothing else mattered and nothing ever had.

To betray or hurt such purity and innocence, when they belonged to a pawn in someone's dirty game, would violate her beliefs. She'd been taught the cause sanctifies the means and had come to not only live by the credo but believe in it as well. She had, however, never hurt someone innocent in the process. Harming Hayley would mean the end of that conviction.

She looked at her watch. Almost eleven thirty. They had a date tonight. Would Hayley remember? Would she call?

Ever since she could remember, she had been loyal to the Organization and her life had been theirs. She'd based her beliefs on what they'd taught her, to never get emotionally involved or attached so she'd never compromise herself or the operation. She'd always lived by the rules, given the Organization her best for taking her in and raising, educating, and training her—manufacturing someone to fix what was wrong with the world.

They'd been the closest she'd ever come to a family. Especially Grant. Joanne Grant had been the one person she'd felt comfortable turning to during those turbulent, lonely years growing up. And Grant had never failed to be there when she needed her. How was she supposed to lie to her family, redefine her already redefined ethics?

She picked up her cell phone and cradled it in her hand. Pierce would be wondering why she hadn't called with an update. But regardless of what she said at this point, the Organization would still not risk that she was wrong. She wasn't holding simply a phone, but Hayley's life. One call about the box and its contents, and Hayley could be only a memory by tonight.

Domino wanted to find the bastards who were trying to hurt them as much as they did, and she would do whatever was necessary to track them down. But she couldn't involve Hayley, and she didn't know if she could lie to them. How ironic, when she'd made a career of living under half truths, fake emotions, and borrowed identities. They had taught her to do and to be whatever necessary to get the job done, but most of all they had taught her to trust her instincts. Remembering that lesson helped her regain her focus, and she made her decision.

She put the scrambler on her phone and dialed Pierce's number. He picked up on the third ring.

"Domino."

"Safe line?" he asked.

"Of course."

"I haven't heard from you in days." Casual words, but she heard the reprimand.

"I don't have anything new on Strike."

"I see."

"Any news concerning her source?" Domino asked.

"Nothing," Pierce replied.

"Do you still suspect an inside job?" Domino watched as Hayley briefly parted the curtains of her room, then closed them again.

"Do you know of any reason why I should?" he asked.

"No, I don't. Strike is clueless. And she hasn't talked to anyone about it, either. She's completely solo on this one."

"Has she been to see anyone else?" Pierce asked. "Is she still asking questions?"

"Not from her house phone."

"It's time we tap her work phone, then."

"I'll do it tonight."

"Call me back tomorrow after you're done," he instructed. "And Domino—we'll be listening in on that line so you can concentrate on surveillance."

She could give only one suitable reply. "Done." She hoped he couldn't hear her reluctance.

❖

11:35 a.m.

After disconnecting with Domino, Monty Pierce asked his co-administrators to join him in his office. He drew the blinds on his spectacular view of the Rockies and the cadre of students tackling the obstacle course in the distance.

Determined to find out whether the leak about the EOO had come from inside the Organization, he'd decided to have Grant, Arthur, and several of his top operatives followed. At least his paranoia had confirmed that Joanne was not the traitor, he thought, straightening his tie. Nonetheless, his directive had produced unsettling results.

David Arthur arrived a little ahead of Joanne Grant, but Pierce waited for both to settle into the chairs opposite his desk to begin. "Looks like we have a problem."

"Was it what you suspected?" Arthur ran his hand absently over his crew cut, newly trimmed. His skin was nearly as red as his hair from all his time in the sun. He was teaching archery, rappelling, and skydiving this semester, among other things.

"Domino didn't mention anything about Strike having gone back to Vasquez or having the tape dropped off at Koster's for enhancement," Pierce confirmed. "She also neglected to mention she spent the night with Strike and followed her to work. Or that she was seen leaving the building holding the same box Strike left with from Vasquez's apartment building. Or that she's currently sitting outside a motel, where Strike has apparently gone to hide out after fleeing her apartment."

"Do we know what's in the box?" Grant asked.

"No. She still has it with her."

Grant got to her feet and went to the window. After a few seconds' pause, she opened one of the blinds and stared out at the school compound and wilderness area beyond. "I don't understand. This isn't like Domino." Pierce allowed her a moment for reflection, because Grant always found it difficult to put their charges in jeopardy. And her fondness for Domino in particular was obvious. "Still, I think we should give it some more time. I'm sure she knows what she's doing."

"We can't risk giving her time," Arthur said, getting to his feet. "She knows the rules. She's been playing by them for the past twelve years. No changing them, no exceptions. Why would she hide all this from us unless something was going on?"

"He's right, Joanne," Pierce said. "I don't like it any more than you do. But we have to face it."

"I won't hear of this," Grant declared, whirling around to glare at both of them. Her vivid green eyes darkened, stark against her white hair. "I know Domino and so do you. She'd never do anything to hurt us. If she wanted to, she'd have led them here already."

"She's not trying to hurt us," Pierce replied. "She might want out, and this is how she thinks she can accomplish that. Or there may be more on the video than we think. Maybe somebody—some fed, some ambitious cop—made her and offered her a deal. She may be trying to save herself, and we're what she has to offer in return. She apparently has her own way of going about this. She hasn't led them here, but that doesn't mean she won't or that she's doing anything to stop them."

Grant turned her gaze back to the campus below.

"We need to eliminate Domino and bring Strike in for questioning," Pierce continued. "We can't take care of her until we find out what she knows. I already have Wasp surveilling Domino. I'll put another operative she won't recognize with him to grab Strike. How do you vote?"

"No." Grant kept her back to them. Her hands were clenched into fists at her side. "We should bring Domino in, too. Give her a chance to explain. If they *are* romantically involved, maybe we can use that to our advantage."

"I'm sorry, Joanne." David Arthur stepped to her but made no move to touch her. His voice softened. "We can't take the risk. We can easily get what we need from Strike. But Domino won't come willingly. She knows the rules for mutiny, and we'll never get her to talk. No, the stakes are simply too high. I vote yes."

Pierce picked up the phone to buzz his secretary. "Nancy, get Wasp on the line, and find out which op in the DC area is available. Then notify all operatives Domino is a rogue. They're to avoid her and notify us if she attempts any contact."

❖

Noon

Hayley peeked out the curtains at the few cars in the motel parking lot. No one was coming or going. Her room had a peculiar odor she couldn't identify, and she certainly wasn't going to open a window, but at least she felt safe for the moment. She hoped she was overreacting, but fear was devouring any remaining optimism.

She'd registered under a false name, used cash instead of a credit card so she couldn't be traced, and parked the Mustang where no one could see it from the street. But she had only bought herself a little time. She was almost out of options. The story that had once seemed so important had become a lethal affair and was going to get her killed. She couldn't involve her family or friends, and she didn't feel safe returning to work or home.

Home. Luka was due to pick her up at her apartment in…she checked her watch. About six hours. She grabbed her cell phone.

"Hey there." She had to work to make the greeting sound casual.

"I was just thinking about you."

"That's what I like to hear. Listen, I'm afraid I have to cancel our date tonight. I got caught up with work and had to go out of town. I don't know when I'll be back."

"Is everything all right?" Luka asked.

"Oh, fine, just very busy. I'll call you when things settle down, okay?"

"Yes, of course. Let me know if there's anything I can do."

"That's sweet, Luka. I'll keep that in mind. Take care, and I'll talk to you soon?"

"I hope so. Bye, Hayley."

Hayley disconnected and went to the window again, pulling the curtain just enough to peer outside. She wasn't sure what she was looking for, but she felt restless and edgy. She would have to go to the authorities. The only question was, where would she go and what would she say? The EOO had ties in law enforcement. And she needed to figure out a way to confess what she knew without incriminating herself too deeply.

The ringing of her cell phone made her jump. The caller ID read *private number.* That meant it was unlisted and someone not in her address book.

"Hello?"

"Is this Hayley Ward?" A man's voice she didn't recognize.

"Yes, who's this?"

"I'd rather not say, Miss Ward. You called a colleague of mine this morning, asking about the Castellano case? He gave me your number."

She'd made a lot of calls. That didn't narrow it down much. "Who is this?"

"Someone who knows something about this organization you've been asking about. But I'm not going to give you my name. These people mean business, and I have a family to think about. I'm taking a chance just by calling you." The man had a whiny voice, and he sounded like a local, with traces of the unique diction common to those who'd grown up around Chesapeake Bay.

"How do I know this is safe?"

The caller finally spoke again. "Safe? What do you mean? Have they gotten to you? Is that why you called my friend? If that's the case we shouldn't be having this talk at all. Good luck, but I can't—"

"Wait!" she said. "Don't hang up. I need help. I think they're after me, and I'm going to the police, but I need someone to back me up."

"Back you up? With the police? Are you kidding? The police can't touch them."

"Then who can?" She gripped the phone tighter. "What the hell am I supposed to do?"

"I know people who can help." The man sounded hesitant. "People with more authority than the police. I turned to them a few years ago."

"Who are these people?"

"They're in the government."

"Who?" she pressed.

"I really can't talk about this on the phone, Miss Ward. Maybe we can meet next week."

"Next week!" She couldn't possibly stay cooped up in a motel that long, jumping out of her skin at the slightest noise. "I don't have till next week."

"I leave tonight for Washington," the caller said, "and won't be back until then."

"How about now?" she proposed.

"That depends. Where are you?"

"Near Baltimore. We can meet at a bar or someplace."

"I'd rather not be seen in public with you," he said. "I don't think that's safe if they're after you. And I don't want you coming near my family or work. It's too risky."

Given all she'd been through, she understood his paranoia. "Why do you want to help me, anyway?"

"Because I've been there, I guess, and I was happy I had someone to help me out," he replied. "I'm willing to advise you, Miss Ward, but I won't risk my safety or that of my family. I'd suggest we meet at your house, but not if you really think they're after you."

"I'm not home. I'm staying at a motel, and honestly, I'm too afraid to tell anyone where. I don't know who to trust."

"That's up to you. Certainly understandable. Once again, good luck and be careful." It was clear the caller was ready to hang up.

"Wait!" He sounded sincere, and she *had* determined her cell phone wasn't bugged. The fact he mentioned the calls she'd made that morning made his callback *seem* legitimate, anyway. She took a deep breath. "I'm staying at the Timbers Motel…"

CHAPTER TWENTY-THREE

12:15 p.m.

Terrence Burrows was in his backyard, sampling some of the food to be served to his guests when his cell phone rang. After he saw who it was, he hurried toward his den and answered it halfway there.

"Yes?"

"Found her, but something's up," Jack relayed. "She's at a motel outside Baltimore. We need to move fast. My guys can be there in about a half hour."

A little of Terrence's anger slipped away, replaced by an increased sense of alarm. Hayley Ward had been tipped somebody was after her. At least the EOO hadn't gotten to her yet. "Did she say anything else?"

"No, only that she doesn't trust anyone. I think she's ready to talk."

He closed the door to his den so no one could overhear him. "Make sure she talks to you. Move fast, but don't take any chances. And Jack, if anything goes wrong, destroy all evidence, including her."

"Understood." The line went dead.

Terrence considered his next move. First, he'd find out what she knew. How she had gotten David Rabinowitz's name. Who else she had talked to. Then he'd offer her to Pierce. *I bet they got close to her—close enough to scare her into running. They want her bad. Real bad.* That was good news, as long as his own men got her first. It confirmed she was the perfect bait for his trap.

❖

12:50 p.m.

Although Hayley was expecting him—had gone back and forth to the window a dozen times, in fact, anticipating his arrival—the knock on the motel-room door still startled her. She pulled back the curtain a couple of inches to study her visitor before she admitted him.

He looked like a guy who lived his life in front of a computer. Slight build, average height. Probably in his early forties, he dressed like a vintage nerd—glasses, white button-down oxford shirt and sweater, trousers hiked too high to be fashionable. Dark hair, slicked down and combed to one side. All he was missing was the pocket protector. He seemed nervous, glancing about as he waited, which reassured her.

She removed the security chain and opened the door.

"Miss Ward?" he asked. "I called you on the phone."

She nodded. Same whiny voice. "Come in."

As he entered the room, she turned and took a couple of steps toward the small table near the front window where she'd set two chairs. Hearing the door click shut behind her, she pivoted, intending to ask him to fasten the chain again, but the words froze on her lips.

Behind the geek stood another man, roughly the same age, but bigger, tougher-looking, in a dark jacket and jeans. Hayley's heartbeat doubled. "What's going on?"

"We need you to come with us," the geek replied.

"Who are you?'

"We're here to protect you," he said.

Hayley didn't like the way the second man was blocking the door. And now she looked closer at the geek. Something wasn't quite right about him. The nervous demeanor had evaporated and he no longer resembled the scared family man he claimed to be. "Protect me from what?

"We can answer all your questions later."

Her pulse accelerated. "I'm not going anywhere. That wasn't the deal. And who's he?" She tipped her head toward the second man.

"We don't have time for this," the second man told the geek.

Her heart was beating so fast she felt light-headed. "For what? What's he talking about?" She took a step backward, then another, feeling the threat like a living presence in the room, and, instead of answering, they both moved toward her.

She turned to the window, two feet away, grabbing at the curtain to throw it open, desperate, an inch from screaming.

As she closed her hand around the drapery material, the second man grabbed her from behind. He was quick, and strong, and he pinned her free arm while the chloroform-soaked rag covered her mouth. She tried to struggle, but her world went black.

❖

When Domino saw the man stop at the door to Hayley's motel room, she went on high alert. She hadn't seen him enter the lot or park. He'd approached on foot from the back side of the building, and he seemed on edge.

She relaxed only slightly when Hayley opened the door and admitted him. Given Hayley's fearful state of mind, the newcomer was likely a friend or relative, certainly someone she trusted without question. Nonetheless she put her hand on the key in the ignition.

When a second man slipped around the corner and into the room, she automatically started the van.

And when she saw the curtains move, yanked hard to the side, it was obvious something was very wrong. She shot forward into the empty space beside Hayley's Mustang.

She grabbed for the ski mask on the passenger seat and bolted from the van, quickly pulling it on just outside the motel room. She retrieved the 9mm Luger P95 from her pants, at the small of her back, and silently turned the knob. The door was unlocked.

As she slipped into the room, she was grateful both men had their backs to her. The nearest one got the butt of her Luger to his left temple and went down without a struggle.

The second man had his arms around Hayley, who was slumped against his chest. When his friend crumpled, he turned—saw Domino two feet away—and dropped Hayley to reach for his gun.

He managed to get it out, but she clamped down hard on his wrist as he began to bring it up to fire. She pivoted, her back to him, and rammed her left elbow into his stomach, then his face, before she knocked him out too, with her Luger to his temple.

She hurried to Hayley, bent over her to check her breathing, and caught a whiff of chloroform, a welcome development under the circumstances.

Domino stripped off her mask, shoved her gun back into her pants, and packed up Hayley's gear. She took it out to the van, then turned the vehicle around so its open rear doors faced the motel-room entrance. No one was in sight.

She hefted Hayley onto her shoulder and carried her out, and a few minutes later they were on the expressway toward Washington. She couldn't be certain no one was tailing her in the heavy traffic, but she couldn't risk any lengthy evasive detours. She had no idea how much chloroform Hayley had been given, but she had started to stir and mumble, and Domino kept an eye on her. She could come to at any time, and she didn't want Hayley to wake up until they were safely inside her condo.

Beside her was Manny's box. Most of the contents were innocuous, but she couldn't take the incriminating Frankie the Fox tape or the enhanced DVD of the Guerrero assassination into her place, where Hayley might be tempted to retrieve them. And she couldn't leave them in the van. Two blocks from home, while stopped at a red light, she fished both items out of the box and destroyed them.

❖

1:00 p.m.

"There's been a development you need to know about." The call came from Wasp, the operative Pierce had assigned to follow Domino.

"Go on," Pierce replied.

"Two men entered Strike's motel room. Domino followed, in a hurry. Not long after, she carried Strike out—who wasn't moving—and they're headed south, toward DC. The two guys never came out of the room, but I got their photos as they went in. One's been ID'ed. Local muscle, no known connections."

"Has your assistance arrived yet?"

"No, not yet."

"All right," Pierce said. "Stick with your target and I'll have him check out the situation at the motel before he rendezvouses with you." Wasp's teammate might be able to extract some information from the two men about who had hired them. But more likely they were just petty losers contracted for the day, who'd be long gone before anyone got there, if they were still alive.

Pierce had long ago accepted that his life could include no emotional attachments. He'd had to order a rogue operative taken out only once before. In both that case and this one, he had experienced deep remorse—this time in particular. For he'd become quite fond of Luka Madison, and Domino was one of the best operatives they'd ever had.

Such a damn shame it had to come to this.

❖

2:00 p.m.

Hayley was still unconscious when Domino pulled into the underground parking garage. She bypassed her usual slot in favor of an empty space near the freight elevator, which she used to transport Hayley up to her condo.

She laid Hayley on her couch, knowing she had to figure out what she could tell her. She'd be coming to any minute.

She was running out of options. *You made your choice when you started lying to Pierce. It's time she learned the truth.* Or at least as much of the truth as she could risk. More than anything, she wanted Hayley to understand her bloody business had a noble purpose. And that she would keep Hayley safe, at any cost.

But she was still terrified Hayley would want nothing more to do with her when she realized the woman she'd made love to, and the woman she'd seen kill in cold blood, were the same person.

Hayley moaned and her eyelids fluttered.

Domino's courage faltered. She jerked on the ski mask again, just before Hayley opened her eyes.

CHAPTER TWENTY-FOUR

Hayley blinked awake, groggy and totally disoriented, with a bitch of a headache and a queasy stomach. And this foul taste in her mouth, acrid, like she...*Oh, fuck.* It hit her, the memory of those last seconds. The two men, coming toward her.

She tried to sit up, alarmed, shaking off the remnants of the chloroform, and looked to her left. She was in someone's living room. Sparsely furnished. The hardwood floor was half-filled with dominos, arranged in an elaborate pattern and ready to be toppled.

An icy chill ran up her back and she froze, listening intently. Though no sound alerted her, she sensed someone standing behind her, watching her, but she was too terrified to look around.

Several seconds passed. Her heart fluttered wildly against the walls of her chest. Almost against her will, she turned her head farther, slowly, and in the big picture window saw the reflection of her captor. A woman, from the shape of the silhouette, dressed in black, with a ski mask hiding her face.

A sudden flash of memory told her it was the same figure that had overpowered her in Manny's apartment.

Then the rest hit her, like a brick to the side of the head. The scar. The domino she'd found in her couch. Luka's hyperalertness and quick reflexes.

The figure began to move and Hayley closed her eyes. Her throat felt constricted, and bile roiled in her stomach. She was certain it was true, but her heart wouldn't let her believe it. And she didn't know which was more terrifying, being wrong or being right.

She had to face what was there, she couldn't sit like this forever. Gathering her courage, she opened her eyes and was startled to find the figure kneeling before her.

They stared at each other for several seconds, not speaking. Hayley put her hand on the mask, reluctant, but her captor nodded yes, and slowly she pulled it off to gaze into familiar blue-gray eyes. The saddest eyes she had ever seen. "Domino?"

When she said the name, Luka bowed her head, looking at the floor as if in defeat.

"Or is it Luka, or neither?" Hayley sat up straighter. "Who are you? *What* are you?" When Luka didn't reply, she demanded, "So that is you on the tape, isn't it? The tape that was sent to me, the damn thing I've been working on all this time. It's all true? This secret organization. This school for…you…you're an assas—"

"Please stop," Luka finally interrupted. "Yes, it's me on the tape, okay?"

It can't be true. Please, no. It just can't. Hayley stared numbly into space. "Who were those men at the motel? Are they from the same organization?"

"No. I don't know them. I had nothing to do with them, but it's obvious someone out there wants to hurt you."

Hayley snapped out of her trance. "Someone else besides you, you mean?" She stood and faced Luka, and when their eyes met, she suddenly remembered the feeling of the gun—hard, cold, pressed into her back. She panicked and glanced about for an escape. The door was twenty feet to her right.

Luka stood a split second before she did, anticipating her next move.

Hayley backed away. "It was you in Manny's apartment. You who came at me—" She stopped. "Did *you* kill Manny?"

"No, Hayley. It wasn't me…us, who killed him. Yes, I was the one in his apartment, *after* we found out he was dead, and I'm sorry for scaring you. I never meant to." Luka's voice was pleading and apologetic. "I was following orders because of the tape." She took another step toward Hayley.

"Stay away from me. I'll give you the tape and everything else I have. Just let me go."

Anguish washed across Luka's face. "Please stop looking at me like that," she said quietly. "I'm not going to hurt you. I couldn't. I'd never have brought you here in the first place if that was my intention."

Hayley looked around, really taking in the entirety of the room for the first time. "Where is here?"

"This is where I live."

"This is your house? Where *is* everything?" No one lived like this—in a room with no furniture, except a couch and a bunch of bookcases. There were no pictures on the walls, no TV, no souvenir keepsakes lying about, nothing personal except the dominos.

Luka shrugged. "I don't need much."

"That's an understatement," Hayley answered matter-of-factly. "So why *did* you bring me here?"

"I'm not sure. But I know you aren't safe out there. We're not the threat, Hayley. Someone else has been following you and sent the two men to the motel to get you. Probably the same people who killed Manny."

Hayley digested this information. "So my best chance of survival is in the company of an assassin? Is that what you're saying?"

"I wish you'd stop calling me that," Luka said. "I'm not—"

"Oh yeah, that's right, you're just an art restorer. Jesus! All the bullshit. The art restorer, the dates, the…everything. All a damn lie."

"I *am* an art restorer," Luka asserted. "But I also…I…I—"

"You also kill, deceive, and seduce."

Luka glared at her with torment in her eyes, and Hayley could see she'd hit a nerve.

"I never planned this," Luka said. "I never intended to hurt you."

"So…what does that mean? You just happened to run into me? You just happened to be at the benefit? None of this was set up? None of this happened because I have this damn tape?"

"Yes, I was at the benefit because the Organization knew you had the tape. I was on assignment. But it wasn't how you think. I never counted on—"

"On *what?*" Hayley spat. "Having to seduce me, fuck me to get your tape, and then do God-knows-what with me once you had it?"

"Please let me explain." Luka threw up her hands as if in surrender. "When we met that night, I didn't know who you were or why I was really there. They simply told me I was to meet someone. Later that evening they informed me that you were the one I was there to see— that you had the tape of the Miami incident, and they wanted to know if you could recognize me from it."

Luka's voice softened. "It was because we clicked, had chemistry, that you became my ta...assignment. I hated that. But I had no choice. I was ordered to stick with you, find out what you knew and who you were talking to, see if you were going to work on this alone."

"But I don't know anything," Hayley shouted. "I have no idea who sent me this tape, and I haven't told anyone but Manny about it."

"I'm aware of all that."

"How?"

"Because your house is bugged, your phone is tapped, and I've been listening in on and shadowing you the whole time. I've been staying at an apartment across the street from you."

That certainly explained Luka's unannounced arrival, without a car, at her apartment the night before. Just as she was going through Manny's box, listening to the tapes about the EOO.

"Jesus Christ! I've had my head so far up my ass with this damn story and you, I didn't notice a damn thing. What an idiot."

"You're not an idiot, Hayley. I'd be doing a bad job if you'd noticed me."

"Yes, of course—you being a pro and all. So tell me, Luka…or Domino, or whatever it is you go by. What were you planning to do with me after you got whatever you needed?"

"I can't talk about that. Besides it's not—"

"What, Luka?" she pressed. "Say it, damn it. For once, be honest. What were…are you going to do with me, besides keep me safe. Isn't that what you said? Which makes complete sense. I mean—that is what assassins do, after all, keep people safe."

They stared at each other in silence.

"My only crime is being on the receiving end of something I never asked for," Hayley said. "I have nothing to do with this mess. Apparently I was on a wild goose chase from the very beginning. And now, all of a sudden, I have assassins after me. What did I do to deserve this?"

"Listen to me, I know you've done nothing wrong, and please stop calling me that." Luka looked hurt, and Hayley didn't know whether she wanted to hit her or comfort her.

"Fucking collateral damage, isn't that what they call it? That's all I am to you. And then there's stupid me, actually falling for you. Feeling things I've never felt before and hoping it was mutual. Jesus. You must have had a real good laugh with that one. Well, you can pat yourself on the back. You gave a hell of a performance."

"Hayley, stop." Luka sank onto the couch, shoulders hunched as though in defeat.

"No, Luka, *you* stop. Stop with the bullshit. You don't have to pretend anymore." She had given her heart, had risked love again, and it had all been a lie. Luka had only been feigning interest. Tears sprang to her eyes, and she wiped at them angrily. "Tell me, are you even gay, or did you have to fake that, too?"

Luka got up and took her by the shoulders. "Look at me, damn it!"

Hayley tried to resist, because Luka was too good at fooling her. She met her eyes, with the coldest expression she could manage.

"I won't do anything to hurt you," Luka began. "Not now, not ever. Yes, I was asked to spy on you. But we weren't going to hurt you if you weren't involved. We don't hurt innocent people, nor do we believe in 'collateral damage.' Yes, I've hurt people. But they were drug lords, mobsters, smugglers, molesters, pedophiles, terrorists, skin traders, and the list of sickos goes on. I didn't enjoy having to spy on you—"

"Yeah, but—"

"Please let me finish." Luka released her. "I hated and loved every minute of being around you. I wanted to kiss you from the instant I saw you, but I didn't want to do that as part of a job. I couldn't handle using you that way. Never mind making love with you and letting you touch me. That just...well...I wanted to, so much, for the first time in my life that it ate me up inside. It terrified me and still does."

Hayley wanted to believe her so badly she ached with the wanting. But her head was spinning from all the lies, and she needed time to absorb everything, sort out where the truth lay.

"Before you interrupted me earlier, I wanted to say I never counted on falling in love with you. But I did. And somewhere along the way, my priorities changed. *I* changed, because of you. I can't alter who I am, or take back what I've done, but I won't let them hurt you. I'll talk to my employers, make them realize you know absolutely nothing. That you're no threat, you were set up. Then I'll find whoever is behind all this."

Oh, is that all? Piece of cake. Hayley felt so overwhelmed and exhausted that the tears began to fall in earnest and she started to shake. She wanted desperately to believe Luka, trust she could make this nightmare disappear. But could she?

The ringing of Luka's cell phone startled them both.

Domino checked the display and frowned as she flipped it open. Very few people had this number. Anyone who called it should have registered with caller ID. The woman on the other end did not identify herself and spoke only three words before disconnecting.

"You're not safe."

Domino knew that voice so well she recognized it immediately. Joanne Grant was one of the very few people she trusted implicitly. She turned to Hayley. "We've got to get out of here. *Now*."

CHAPTER TWENTY-FIVE

2:30 p.m.

"Where are we going?" Hayley asked as they rode down to the parking garage in the freight elevator. "What was that phone call all about?"

"We're going to my boat," Domino replied. She didn't think the EOO knew of *The Seawolf*, but she couldn't rule out the possibility. Still, if they got aboard and out on the water, they should be relatively safe for a while. Long enough for her to consider their next move. Joanne's call could mean only one thing. The EOO was aware she was no longer following protocol and was acting on her own. Pierce considered her a rogue operative. "That call was a warning we're not safe at my condo." She didn't want to tell Hayley that now her own people were after both of them. She already had enough to deal with.

The knowledge the Organization considered her a traitor saddened her. She didn't regret her actions, but she knew things were certainly more dangerous now than ever.

She didn't expect the EOO to make a move on her at her home or at the marina, and certainly not in broad daylight, because it would raise too many questions, bring attention and heat down on them, which was exactly what they were trying to avoid. Then again, she'd never been on the wrong side of the Organization, and she knew Pierce considered a rogue operative the most dangerous threat of all. He might go to any lengths.

As the lift slowed to stop, Domino pulled her gun from beneath her jacket. "Stay back," she whispered right before the doors opened. She exited first, glancing about for trouble and keeping Hayley behind her. Her senses were finely tuned for the slightest hint things weren't what they should be, but all seemed quiet.

The van wasn't safe—it was an EOO vehicle—so she led Hayley to her own car and seated her, then slipped around to the driver's seat and started the engine. They pulled out of the garage, with Domino glancing constantly from street to mirror to passersby, analyzing everything.

Hayley could see their danger in Luka's hyperalertness and rigid body language, and she started looking around as well, not knowing what exactly she should be watching for. If this woman—who always seemed to have everything under control—was worried, then she must have good reason. She wanted to ask what the threat was, but knew instinctively that now wasn't the time to distract Luka with questions.

The closer they got to the Potomac River marina where *The Seawolf* was moored, the more congested traffic became. The waterfront had a good view of the massive fireworks display on the National Mall, and the holiday crowds were staking out their spots early. Families and couples in red, white, and blue, carrying picnic baskets and lawn chairs, overflowed the sidewalks on either side of them. Domino should have anticipated this situation; the holiday events in DC on the Fourth of July were legendary, but since she'd always spent the occasion alone, or working, they surprised her.

"So many people," Hayley remarked warily as they crept along, still a half mile or so from the boat.

In an effort to cheer her, she replied, "There can be safety in numbers," which was generally true. But the rules often got bent when the threat was large enough, and whoever else was after Hayley had, earlier that same day, demonstrated their willingness to take unusual risks if the opportunity arose.

When traffic stopped, she decided it was smarter to walk the rest of the way. Staying in a vehicle that couldn't move made them too vulnerable. She parked at her first opportunity, at a bank closed for the holiday, and they got out.

Smiling, jovial faces surrounded them, but she was in anything but a celebratory mood. She led the way, threading through the crowd, keeping Hayley behind her. Scanning faces as she went, she tried to anticipate any hint of danger or someone who didn't belong.

They made it about halfway and were in a small park packed nearly shoulder to shoulder, when she spotted him through the crowd, about fifteen feet away. A man, about thirty, was pushing his way in their direction, studying the people around him in much the same way she was. At first, she could see only his face and part of his upper torso, but something about him said he wasn't just a reveler who had temporarily lost his wife or girlfriend among the masses.

He cupped his hand near his ear briefly and said a few words, then turned his head in her direction. Their eyes met, and he gazed past her to Hayley. She could see recognition on his face as he came straight for them.

Several things registered as he closed the distance. He wasn't alone, and he wasn't holding a gun, which meant his unseen accomplice *was*, and he was coming toward them so purposefully he clearly thought by the time he reached them, she would be no threat.

She reacted before he'd traveled two steps, shoving Hayley hard, away to her left, as she ducked right, and the bullet passed between them, grazing a middle-aged mother of three.

The woman screamed as red blossomed above her temple; she clutched at it as the toddler in her arms started to cry.

"She's been shot," someone yelled. People scattered in a panic, shoving and pushing.

The chaos of the crowd slowed the man momentarily as he pushed toward Hayley, but only a few feet separated them now.

"Hayley! Run," she shouted as she drew her gun. Someone slammed into her from behind, trying to flee, and she was thrown off balance. When she recovered, she saw the man grab a redheaded woman, and she thought for an instant he'd gotten Hayley. It was an easy mistake in the bedlam—the two women were roughly the same height, and both were dressed in red. But it wasn't Hayley—she'd gotten away, enveloped by the crowd.

When the man realized his error, he looked around for the real Hayley, then reached into the pocket of his windbreaker as he turned back to Domino. She took off, back toward the parking lot to divert him from Hayley's direction, roughly shoving through the panicked crowd as she tucked her gun back into her pants, out of sight.

She heard screams behind her as he pursued, and a man shouted, "Gun! He's got a gun."

Domino accelerated, trying to keep low, but she didn't return to her car. If she'd been followed here, they might have messed with it, so she stayed in the crowd, moving toward the busy main street. When she glanced back, she didn't see him, and the crowd was thinning now, calmer, so she slowed her steps to be just another holiday reveler wondering what the hell all the shouting was about. Two cops ran by her, toward the bedlam she'd left, and she heard the first sounds of sirens in the distance.

When she reached the main intersection, she paused at the curb deciding where to start looking for Hayley.

The roar of an engine and shouts to her right made her turn in that direction. Several cars away, a black Mazda Miata had jumped the curb, pulling out of the bumper-to-bumper traffic and half onto the sidewalk, and was headed right at her.

She didn't recognize the driver, but he had one hand on the wheel and a gun aimed straight at her in the other. She pivoted, intending to retreat to the safety of the crowd, but spotted the other man—the one she thought she'd lost—not twenty feet away and closing fast.

As the light changed to red, stopping traffic, she turned back to the street and saw her opportunity. A guy sat on a motorcycle in the far lane at the front. She ran to him. Though she hated to do it, she pulled her gun with one hand and put it to the man's neck, while she yanked the key from the ignition with the other. "I need the bike."

He looked at her like he was about to tell her to go to hell, so she pressed the gun harder against his throat and saw the flash of recognition cross his face as he realized what it was. He opened his mouth to speak, but she cocked the gun near his ear. "Now," she barked.

He hustled off the seat, and even before he had both feet on the ground, she was astride the bike and firing it back to life. She shot through the red light and heard a squeal of tires from her left as the Miata came off the pavement after her.

❖

Hayley had been so on edge and ready to bolt throughout their trek to the boat that when all hell broke loose and Luka told her to run, she reacted instantly, taking off in the opposite direction as fast as she could shove through the crowd.

She'd gone a hundred feet and had begun to believe she'd gotten away, when someone abruptly bear-hugged her. Before she could react, she felt a sting in her shoulder and the man who'd grabbed her said loudly, "Honey, I think you've had too much to drink."

Hayley barely glimpsed him before she collapsed.

CHAPTER TWENTY-SIX

3:45 p.m.

W e have her."
Hayley blinked fuzzily, disoriented, trying to shake off the effects of whatever they'd injected her with. The quiet voice came from behind her.

"No, there was a problem at the motel. Someone interceded and got her out of there—taking two of our guys out in the process. But the third—the driver—followed them to DC, and we got her about an hour ago. She's in a secure location."

Cool air was blowing on her from somewhere above. And she was lying on something hard.

"It was a woman. And from the description, it sounds like the art restorer who strong-armed the private detective we had following them." A pause. "Okay. She should come to any time. I'll let you know."

Hayley tried to lift her hands and discovered they were bound together. Then she realized her legs were, too. She craned her head, trying to scan the room, but the place was dimly lit, with no visible windows.

A dark silhouette walked past her field of vision. Then the lights came on, bright and blinding, and she shut her eyes against the sudden glare. When she opened them again, a woman was looking down at her. Tall, five-eight or better, and trim, with green eyes, and straight, dark brown hair that fell nearly to her waist. She'd pulled her hair back, which accentuated the one feature that kept her from being model-attractive—a scar, about an inch and a half long, from just beneath her left cheekbone to the corner of her mouth. She wore black jeans, a long-sleeved black T-shirt, and a blank expression.

"Where am I?" Hayley asked.

The woman stood at her feet. "You're not here to ask me questions, Ms. Ward. You're here to answer mine."

She looked around again at the small room with bare white walls and ceiling, the table she lay on, and four chairs. No windows, just the vent right above her. It reminded her of an interrogation room in a cop shop—she'd been in a few while covering stories.

The woman was blocking the only door. A device next to it didn't look like anything she'd ever seen, just a metal rectangular box with a protruding platform at the bottom.

"I want to know what led you to David Rabinowitz," the woman said.

Rabinowitz. The political advisor on Manny's list of names. Is that who had sent her the tape? "Who are you?" she asked.

"Someone not known for their patience. So don't make me repeat myself."

"I don't know any David Rabinowitz, okay? His was only a random number I dialed—one of many—off a list I found."

The woman stared at her, unblinking, waiting for her to continue.

"I left my number with him." Was that only this morning? *How long have I been unconscious?* So much had happened it seemed like days. "That's all I know."

Still the woman merely stared at her, unmoving.

Bile burned in her throat, and she tried to will her hammering heartbeat to slow. *What the fuck does she want?* "Listen, I'll answer your questions, but get me off this, will you? It's killing my back and I think I'm going to be sick."

"No."

"Jesus Christ, look at me." She was almost shouting now. "It's not like I can go anywhere. You've got me trapped like some kind of lab rat."

The woman seemed to consider her words. Then she helped Hayley up and off the table and into a chair. "Go on."

So much adrenaline was pouring through her, she was almost dizzy. "I called Rabinowitz and a bunch of other numbers. Someone called me back later and said they could protect me from the EO… from a certain organization. I trusted this man to help me and told him where I was. The next thing I know two guys show up, and I'm being drugged and out cold. Look, I don't know what's going on, what all this means or why I'm here, and I don't care to know. This is scaring the shit out of me, so if you just let me go, I won't say anything to anybody." It was hard to catch her breath, as if there weren't enough oxygen in the room.

"And?"

"And what? That's all I remember." Her lungs ached. She was panting now, close to hyperventilating. "I'm not feeling well."

"Where were these guys when you woke up?" the woman asked.

"I don't *know*." She struggled against the tape on her wrists, panic squeezing her from all sides.

"So they drugged you and walked away?"

"I don't remember. Listen, my hands are really starting to hurt. Please. Can you get this tape off me?"

"Who was the woman who knocked out those men and got you out of the motel?"

Jesus, they know about that. They saw Luka. Her chest seemed to constrict even more. "I was out cold, how should I know? You seem to know more about it than I do. Look, I can't feel my hands any more, and I—"A coughing spasm seized her. "God, I feel sick. I can't breathe, and I feel like I'm gonna throw up. What the hell did you inject me with?" Bile rose again, and she choked it back, gagging.

"Damn it." The woman knelt beside her and removed the tape from her hands.

"Please," she said, rubbing her wrists. She was wheezing. "I need water."

"You'll be fine."

She leaned forward awkwardly, trying to put her head between her legs, and started to gag again. Coughing back the acrid taste in her mouth, she looked up at the woman. "I need water, damn it!"

The woman stood and went to the door. Hayley noticed a gun tucked into the back of the woman's pants and watched as she put her palm on the small platform that protruded from the device next to the door. The door unlocked with an audible click, and the woman pushed it open.

"Dennis, get in here," she called loudly, and almost immediately a man appeared in the doorway. Thirty or so, slender, about the same height as the woman. "Bring me a glass of water."

When he returned in a couple of minutes, he addressed the woman just loud enough for Hayley to hear. "You got a call, Jack. Your friend wants an update ASAP. And he wants to pick her up tonight."

"All right." Jack handed her the glass. "You have your water. No more stalling. I'll be back, and when I am, you're going to be a lot more forthcoming, Ms. Ward. You're going to tell me all about your friend, all about this list with David Rabinowitz's name on it. And you're going to give me the names of everyone you've talked to about the tape that was sent to you."

❖

4:00 p.m.

Senator Terrence Burrows felt smug as he stood at the window of his den, smoking a cigar and watching the festivities in his backyard. Red, white, and blue bunting and flags festooned the privacy wall enclosing the estate, the pool was full of splashing children, and one of his aides was manning the barbecue, grilling steaks, ribs, and chicken for his well-heeled guests.

It was indeed a day to celebrate. He had contained the threat and would soon eliminate both Hayley Ward and the EOO leadership so he could finally accomplish his quest for the Oval Office in peace.

When his secure line rang with Jack's callback, he answered with, "I'm listening."

"Doesn't look like she knows anything about you," Jack began. "Says she got Rabinowitz's number randomly, from a list, along with several others."

"What else?"

"I'm still questioning her, but she's scared, and apparently she's telling the truth when she claims not to know much. She's not a serious threat to you."

"Good work," he replied. "I'll pick her up in three or four hours."

"I'll be expecting you."

He disconnected and dialed Pierce's number. "I have your meddlesome journalist."

"I didn't ask you to go after her," Pierce replied.

"That's right. I decided to do it anyway." Terrence injected the right amount of righteous anger into his voice. "I couldn't take that kind of risk. And it's a good thing I did, Pierce. She was about to go to the police."

"Where is she now?"

"Somewhere she can't talk or create any more problems."

"I need her alive," Pierce said.

"That's up to you, but I don't see why." He puffed on his cigar. "I didn't even have to try, and she gave up names and locations," he lied. "She knows too much, and she's afraid. Dangerous combination."

"I said I need her alive," Pierce repeated. "We'll see to it that she doesn't talk, but first we need some answers. Where can we collect her?"

"You can't," he said. "I'll deliver her to you personally. I don't want anyone else involved, Pierce. None of my people, and especially not any of yours. I can't risk having one of your operatives recognize and then blackmail me. Besides, I need to hand over the information Grant asked for concerning the China delegation. You might as well bring her along, because we need to talk specifics."

"Fine," Pierce said. "It's a four-hour flight to get to you. Where and when?"

"At an abandoned office building." He gave him the address. "Go to room 512. I'll see you there at eight thirty. I hope you appreciate my help with—" He heard the click of Pierce disconnecting, then a dial tone. Arrogant fuck, he thought. But then he smiled because he wouldn't have to put up with this shit after tonight.

The timing couldn't have been better. All the necessary accoutrements for tonight's lethal festivities were in the trunk of an old Buick Jack had acquired for him. He would celebrate his independence tonight from his shackles, and the fireworks in the capital would be the perfect backdrop.

❖

The Mazda Miata was fast and maneuverable, and its driver skillful, but Domino had the advantage on her stolen speed bike in the slow, congested traffic near the marina. She darted between the lanes of cars, narrowly missing mirrors, hearing curses and shouts on either side, while the guy in the Miata tried to parallel her on the wide sidewalk, scattering pedestrians and street-food vendors and plowing

KIM BALDWIN & XENIA ALEXIOU

through lawn chairs, newspaper racks, trash bins, and anything else in his way. She gained ground quickly, but couldn't shake him entirely.

Seeking an avenue of escape, she paralleled the Potomac, hearing sirens closing in. Ahead she spotted a pair of office buildings that filled a city block, with a pedestrian walkway between that looked too narrow for the car to follow, so she braked, swerved, and shot through it, nearly losing control halfway when she suddenly reached a series of wide steps. They led down to a small, bench-filled plaza in the shadow of the buildings, where office workers could smoke or eat their lunch alfresco.

On the opposite side, more steps led up and out to the main street north of the buildings, where she guessed her pursuer would try to pick her up again. She bounced down the half-dozen stairs to the plaza level, where she had room to turn the bike around, then roared up them again to head back the way she came.

When she emerged from between the buildings, the Miata was waiting for her. This guy was good. Too good, which led her to believe he was another EOO op.

She gunned the bike and took off eastbound, the sports car in pursuit. Traffic was sparse now, and he was able to keep closer, dodging around cars with her, at one point so near she could see his gun out of the driver's side window, readying for a shot.

Ahead, the road ended as it bisected another. Taking a left would lead her back toward the marina—certain to be filled with cops by now—but to the right, the road was closed, under construction. Wooden barricades with flashing lights blocked all of the pavement and sidewalk.

She barely slowed as she took the corner, leaning the bike over so far the foot peg scraped the pavement. Then she plowed through the barricades, pieces of wood flying in all directions. One cut through her jacket and into her side, but she barely felt it.

She fought for control as the bike barreled through a patch of sand beyond the barricade, the Miata not far behind. Then, no road at all, only a grid of steel where the concrete would be laid, impassible for either of them. The only alternative was a narrow alley to her right, so she braked hard and smelled burning rubber as the bike shuddered to make the turn.

The Miata fell a bit farther back. The driver had to slow severely to follow her down the cramped space.

She was a hundred and fifty feet down the alley when she saw the enormous dumpster ahead and, beyond it, a brick wall. She hit the brakes a few feet before the wall and twisted the throttle, turning the bike on its axis until it faced the Miata, which was accelerating toward her, closing fast.

She took in her surroundings and saw only one possibility. She twisted the throttle and headed straight for the car. They were forty feet apart, then thirty. She stood on the pegs and jumped off when she reached the dumpster, slamming onto the metal top with a bone-jarring impact that knocked the wind out of her.

The bike slid down the alley toward the Miata, and she heard the squeal of brakes and the deafening sound of metal and glass as he crashed into it, then spun toward the dumpster.

He hit it just as she jumped for the fire escape, hanging on by one hand.

Domino pulled out her gun and dropped onto the roof of the Miata as it stopped beneath her, then lay prone, hanging over the side at the driver's side window. Her pursuer's hand closed on the gun on the seat beside him. As he brought it toward her, she shot a hole in the window, then shattered it with her fist.

Her reflexes were only a hair faster than his. She had her gun to his head before he could fire. "You have a good shot at me right now, but I have an even better one. Don't fuck with the odds. Drop the piece."

Instead, he shifted to take a shot, so she fired right next to his face and shattered the passenger-side window. He froze.

"Next time I won't miss," she said. "Throw the gun out of the window I just opened for you."

Slowly, he complied.

She slid off the car, her gun trained on his head. "Keep your hands on the wheel where I can see them."

When he obeyed, she walked around the car to retrieve his gun, still aiming her own at his head. At the back of the vehicle, she put two of his bullets into the rear tires, ejected the magazine from his gun, and stuck it into her pocket before tossing the weapon beneath the car. Then she ran like hell.

Under normal circumstances, she'd have taken care of him for good. But he was almost certainly EOO, and she still hoped to work things out with Pierce and return to the Organization.

A half mile from the alley, she slowed, considering what to do next. Her jacket was torn, as was the shirt beneath it, and badly bloodstained. She had a deep cut from her encounter with the barricade, which needed dressing. And the police were looking for her by now. A lot of people could have described her, which was another reason to change her appearance.

She also wanted to call Pierce, and she had to do it from her cell phone. He wouldn't pick up if she used a phone not in the EOO database. But if they were trying to track her, they could use her cell to do so, so she had to call from a busy place where she could get lost quickly.

She needed some kind of department store. After taking off her jacket, she folded it to hide the tear, then draped it over her arm and against her injured side to hide that, too.

It took her fifteen minutes to find a subway stop and she recalled a Macy's nearby, at Twelfth and G Street, so she got off at the Metro Center stop and headed for it. The store was busy with holiday shoppers, but she found a quiet corner where she tried her call to Pierce.

When the line connected, a recording told her the number she had dialed was no longer in service.

The finality of the situation hit home. She was on her own, and the only family she had known weren't just rejecting her, but were out to kill her. Though solitary all of her life, Domino felt more alone than she could remember.

She had to contact Pierce and explain the situation. *There must be a way to make him listen.* Otherwise, they wouldn't stop until they caught up with her, and she couldn't run for the rest of her life.

Next, she tried Hayley's number, hopeful she'd gotten away and was somewhere safe. But she'd had too many surprises today to be sure of anything. The phone rang five times, then went to voice mail. "Hayley, it's Luka. I hope you're safe. Call me and I'll come get you."

Twenty minutes later, she emerged from the store, her side patched up and wearing a new T-shirt, ball cap, and sunglasses, and she had nothing to do but wait.

❖

A myriad of questions swirled through Hayley's mind after the woman left her alone. Who the hell were they going to turn her over to? Rabinowitz? And for what purpose? She took a long drink of the water and several deep breaths. *Don't panic.* She couldn't merely sit around and wait for whatever was going to happen. It didn't seem to matter she didn't know anything. Someone had a plan for her, evidently, and she wasn't going to change their minds.

Only Luka believed that she knew nothing about this affair. She had said she would find a way out of this mess, but where was she? *How do I find her, or help her find me, when I don't even know where I am?*

She peeled off the tape binding her ankles together. Getting out of this room was her first objective. Then she'd try to figure out where she was, find a window or something, and see if she could locate a phone to call Luka.

Hayley stood and felt dizzy. She had to hold on to the table to steady herself. After a minute, she took a few tentative steps. Better. Her breathing had started to settle, thank God. And her heartbeat was a little more normal. She'd had panic attacks before, never this bad, but she'd never had these kinds of reasons to panic.

She forced herself to take several deep breaths. Slow and steady. Yes, she was definitely feeling better. *Keep a cool head. Think.* She'd had to talk herself in and out of situations before.

Footsteps approached outside, and another rush of adrenaline poured through her. Without thinking, she picked up the chair she'd been sitting in and stood behind the door. She heard the click as it unlocked and raised the chair above her head.

The next few seconds happened in slow motion. The door started to open. She expected Jack, but instead the guy who'd brought her the water said, a millisecond before he came into view, "Yes, sir. Jack told me to contact you with an update—"

She brought the chair down hard and fast on the side of his head. He stumbled and fell to the side, off balance, dropping his cell phone, and before he had time to recover, she brought the chair down on his head twice more. The man lay on his side, unmoving, the butt of a gun sticking out of the rear waistband of his jeans.

After she retrieved the gun, she picked up the cell phone. It had disconnected, but still worked. She was tempted to call 911, but hesitated. She still didn't know who to trust, and her gut told her to let Luka try to help—that she was in the best position to take care of whoever was after her.

But better to get the hell out of there and somewhere safe first. Jack could walk in any minute, and whoever was on the other end of that call knew it had disconnected. What was she going to tell Luka, anyway? That she was in a room without windows somewhere?

She turned to leave. *Shit.* Somehow the door had clicked shut again. She remembered how Jack had gotten out and was about to put her own hand on the device near the door when she realized it probably worked with print recognition. Placing the wrong palm there might set off an alarm.

The guy on the floor evidently had clearance. She stuck the gun into her pants and flipped the man onto his back. Grabbing him by the wrists, she dragged him to the door. First, she tried to lift him by his right arm, twisting it to maneuver his palm into place. But the man was dead weight.

Leverage. That's what she needed. Using the man's belt loops, she turned him onto his stomach and straddled him, lifting him by the armpits, using her knees to keep his upper torso off the ground until she could wrap one arm around him while she positioned his palm on the device with the other. The struggle took all her strength, but it worked. *Click.*

Hayley dropped the man and took the gun back out. The safety was off, ready to fire. When she'd moved away from home and into her first apartment, her brother had insisted on teaching her how to shoot a gun and had urged her to get one for her personal protection. But she'd never felt particularly comfortable with firearms, though she was glad to have one now. She'd use it if she had to, to get out of here. Gripping it tightly, she headed toward the door.

CHAPTER TWENTY-SEVEN

4:40 p.m.

Hayley pushed the door open a few inches and listened. Nothing. She peered out at a hallway that had a doorway to the left about fifteen feet away and another door at the end. Of the two windows, the nearest one was to her right a body length away.

Quietly, she headed down the hall to the first window, her heart thumping wildly, straining to hear anything from the room ahead. The Washington Monument stood in the distance, stark white against a brilliant blue sky. Otherwise she seemed to be in an industrial area, unfamiliar and largely deserted, no traffic or pedestrians. And no signage to help her determine exactly where she was.

She hugged the left wall and crept to the room farther down, with its door ajar and no sound from inside. She peered inside, the gun shaking so much she worried about shooting herself in the foot.

No one was there. She released the breath she didn't realize she'd been holding.

It was an office, with a cluttered desk, a small TV, file cabinet, and coffee maker. She searched the desk for an invoice or anything to help determine her location. No help there, but she was alone, at least for the time being. Time to call Luka.

She pulled out the cell phone, the one the woman had been using, she realized, and dialed Luka's number. When Luka answered, she kept her voice low. "It's Hayley. I'm in a shitload of trouble, and I can't talk long."

"Where are you?"

"I was kidnapped. I'm in DC. I can see the monument in the distance, and I'm surrounded by factories, but that's all I can make out.

I've got a gun, they might find me any minute. They're supposed to turn me over to somebody tonight." She knew she was ranting, but her time was limited.

"Hayley, listen to me. I'm coming to get you. Try to breathe," Luka said. "Are you on a cell phone?"

"Yes. It belongs to some woman named Jack. Oh, she was talking to someone, her boss, I think, when I woke up. The number should be in her list of received calls. I'm going to put you on hold so I can get to it."

"Don't call it!" Luka said. "Get the number and read it back to me."

The most recent received call, in fact, the last several calls, read private number. It wouldn't display the number of the caller or allow a callback. She checked the list of dialed calls, too, with the same result. *Fuck.*

"No luck. They all say private number. I don't think there's any way to retrieve it."

"Keep it turned on," Luka said. "It'll help me locate you. Hide it wherever you have to but keep it on. And Hayley, just in case, clear the list of dialed calls so they won't know you contacted anyone."

"Okay. I'm going to try to get out of here," she said. "Should I call 911 first?"

"No. It's not safe. Wait for me. I'll be there soon."

"Okay, Luka. I'm going to hang up. I'm afraid someone might hear me."

"Be careful."

"Hurry." She ended the call, cleared the list, and shoved the phone in her pocket.

"Hey," came a male voice from her right. "What the hell?"

Hayley had taken her eyes from the doorway for only a second, and she hadn't heard him approach, but suddenly a man stood there, the guy who'd subdued her at the marina—as shocked to see her as she was to see him.

But she had her gun out, and he didn't. Yet. He started to reach for his, so she brought hers up in his direction without thinking, gripped it with both hands because she was shaking so much, and fired. Twice.

She wasn't aiming at any particular body part, simply trying to shoot before he did. The first shot missed, but the second hit him in the leg and he went down. The wound wasn't serious enough to keep him from being a threat, but he was no longer as intent on getting his own gun out as long as she still pointed hers at him.

"Don't move." She kept both hands on the gun as she edged toward the door. He was blocking it, so she couldn't give him too wide a berth, but he remained still as she passed by because she kept the gun trained on his head.

"Very slowly now," she said once she got to the door, out of reach, "take your gun out and slide it over here."

He silently did as she instructed, and she picked up the weapon and stuck it in her pants before she bolted down the hall and through the door.

She ran headlong into Jack and a third man, running to investigate the shots she'd fired, and she had no time to react. They subdued her easily, retrieved both guns and the cell phone, and returned to the interrogation room just as the guy she'd knocked out was coming to.

❖

5:00 p.m.

After Domino hung up, she searched for transportation. In the secluded corner of a Metrorail parking lot she switched license plates on two cars, then hotwired a Toyota Corolla, a very popular model in the greater metropolitan area.

Her next step was to track Hayley, and for that she needed help. She couldn't return to her home or the surveillance apartment, so she didn't have the equipment she needed. If Pierce's number was blocked, he would have instructed everyone in the EOO not to contact or acknowledge her. But hopefully one person would ignore that order. Mishael Taylor, another ETF. They had been brought into the EOO at the same time, been in the same classes and grown up together. And though personal attachments of any kind had been discouraged, hopefully their bond would transcend loyalty to the Organization.

She tried Mishael's private number, which forwarded to voicemail. *Damn.* "It's Luka. I need a favor…as a friend. Call me from the office, ASAP. Don't let them know I've contacted you. They have this all wrong, Mishael, and I need to make it right."

More waiting. God, she hated waiting. She paced and stared at her cell phone, willing it to ring, wishing she hadn't given up smoking.

❖

As Jack retied Hayley's hands and feet, the guy she'd hit over the head glared at her with a boy-do-I-wish-I-could-kill-you look. Through the open door, Hayley could hear the man she'd shot cry out in pain, then the sound of approaching footsteps. It was the guy who'd helped Jack end her bolt for freedom.

"Dennis says he thinks she was on your phone when he walked in," the man reported.

Jack took out the phone just returned to her, checked the menus, and frowned. "Dialed numbers have been erased," she said, more to herself than him. "Who did you call?"

Hayley remained silent. *Hurry, Luka. Hurry.*

"I said," Jack repeated, clearly at the end of her patience, "who did you call?"

"I didn't," Hayley said. "He came in as I was about to."

"She's lying," one of the men said.

"No shit," Jack said wearily. "Undo her feet. We have to move her, fast. Cops may be on their way. Let's go."

❖

6:30 p.m.

It took ninety minutes for Domino to get the callback from Mishael.

"What the hell's going on?" her friend asked.

"I'm not certain, but I need your help to find out."

"I sure hope you know what you're doing," Mishael said, "because they're—"

"I know." She was heading back to the car. "I'll explain later. We don't have time. I need you to locate a cell phone through the GPS. The last call received on my number."

"It'll take a few minutes. Was the ID concealed?"

"Yes."

"Hang on. I'll hack into your provider, then find and hack the caller's ID."

"They'll be able to track this phone call as well," Domino said. "You need to delete our conversation from the record."

"Give me some credit, will ya? Have I given you the impression I'm looking for that kind of excitement? Hold on a minute. Okay, let's see. Here it is. The cell's IMEI number and the card's SIM are registered to a Jaclyn Norris."

She started the engine and pulled away from the curb. "Locate it."

"I'm on it." Mishael hummed off key. "Bingo," she said. "Can't give you an exact location, Luka, the signal's too weak. Too much concrete in the area. I can get you within a quarter mile or so." She gave Domino the street names.

"Thanks, Mishael. I owe you."

"And don't you forget it. Be careful."

She disconnected and sped toward the area.

It took more than a half hour to reach an industrial district, full of factories and warehouses, all of them apparently closed for the holiday. It fit Hayley's description, but Domino couldn't tell exactly what building she was in.

She drove slowly up one street and down the next, seeking a clue.

❖

They blindfolded Hayley when they moved her but didn't take her far. In five or ten minutes they stopped again. One guy holding each arm, they led her into another building, tied her to a chair, and left her alone, still blindfolded.

Then all was silent, giving her too much time to think and an eternity to be afraid. Could Luka find her, now that they'd moved her? She should've called 911. Who was coming to pick her up? And what did they plan to do with her?

After another two and a half hours she got her answer. By that time, fear had blossomed into terror, and her hands and feet were numb from the bindings.

The door opened, then closed. Someone approached, though he didn't speak right away, as if studying her. "Good evening, Miss Ward," he said at last, with a chillingly friendly tone. "You've been a very busy woman since I sent you that tape, haven't you?"

CHAPTER TWENTY-EIGHT

"Who are you? Why are you doing this?" Hayley asked. The man was engaged in a task of some kind, very near. She heard a zipper open, then other sounds she couldn't identify.

"Who, what, where, when, why. Always the reporter," the man replied. "But not today. Today I get to ask the questions."

She jumped when his hand touched her shoulder.

"How did you find David Rabinowitz? Did you get his name from Detective Vasquez?"

He knew about Vasquez. Her alarm increased. *Did he kill Manny? Just for talking to me? Jesus.* "He was on a list of names and numbers in a case file of Manny's," she replied. This man obviously knew quite a lot about her already. "I called a lot of them. I don't know why he's so important to you. I don't know anything," she said, unable to keep desperation out of her voice.

"Who else have you told about Rabinowitz?"

The distinct sound of duct tape being pulled from a roll came from her left. He placed something against her stomach and her panic ramped up, especially because she couldn't see.

"What are you doing?"

"We're on *who*, not *what*," he replied calmly. "Who else have you told about Rabinowitz?"

He pressed firmly against one of her shoulders, then the opposite hip. The sound of more duct tape being ripped filled the silence, then he pressed against the other shoulder and hip. He was taping something to her—something hard—against her stomach. Rather large. *Damn this fucking blindfold.*

"No one," she said. "I haven't talked to anyone except this ex-cop called Manny Vasquez. And he didn't tell me anything."

"And he certainly won't be telling you anything now, after his unfortunate accident," the man replied cryptically, as he pulled off more tape. Then he moved behind her and pushed her to lean forward, and she could tell he was wrapping the tape around her middle. So tight it squeezed her if she tried to take a deep breath.

"What about Luka Madison? You didn't tell her? She was the one who helped you out of the motel, wasn't she? Who is she?"

Fuck. He knew about Luka. But apparently not that she was connected to the EOO. Something about the man's speech niggled at the periphery of her awareness. He sounded vaguely familiar. But she knew he wasn't David Rabinowitz. His voice had been much higher, with a trace of New York.

"Someone I've been dating. That's all. She's no one," Hayley said. "I haven't told her or anyone else about this. I promise if you let me go, I won't tell anyone this happened. I won't go to the police."

"No. You won't be telling anyone about this. Not the police. Not the EOO. Not anyone."

The ominous declaration redoubled her fear.

"Time for the *who*, Hayley." His hands fumbled at the back of her head, untying the blindfold.

Her breath caught in her throat.

Senator Terrence Burrows. Not only was his face splashed across numerous magazines and newspapers every other week, but she'd interviewed him once, had been impressed with his clear vision of where he wanted to go and his determination to get there.

She remembered thinking at the time how much alike they were.

Burrows didn't look like the typical presidential candidate right then, however. In place of his ever-present, perfectly pressed blue suit, he wore blue jeans, a T-shirt and windbreaker, and baseball cap.

Hayley had barely digested this information when she glanced down at her stomach and saw what he had taped there.

A bomb.

"Holy fuck!" In a blind panic, she fought desperately at her restraints, kicking and pulling at the tape.

"Stop that." He laid a hand on her shoulder and squeezed so hard she winced. "You don't want to upset the bomb and start the fireworks early, do you?"

The words froze her in place. "You son of a bitch," she shouted. "Why? I'm no threat to you, Senator."

He ignored her as he untied her from the chair and stripped the tape off her ankles so she could walk. Then he yanked her to her feet with a firm hand on her elbow. From a duffel bag at her feet, he withdrew a woman's jacket, pulled it around her, and snapped it shut to hide the bomb. Finally, from his pocket, he withdrew a small remote control, black plastic with a single red button in the center. "See this? If you try to run or do anything foolish…well, I think you know what'll happen. Now, let's go. We have an important appointment, and we don't want to be late."

"Where are you taking me?"

He tugged her along, out of the small windowless room they were in and down a hallway. Jack and her goons were nowhere in sight.

"I knew you'd get to the *where* about now," he said. "Patience, Miss Ward. All your questions will be answered soon." They came to a steel door, and he paused there to look outside before proceeding.

She had lost all sense of time, but she could see it was fully dark.

"You're going to meet the objects of your quest," he said as he put her into the passenger seat of a car waiting outside. The old, battered Buick wasn't at all the type of car she would expect the leading candidate for the presidency to drive. He'd planned this all very carefully, she realized, and was making sure he didn't attract any attention. Not that there was much chance of that. They were still in the warehouse district with its deserted streets.

As he started the car, he turned to her with his polished politician's smile, and she realized he was actually enjoying this.

"Do you know why I picked you to take those bastards down?" he asked. "You want the inside story, don't you? I thought you, of all candidates, would understand I won't let anything stand in my way. Do you understand? *Nothing!*"

His voice grew louder and his up-until-now calm demeanor cracked. "I've paid all my debts to these people. I've worked too fucking hard to get where I'm going, and I know you of all people appreciate hard work. The hunger and drive for success. You see, Hayley, you and I, we're the same. Get the job done, no matter who or what. I liked that about you when we met. That's why it had to be you. I knew once I sent you the tape you wouldn't let go of the story until you had something. And I was right. But you took a direction you shouldn't have."

"Listen, I don't care about your involvement, whatever it is. Please let me go." Tears streamed down her face, but Burrows didn't seem to be listening. "I don't care about the damn story."

"That really doesn't matter anymore, Hayley." He was suddenly calm again, and this Jekyll-and-Hyde thing terrified her even more. "After tonight, nothing and no one will stand in my way."

He was quiet as he maneuvered through mostly side streets, devoid of heavy traffic, heading out of the city. They drove for a half hour or so, until they came to a single ten-story building on a stretch of lonely road. It looked abandoned. The nearest possible help was a convenience store a mile or two away.

The parking lot near the building held one car, and they pulled up beside it. From that angle, Hayley could see one light on the fifth floor.

"We're here," the senator said. "Don't move."

Hayley was terrified, but didn't see any alternative but to comply.

Burrows threw his duffel bag over his shoulder, then came around to her side and pulled her from the car. She allowed him to lead her into the building.

❖

Domino sat with her lights off in one of the factory parking lots, staring up into the only lighted windows in the district. A pair of them, on the second floor of a company that made office furniture. She was considering how she would enter the building when she saw the headlights of an approaching car.

It was an older-model Buick, and it stopped, not at the building she was watching, but at the one next door, and the driver got out and went inside. He had his back to her, and it was dark, so she couldn't see his face. But he was large, and he was carrying some kind of bag.

After a couple of minutes, two people emerged. A different man, shorter, and a woman, who got into a car parked nearby and drove away.

She was certain Hayley was there and had to fight the urge to rush inside. But rescuing her wasn't enough. Hayley had said someone was coming to pick her up—for what purpose, she didn't know.

Neither she nor Hayley would be safe until she found out who was behind all this.

She didn't have to wait long. Ten or fifteen minutes after the first man went in, he came out again, leading a woman by the arm. Hayley. She glimpsed her face as they passed under the weak light outside the door. But the man had a baseball cap on, and his face was hidden in shadow. She didn't know if it was the guy they had been after or merely his lackey.

The man put Hayley into his car and they drove off. She gave them a good head start but kept them in sight and followed with her headlights off.

❖

"Keep your mouth shut," Senator Burrows told Hayley as he pushed her ahead of him up the stairwell of the abandoned building. They ascended five floors, then walked down a dark hall, past several open doors, toward the only lit room. That door was closed, but she could see the illumination spilling from beneath the threshold.

Burrows yanked her to a halt a few feet away and pulled out a small pen flashlight to ensure the bomb was still concealed beneath her jacket. Tying a cloth around her mouth, he whispered in her ear, "You'd better do as I say." The odor of his sweat tainted the scent of his cologne, a sign he wasn't quite as composed as he appeared.

They proceeded the rest of the way, and he knocked sharply on the door.

When a male voice answered, "Come in," Burrows placed Hayley in front of him and slowly turned the knob, then gently pushed her forward.

The room had once been an office of some kind, with a couple of battered desks and three chairs. An ancient radiator ran along one wall, and scraps of paper littered the floor.

Two people, a man and a woman, were waiting for them. Well dressed, they looked to be in their fifties, and both wore serious expressions.

"Here she is, as promised," the senator said from behind Hayley.

"We'll take her from here," the man inside said. He was leaning against one of the desks, watching them.

"And the information I asked you for?" the woman added.

Burrows didn't answer. Instead, he stood in front of Hayley, his back to the two strangers, and unbuttoned her jacket. "The plan has changed," he said, before stepping aside so the pair could see the bomb taped to her stomach. Six sticks of dynamite, wires, and a round, metal detonator. There was also a digital clock, but the display area was blank.

Before either could react, he raised his arm to let them see the activation device in his palm. "One fucking move, one word, and we all go up together." The Hyde side had reappeared. "Now, stretch your arms out in front of you. Slowly. Very slowly."

As they followed his order, he opened his duffel bag and pulled out a knife. All the while, one hand remained on the detonation device. He cut Hayley's restraints, then shoved three pairs of handcuffs into her hand. "Cuff them to each other."

Hayley was shaking uncontrollably, and her heartbeat was so loud in her ears she heard him as through a tunnel. The cloth in her mouth gagged her, and she shook her head no. It was pure instinct. Burrows's plan was clearly careening toward its conclusion, and she didn't want to get there any faster than she had to.

"Come on, Miss Ward. It's simple enough. Start by cuffing his hand to the radiator. Then him to her, then her to the radiator. Now move."

Hayley's vision blurred as tears flooded her eyes. She stumbled toward the pair and followed his instructions. When she finished, Burrows motioned her to step to the side and checked that the restraints were secure. Then he patted them down. Both were wearing guns, which he removed and stuck into his jacket.

Once satisfied they were no threat, he seemed to relax. He stood before the man, their faces inches apart, and smiled at him with a smug expression. "So, our agreement isn't the kind that expires. Isn't that what you said, Pierce?"

"You're never going to get away with this," Pierce replied.

"Don't tell me what I can and can't do. I've had to listen to that shit all my life. But you know what it comes down to? This moment. Right here, right now. Doesn't it, Pierce? And it looks to me like I am going to get away with it. And you know why? Because I take care of my own business. I don't have to resort to trained monkeys to do it for me."

"You old pathetic fool, you don't really think you're going to become president, do you?" Pierce goaded him.

"Shut the fuck up," Burrows shouted. He turned to Hayley. "You, grab that chair and put it in the middle of the room. Now."

She was so on edge she jumped at the command. As she picked up the chair he was pointing to, she told herself to take deep breaths to keep from hyperventilating, but each effort met resistance when it reached the tape around her middle, reminding her of the dynamite she carried.

She placed the chair where he asked, and he reached into the duffel bag for his roll of tape. "Sit. And don't move."

What could she do? Burrows held up the detonator, his thumb twitchy on the red button.

She sat in the chair, and he taped her to it. Hands and feet. Absolutely secure. No chance for escape. While he was occupied, she looked beyond him, to her left, at the other two surreptitiously trying to free themselves from their handcuffs, but they weren't having any success.

Finally the senator picked up his duffel bag and walked to the door, then turned back to look at them. "Well, aren't you going to wish me good luck?" Without waiting for an answer, he raised his hand, making sure he had their attention before he pressed the button then quickly departed, closing the door behind him.

They all braced for an explosion, and when none immediately occurred, they all stared at Hayley's stomach. The digital clock on the bomb had come to life and now read 7:58…7:57…7:56…

Hayley gaped in horror, then started thrashing furiously against her bindings.

In unison, the other two shouted, "No! Stop! Don't! You may set it off."

She didn't entirely end her efforts, thinking they were all done for anyway and a few minutes one way or the other didn't matter much, but their warnings did make her minimize her movements. She worked to free her hands, but Burrows had done a thorough job, and she couldn't loosen the duct tape.

"Any luck?" Hayley heard Pierce ask the woman.

"None," the woman replied. "Can't reach. Any ideas?"

"I think we're screwed," he said.

CHAPTER TWENTY-NINE

D omino had been careful to keep her distance from the beat-up Buick sedan, especially when it ventured onto side roads free of other traffic. Once they were well out of the city, she dropped back a couple of miles, keeping her headlights off when she thought she might be visible. A few times she was afraid she'd lost it, thought perhaps it had turned into a driveway or two-track, for that was almost all they were passing now. But eventually she'd see the red tail-lights in the distance when the road straightened out, and she would relax again.

After a half hour or so, she was in a fuck-I've-lost-it panic. She hadn't seen the Buick for several very long minutes. First she sped up, then concluded she must have passed it, so she turned around to retrace her route. Only approaching from the opposite direction could she see a gleam of light in front of the dark hulk of an abandoned building. Two cars were in the parking lot, and just as she slowed to a crawl, one of them, the Buick she'd been following, roared to life.

She hurriedly pulled off the road as far as she could, bouncing across a flat patch of meadow into some thick brush. The Buick flashed by, so fast she couldn't tell whether Hayley was inside, but her gut told her no. He was merely the delivery man, and Hayley was with whomever the other car belonged to, inside the building.

The man's rapid departure set off a torrent of alarms within her and she hit reverse, barreling from her hiding place and down to the building. Throwing caution aside, she jumped out of her car. The external door was unlocked, and she raced up the stairs three at a time and burst into the only lighted room.

She registered everything in a millisecond. Pierce and Grant, handcuffed together to a radiator. Hayley, looking bedraggled, face stained with tears, gagging on the cloth around her mouth as she tried to shout. The bomb taped to her stomach.

"Please, help us," Grant shouted. "Hurry!"

But she was already moving and ignored Grant and Pierce to kneel before Hayley, examining the device. The clock was counting down, 4:12…4:11…4:10…*No time.*

Hayley jerked against her bindings, her cries muffled by the cloth in her mouth, and Domino immediately placed both hands firmly on her thighs. "No, Hayley, don't. Don't move or you may set it off."

She studied the bomb's construction. *Damn.* It wouldn't be easy to disarm. In place of the usual red and black, or red-blue-green wires leading to the detonator and timer were yellow, brown, and orange.

Cutting the wrong wire—the timer wire instead of the power wire—would only accelerate the timer and explosion. She suspected the bomber had also rigged it with back-up power, too, just in case, which meant the bomb might look like it had been defused for a few seconds, then go off anyway.

She shouldn't take that chance but had no other choice. She reached into her pocket for a knife.

"Sit very still," she instructed as she removed Hayley's gag and cut through her restraints, then began to carefully sever the tape used to attach the bomb to her body. "You're going to be fine. I promise."

Hayley trembled beneath her hands. "You've never broken a promise?" she asked hopefully.

"No, never." She sliced through the last of the tape. "I've never promised anything to anyone." She glanced into Hayley's eyes, then reached for the bomb.

As she placed the device gently on the floor beside the chair, she noted the display on the timer. 2:59…2:58…2:57…

Hayley stood and started for the door, tugging at her. "Come on!"

"I can't leave them, Hayley. I'll be right behind you. Go."

Domino pulled her gun, rushed to Pierce and Grant, and in two shots severed the chains that bound the handcuffs to the radiator. "Run," she shouted.

Still linked together, they raced awkwardly after her.

Hayley was on the stairwell just ahead, stumbling down awkwardly, stiff from her long confinements. Domino caught up to her and pulled her along, mentally calculating how much time had elapsed, not at all sure they would make it.

They were just past the fourth-floor landing when the bomb detonated.

The building shook and the staircase began to crumble around them. Hayley stumbled and fell, but Domino yanked her to her feet and got her moving again as thick dust and smoke enveloped them. Chunks of debris crashed down. One solid lump careened off Domino's shoulder, and she cried out but kept moving, one hand on Hayley's elbow, the other on the rail, blindly descending as fast as possible.

As they reached the second-floor stairwell, a portion of the ceiling caved in, narrowly missing them. They stumbled over it, choking on the omnipresent dust and debris and the thick cloud of black smoke from a fire they couldn't see. By the time they reached the door to the outside, Domino realized Pierce and Grant were no longer behind them. Cuffed together, they would be moving much slower. If one had been injured or trapped, the other would be stuck there too, to die.

Looking up, sucking in deep lungfuls of sweet, clean air, she saw that the fourth, fifth, and six floors were blazing and the fire was spreading fast.

"Stay here, Hayley. I'm going back in to get them," she said, but as she turned to leave, Hayley grabbed her.

"No, you can't. It's too dangerous."

She shook her off, gripping her by the shoulders. "I have to, Hayley. They're my family. Stay here, no matter what happens. I'll be right back."

❖

Three miles from the abandoned building, Senator Terrence Burrows stopped by the side of the road and got out, checking his watch. Right on cue, the explosion lit up the sky, followed by the distant orange glow of a fire. Smiling to himself, he climbed back inside and started the engine. *And they said I don't have what it takes.*

Once he got back to the city, he'd ditch the beater of a car Jack had procured for him and take a cab back to his Lincoln Town Car. He'd missed the big show on the National Mall, but his own fireworks display had been more than satisfying.

❖

Domino found them between the second and third floors. Pierce was trapped beneath a huge chunk of the collapsed ceiling, and both EOO bosses were coughing, shouting, trying to free themselves. The smoke was so thick they were desperate for air, and Domino's lungs burned as she tried to lift the slab of concrete. Even with Grant's help, they couldn't budge it. She spotted a long piece of metal and quickly wedged it at the edge of the block, then managed to lever the slab enough for Grant to pull Pierce free. His left arm and leg were cut and bleeding badly, but with Domino on one side and Grant on the other, they managed to make it outside, debris still falling around them.

They all collapsed on the concrete, coughing and retching from the smoke, eyes burning.

Pierce threw his free arm around Grant in an awkward embrace. "Thank God you're all right."

Hayley echoed the sentiment, hugging Domino from the side as she fought to regain her breath. Above them, the fire raged, lighting up the night sky. After a minute or two, Domino and Hayley rose to watch the building begin to collapse inward.

Grant struggled to her knees beside Pierce. "Get these off us," he told Domino, holding up the handcuffs that still bound them together.

"And then what? Am I supposed to let you go so you can continue to hunt me down like an animal? My loyalty will only stretch so far."

"You know the protocol for rogues. You didn't leave us a choice."

"I've been with you all my life." Domino stood over him, then turned toward Grant, remembering her anonymous warning. The look that passed between them was a mutual acknowledgment of their long-standing bond. "Do you think I'd do anything to hurt you?" she told Pierce. "It's unfortunate the sentiment isn't mutual."

"Then what exactly were you doing?" he asked. "In the beginning, I had you followed only as a precaution—because I thought this might be an internal matter—and later because you started to withhold information. We knew Strike was getting close, and we saw you sit back and not only do nothing about it, but protect her as well."

"If you had me followed, then you know I retrieved all the evidence she had against us," Domino said. "Yes, I protected her, because although I got to the evidence before she ever saw it *and destroyed it*, I couldn't take the chance you'd still want her eliminated. She's an innocent—and that's not what we're supposed to be about. But I have nothing to do with whoever is behind this."

Hayley said, "Senator Terence Burrows was behind it, Luka. He had me kidnapped. He put the bomb on me and brought me here. He admitted he sent me the tape hoping I'd uncover the EOO, but apparently he's got some connection to them, some debt he wanted out of, and I got too close to finding out about it. So when things went wrong, he decided to use me as bait to lure them here, and well…you know the rest."

"I should have suspected him," Pierce said. "He'll have to be taken care of."

"I told you Luka would never harm us," Grant said.

"We have to get out of here." Pierce groaned as he tried to sit up. "The police will be here soon."

"I have a plan." Domino pulled out her gun. "But we need to take my car and leave your rental here. I'll explain on the way." She told Pierce and Grant to stretch their arms away from each other and shot the chain linking their handcuffs. They helped Pierce to his feet and into the back of her stolen car.

"How do we know the journalist won't pursue this?" he asked as soon as they were on the road back to Washington.

Hayley turned around in the passenger seat to face him and Grant. "I won't harm Luka, and if that means taking this to my grave, that's exactly what I'll do. After today, I don't give a damn about this story. I just want my life back."

❖

As soon as he walked into his den, Senator Terrence Burrows clicked on the late-night local news and waited anxiously for some reference to the explosion. It was soon one of the top stories. Although the location was remote, a news crew had managed to arrive before the fire was fully out. The video was dark, but it appeared as though the ten-story building had become roughly three floors of burned rubble. Especially satisfying was the cutaway shot of the automobile found parked at the site.

"An explosion rocked an abandoned office building thirty miles southwest of the capital this evening," the newscaster announced. "Authorities are searching the wreckage, but they say several floors collapsed on top of each other, so it will take some time to determine whether anyone was inside at the time of the blast. A rental car found at the scene had been leased earlier in the evening at Reagan National Airport, but the name of the person who rented it is being withheld pending notification of relatives. No cause for the explosion has yet been determined."

He lit a cigar. Tomorrow he'd treat himself to a night out and celebrate his accomplishment. *Nicely done, Terrence.* He imagined he was hearing the voice of his father and could almost believe it was so. *Yes, indeed. Nicely done.*

❖

"What about the tape? The original," Monty Pierce asked, looking from Hayley to Domino. "Has that been destroyed?"

They'd parked in the lot of a closed convenience store, a safe distance from the scene. "No. I still have it," Hayley replied. "But I'll get it for you."

"I'll deliver it to you personally," Luka promised, glancing in the rear-view mirror at Pierce. "We're not going to discuss this any more. She's been through enough. No one touches her. Is that understood?"

Pierce met her eyes in the mirror. "Yes."

Beside him, Grant said, "You have my vote, Luka."

"You want me to drop you in Arlington?" she asked. Pierce needed medical attention, but a trip to the hospital would raise too many questions. He could get someone to come to his house, but she wasn't sure how he felt about being taken there since Hayley was with them.

"Yes," he replied. "Close by."

She nodded and started the car. They were silent during the forty-five minutes it took to reach Arlington. She parked on a side street around the corner from Pierce's house and got out with him and Grant, telling Hayley to stay put.

As they headed down the block toward Pierce's home, Luka pulled out her cell phone and handed it to him. "Order them to abort both targets."

While he was on the phone, Grant drew her aside. "I hope you know what you're doing, Luka."

"I do. Like I said, she's innocent."

"I don't doubt that any more." Grant regarded her steadily. "I'm talking about your feelings for her, and don't try to deny it. I've known you too long. People like us live in the shadows, Luka. We stay away from romantic relationships, for good reason."

"Joanne, I appreciate that you've always looked out for me," she said. "And continue to do so. You were the only one who ever did, you know. Put me first, treated me like a human being instead of a weapon to be allocated. You were taking a big personal and professional risk when you warned me. I'm very grateful. But after all Hayley has learned about me in the past twenty-four hours, you don't need to worry about any romantic involvement." She wished it could be different. "After tonight, she'll want nothing more to do with me."

"It's probably for the best," Grant replied. "You know that." She laid a hand on Luka's shoulder. "By the way, I haven't thanked you for saving our lives."

"I was happy to repay some of my debt," Luka said. "For making all those years growing up a lot more tolerable."

Pierce finished his conversation and handed Luka the phone. "I heard some of that. I suppose I should thank you as well." Without waiting for a response, he turned to address Grant in an uncharacteristically gentle tone of voice. "You sure you're okay?"

"Yes, Monty, I'm fine. Stop fussing over me."

"He's enjoyed fussing over you for years," Luka observed. "Why stop now?"

The two of them looked at her in surprise, then at each other. Even in the dim light of the nearby streetlight, she could see Pierce's face redden.

"You're the one who needs fussing over." Grant put an arm around Pierce's waist. "Let's get inside and patch you up."

"And make some calls," Pierce said. "We need to take care of our friend the senator ASAP."

"I want to take care of this one personally," Luka said. "And I don't want to waste time with discussions. As far as he's concerned, all three of you are dead. And we're going to let him hold on to that idea. That's why we needed to leave your car. It'll help convince him and give us time."

"Does that mean you're still with us?" Grant asked.

"I never left."

Pierce looked at her thoughtfully. "In that case, I have an assignment for you, Domino…"

CHAPTER THIRTY

10:30 p.m.

W hat a day, huh?"
Hayley laughed at the statement and didn't slug her, which was a good sign.

"I almost wish I could write an article about this—not that anyone would believe it. But I really don't want to risk another experience as a human bomb. Once was more than enough." Though Hayley's tone was light, Luka knew the horrific nightmare she'd been through had shaken her badly.

"Really, Hayley…how are you doing?" she asked gently.

Hayley let out a big sigh and leaned back against the headrest. "Ow," she said, immediately bending forward again to rub her skull. "I hurt all over. Even where I didn't know it was possible to hurt."

"I'm taking you to my place for tonight and perhaps a couple of days. You'll be safe there. You can't go anywhere familiar until we've dealt with Burrows." She could finally take her to her home without having to think of her as a target. Without having to be Domino or anyone else but herself. The thought elated and saddened her at the same time, because although she could be herself without guilt, she also knew that it was too late to make a difference to Hayley.

"What do you intend to do with him?"

'I can't talk about—"

"You know, forget I asked. I don't want to know, and frankly I don't give a damn. He deserves whatever he gets. And boy, safe sounds like a wonderful place to be." She yawned, closed her eyes, and settled back against the seat.

"I'm glad you're all right with staying with me." Luka glanced at her, wanting to say more, needing to know whether Hayley would ever agree to see her again once the danger was past, but her breathing was already slowing. Now wasn't the time.

After they drove over the bridge into DC, Luka found a quiet street where she could ditch the stolen car, around the corner from a cabstand. She roused Hayley, and they taxied the rest of the way to her condo.

As they rode the elevator up without speaking, they stood at a distance from each other, Hayley leaning against the wall. She tried to suppress a yawn, and Luka finally took her eyes off the gray elevator door to study her. She looked pale and exhausted under the fluorescent lights, and for the first time that evening Luka realized how close she had come to losing Hayley. The thought made her sick to her stomach, and the feeling intensified with the realization that she'd lost her anyway.

"Can I get you anything?" she asked once they were inside. "Coffee? Something else to drink?"

"No, thanks," Hayley said sleepily. "I just need to crash for a while."

"Of course. Give me a minute and I'll get things ready for you." She hurriedly changed the sheets and dug through the drawer in her bathroom for an unused toothbrush. By the time she finished, Hayley was asleep on the couch.

She bent to wake her, but instead gently lifted her and carried her to the bed, then stood debating whether to undress her to make her more comfortable. Her clothes were filthy so it should have been an easy decision, but the uncertainty of how Hayley felt about her after the last twenty-four hours made her hesitate.

She stripped off Hayley's red blouse, now mostly gray from the dust of the explosion, and her torn, stained jeans. Beneath were the lacy red bra and panties she'd watched Hayley put on that morning after their night of lovemaking. At the memory, she felt a twitch of desire low in her stomach.

As she stood there, lost in Hayley's near-nudity, Hayley opened her eyes groggily.

Luka averted her gaze and quickly reached for the blanket to cover her. "Sleep now," she said gently. "And I'll see you in the morning."

"Where are you going?"

"I'll take the couch. It's fine, it's—"

"No, stay with me. I want you here."

Luka tried not to read too much into the soft plea. Hayley was simply afraid, and who could blame her? "All right," she said, against her better judgment. She wanted to lie next to Hayley more than anything, wanted to escape again from everything that was wrong, in the embrace of the woman who made it all feel right. But she knew the embrace would not be there as it had before, and that in a few days Hayley would be gone forever. Sharing a bed with her tonight would make it so much harder for her to say good-bye.

She sat on the edge of the bed and pulled off her boots, then stripped off her shirt and stepped out of her jeans. When she turned toward Hayley, Hayley seemed a bit more awake. She was watching her and had the bed sheets turned back, waiting for her.

After Luka stretched out beside her and covered them both, Hayley moved easily into her arms as though they'd been doing it forever. She fell asleep with Hayley's soft breath against her chest.

❖

When Hayley woke, it took her a full minute or two to remember all that had happened and to realize she was lying in Luka's bed, wrapped in her arms.

Luka was still asleep, and it wasn't light out yet, so she remained where she was, sorting through all she had learned about the woman she had so completely fallen in love with, despite all obstacles.

She didn't doubt that much, but there was a lot she didn't know. The last time she was here, Luka had said she loved her, that she'd never felt this way before. *And she's certainly risked her life more than once to rescue me.* She had even gone against the EOO for her. Shouldn't that be more than enough to forgive the lies and deceptions?

The moment she learned that Luka was Domino, realizing their relationship was based on lies had shocked and horrified her—especially the fact she'd been Luka's assignment. Knowing that Luka and the EOO had followed her, spied on her, and listened in on her phone calls made her feel vulnerable and violated.

But Burrows was the culprit here. The EOO had merely reacted to his plan to bring them down. And Luka wasn't the cold-blooded assassin she'd been led to believe, but a woman assigned to track down—*what was the word she used?*—the sickos, drug lords, pedophiles, skin traders. Those the law couldn't touch.

Hayley had covered enough stories to know how many times the worst of humanity escaped justice through some legal loophole, only to kill or molest again. How was Luka any different from a cop on the street, really? Weren't their intentions the same? To make the world a better, safer place?

By the time the sun came up, she had forgiven the deceptions and accepted the lethal occupation Luka had chosen. If they were to build some kind of future together, it wouldn't be easy to watch her leave on an EOO assignment knowing first-hand what kind of danger she'd face. No doubt they would have a lot of secrets between them still, regarding where Luka went and what she did.

Luka certainly was resourceful and able to keep herself safe. And Luka seemed ready to be honest with her now about the things that were most important, such as how they felt about each other.

But, did Luka want a future with her as much as she wanted one with Luka?

It was time to find out. Luka had stirred and Hayley tentatively touched the bruised shoulder peeping from beneath the sheet. "You're hurt."

❖

A hand gently caressed Luka's side, below the bandage covering the wound from her encounter with the barricade. She opened her eyes to find Hayley lying on her side, propped up on one elbow, watching her.

She peered down at the bandage, bloodstained again from her exertions the night before. It was her worst injury of several. As she moved to sit up, the ache in her side competed with the pain in her shoulder from where the ceiling had hit her, and she winced.

"We need to take care of that," Hayley said. "I was a nurse, you know."

"I remember." Luka met her eyes, trying to gauge what Hayley was thinking. Her eyes twinkled, but her expression was unreadable.

"I imagine in your line of work you keep a pretty well-stocked supply of bandages and first-aid supplies, am I right?"

"Yes." Hayley's reference to her "line of work" in such a matter-of-fact way was a positive development.

"Thought so. First step is to get you cleaned up." Hayley got out of bed and went to the doorway. Her tone was all business, but she had a half smile on her face. "A long, hot bath. *Now*, Luka. Come on, let's go. You took care of me, now it's my turn."

"You got pretty banged up, too." Luka followed Hayley toward the bathroom. Indeed, Hayley had an array of small cuts and scrapes, and a couple of rather impressive bruises, but she acted as though they weren't bothering her. They were both filthy from the explosion, their hair more gray than the color they'd been born with.

"You're worse. So you're first," Hayley said. She preceded Luka into the bathroom and turned on the hot water. "I don't suppose you're the bubble-bath type?"

"Sorry, no."

"I'll put that on my shopping list, then." She turned to the medicine cabinet and perused its contents. "Now climb in there while I see what you've got to fix you up."

Luka stripped off her black bra and thong underwear, then pulled off the soiled bandage and slipped into the water. The old-fashioned, claw-foot steel tub was large enough to stretch out comfortably in. It did feel wonderful. She leaned her head back against the curved side, closed her eyes, and let the hot water work its magic.

Behind her, she heard Hayley pulling things out of the cabinet— probably gauze, tape, antibiotic ointment, and who knew what else.

The next thing she knew, Hayley was in the tub with her, facing her from the opposite side.

"Mind sharing?" Hayley crooked an eyebrow mischievously and splashed her like a kid in a wading pool.

Luka had never experienced much light-hearted fun, and she certainly didn't expect it from Hayley this morning, so she wasn't sure how to react. "Uh…sure," she stuttered.

"Turn around and let me wash your hair," Hayley commanded as she reached over the side for a bottle of shampoo.

Luka wasn't about to argue. She spun around, and Hayley carefully pushed her below the surface to wet her hair.

Hayley snuggled up behind her, knees bent, cradling her body between her legs. Her nipples brushed Luka's back, and then she was massaging her scalp with skilled hands, taking her time. Hayley's lips brushed over the bruise on her shoulder, then along the side of her neck.

She fought the urge to squirm. *Christ.* Involuntarily, she tilted her head slightly to allow greater access to the sensitive skin beneath her jaw. The brush of Hayley's lips became small bites and nips.

The sensation was driving Luka crazy. The water wasn't the only thing making her wet. The urge to kiss Hayley became intolerable, so she tried to turn in Hayley's direction and grimaced at a stab of pain in her side.

"Does it hurt that much?" Hayley asked.

"Wanting to kiss you hurts more."

"That smooth talker's back, I see. Well, that kind of pain is easy to remedy." Hayley shifted so Luka didn't have to twist too far, and their lips met. Luka lost herself in the slow welcome, finding the answer she needed, had been aching to hear. She knew, in that sweet exchange, what they'd built was real and lasting, and Hayley had somehow found a way to accept everything.

"Hayley, I hope you…we…" she began, when their mouths parted.

"Shh, Luka. We'll work it all out," Hayley said, before kissing her again on her neck, and again.

"It must be difficult for you to understand and accept what I've done, what I have to do, because that's not going to change," Luka said shakily. "Let alone that I'm horribly ill-equipped with how to deal with falling in love and sharing a life with someone—"

"Luka." Hayley hugged her close. "I don't claim to understand everything you do, but you've helped me realize its necessity. I can't say I like it, but not because I think it's wrong to use lethal force when there's no other way. I just worry about your safety—even though I know how resourceful and brave you are. I don't want anything to happen to you." She punctuated this sentiment with a kiss in the middle of Luka's back. "As to your inexperience with love and relationships, well, as long as you want a future together as much as I do…" She let the question hang in the air, waiting for confirmation.

"You know I want that, Hayley. More than I've ever wanted anything. For the first time in my life, I feel like I belong to someone. Something I suppose I've always wanted but never believed I could have."

"Then stop worrying. We'll figure it all out together," Hayley said, hugging her tighter. "Because that's what you do, when you're in love. And I'm so very much in love with you."

"I love you, too, Hayley." Though Luka was unfamiliar with this kind of intimacy, it came very naturally, and she allowed herself to fully enjoy being here right now.

They washed each other, kissing and caressing, neither feeling the chill of the water as the heat between them increased.

"Let's patch you up and maybe continue this somewhere else?" Hayley whispered in her ear before nipping her lobe lightly.

"I say we leave the patching up for later," Luka replied, "and skip to taking this somewhere else."

"Patience, Luka. Patience." Hayley showed her dimples.

They got out and Hayley expertly tended to Luka's side and shoulder, Luka stealing kisses, and then she returned the favor, cleaning and bandaging the abrasions on Hayley's back and sides.

When they were done, Hayley led her back to the bedroom. "Look at these sheets. Maybe we should—"

Luka picked her up, carried her to the couch, and laid her on it. "Sorry, Hayley," she said, looking into Hayley's eyes as she positioned herself above her and gently urged her legs apart. "You can't walk around naked like this and expect me to spend time changing the linens when I could be making you come."

"Jesus, Luka," Hayley moaned, throwing her head back as Luka kissed her way down Hayley's body, pausing to lick, nip...fevered bites on the swell of her breasts before she sucked each nipple to full erection.

Hayley's nails raked along her back as Hayley began to writhe beneath her, and then her hands were in her scalp, pushing her lower, insistent. "Please, Luka. I need you there."

She pushed Hayley's knees up and spread them apart, then stroked her tongue the full length of Hayley's sex, eliciting a long groan of pleasure that shot through her and doubled her own arousal.

Luka tried to go slowly, but their long foreplay in the tub and her desire to express her love made her unable to restrain herself. Hayley exploded almost at once, as did she. But they had all day together to share their bodies in every way imaginable, slow and fast.

A little before six that night, Pierce called with details of Burrows's plans for later that evening.

CHAPTER THIRTY ONE

As one of the most powerful men in Washington, Senator Terrence Burrows had developed the kind of contacts that ensured he could always find a private pleasure party when he was in the mood for one. And he was certainly ready to celebrate tonight. Some aged whiskey, a Cuban cigar or two, an hour with one of the upscale escorts sure to be provided—their discretion guaranteed—and then a few hands at high-stakes poker.

This evening's entertainment was in the Bethesda mansion that was home to one of his regular gambling buddies, a media magnate with a talent for providing his guests with beautiful blondes.

The walled estate had an elaborately landscaped yard that included a prize-winning rose garden stretching the length of the rear exterior. An elaborate iron balcony extended from the master bedroom on the second floor, and the grand foyer consisted entirely of Italian marble. A dozen guests were invited this evening, most of them politicians and other Washington insiders, but also a few industrial CEOs, and one young Internet entrepreneur who was spending his millions almost as fast as he was earning them.

Terrence had a couple of glasses of whiskey while he ambled among the rooms, admiring his host's collection of big-game trophy heads and studying the competition he would face later that evening at cards.

"Do you feel like company, Senator?"

The voice behind him was velvet, and as he turned, he hoped the face and figure matched. He wasn't disappointed.

She wore a classic black dress, tasteful but sexy, that showed a generous amount of cleavage and ended mid-thigh. Her matching black heels emphasized her finely toned legs.

Normally he had a weakness for blue-eyed blondes, and this one had dark hair and brown eyes, but she was breathtaking, and she was giving him a seductive, fuck-me look that made him instantly hard.

"What kind of company did you have in mind?"

"Whatever you're in the mood for," the woman said. "We can sit here and you can tell me about your day, or we can go somewhere private and you can tell me what I can do for you."

"I've had a productive day and that just about describes it," Terrence said. "Now how about we go somewhere and I tell you what you can do for me?"

"My pleasure."

He put his arm around her waist and led her to the room his host had reserved for him, a ground-floor guest room. Once there, he stepped aside for her, then followed and shut the door. The room was simply but elegantly furnished. To the right was a queen-sized bed with a cream duvet, bookended by matching oak nightstands. Tiffany-style lamps cast a soft amber light.

Straight ahead was a large window with a view of the gardens, and to the left of that, an antique oak dresser. The curtains stirred as the fresh, sweet scent of roses wafted in. The woman had taken a couple of steps to the right, in the direction of the bed, and waited there for him.

Terrence walked up to her and pushed her against the wall beside the door, his thigh firmly between her legs. He reached down to put his hand there, but she stopped him.

❖

"Not yet, Senator." Domino distracted Burrows by putting her hand to his crotch. He was stone hard and ready.

He groaned and stepped back, smiling with approval. "So you like games. Take your clothes off and lie on the bed," he ordered.

She nodded and walked to the foot of the bed while Burrows headed toward the dresser. Sensing he was behind her, Domino glanced over her shoulder and confirmed he was standing with his back to her. Moving swiftly and quietly toward him in four steps, she came up behind him just as he removed his wedding ring.

The second the ring hit the dresser top, she had his head in her hands, one on his chin, the other on the back of his head, twisting his neck until he couldn't move, the pressure intense.

A couple of more inches was all it would take. But she had a message to deliver. "If you can't play by our rules, Senator, then you shouldn't play at all."

She was about to finish him when someone knocked on the door and a woman's voice called, "Terrence? Can I interrupt? It's important."

Domino stretched him to the limit, until she could see the pain in his eyes. "Tell her not now," she ordered quietly.

"Not now, Maria," the senator called.

To her surprise, the knob turned and the door began to open anyway.

The rest happened in the time it took to draw a breath.

Domino reacted according to her training—pure reflex, no thought. As she wheeled toward the door, she reached beneath her dress for the revolver strapped high on her thigh, just beneath her ass, and had it pointed toward the door before it was fully open. She wrapped her left arm around the senator.

"Jack," the senator shouted when he saw Domino's weapon, "she's got a gun!"

The woman in the doorway held a gun, too, and fired without hesitation. But Domino was in motion, pulling Burrows in front of her, making him a human shield, and the shot hit him square in the chest.

Jack froze for a second, and Domino threw the senator's body to the side, dove for the window behind her, and disappeared into the dark night.

EPILOGUE

Valletta, Malta
Seven months later

Luka stripped off her latex gloves and stretched, arching to relieve the tension between her shoulder blades. She was always a little sad to complete a restoration such as this, despite the gratification of seeing the original artist's work finally restored to its former vivid glory. But the chill of the January morning in the massive Co-Cathedral was apparent as soon as she stopped working, despite the extra layers beneath her coveralls. So she quit appreciating her handiwork in favor of coffee and a warmer environment.

She packed up her gear and had made it halfway down the scaffolding when the voice beckoned her from behind, loud enough for her to hear, but not enough to disturb the priests, preparing for the morning mass.

"I really hate it when you sneak out of bed like that, you know. I'd have come to keep you company."

Luka glanced over her shoulder as she continued climbing down. Their months together had not diminished her thrill when Hayley looked at her—her eyes shining with love, her dimples framing the crooked grin that said she was remembering their passion of the night before.

She released her grip a body length above the floor and landed lightly on her feet in front of Hayley. "I felt guilty for keeping you up so late. I didn't have the heart."

"Well, for the record, and you can quote me on this, you never have to feel guilty about waking me up. When it comes to spending time with you, I love to be kept up late and wakened early."

"Got it, chief." Luka smiled, set down her bag of gear, and opened her arms.

Hayley stepped into her embrace and hugged her tight before she gazed up at the ceiling where Luka had been working. "It's wonderful, Luka. Breathtaking. All finished?"

"Just," she replied, following Hayley's eyes to the fresco. "It's always bittersweet, though, to complete a job like this." She sighed, then gazed at Hayley. "But less so this time, because I have something great to look forward to."

"Yeah." Hayley squeezed her tighter. "Tibet. Can't wait."

"I don't suppose you can extend your leave of absence for another month?" she asked. "We could see a little more of Asia. Spend some time in China, or India. Wherever you like—" Luka's cell vibrated against her hip. "Sorry, my phone." As Hayley released her, she checked the caller ID and was surprised to see a European area code. "Hello," she answered cautiously.

"Isn't payback a bitch, especially when the bitch calls to collect?" It was Mishael.

"Do I need to bail you out? Have they finally arrested your ass for exceeding the speed of light?"

"No, that's in next week's agenda. Are you still in Malta?"

"Yup, and about to leave for Tibet," she replied, smiling at Hayley.

"Can Tibet wait? I need your help ASAP."

"Work?"

"Sure as hell not pleasure." Mishael gave her an address.

"Are you in trouble?"

"In more ways than one. How soon can you get here?"

"One moment." She covered the mouthpiece and looked at Hayley with apology, but Hayley simply nodded.

"I'll be there in a few hours. Call you at this number when I get there."

"Oh, and by the way, do you think I'm a self-absorbed, arrogant pain in the ass?"

"No, no, and yes." Luka was amused and surprised at her friend's apparent insecurity. "Why?"

"Just something someone recently accused me of. Obviously they don't know what they're talking about."

"Obviously." Luka tried not to laugh.

"Anyway, see you later." With that Mishael ended the call.

Luka took Hayley's hand, and they started out of the cathedral.

"How long will you be gone?" Hayley asked.

"I'm not sure. But you'd better head back to the States."

Outside, on the steps, Hayley stopped and faced Luka. She took both her hands in hers and looked at her with obvious concern. When she finally spoke, her voice was barely a whisper. "You are coming back, right?"

Luka kissed her. "Better yet, I'll be coming back…home."

About the Authors

Kim Baldwin has been a writer for three decades, following up a twenty-year career in network news with a much more satisfying turn penning lesbian fiction. She has published five novels with Bold Strokes Books in addition to *Lethal Affairs*: the intrigue/romances *Flight Risk* and *Hunter's Pursuit* (a finalist for a Golden Crown Literary Society Award in 2005) and the romances *Force of Nature, Whitewater Rendezvous,* (a GCLS finalist in 2007) and *Focus of Desire.* She has also contributed short stories to five BSB anthologies: The Lambda Literary Award winning *Stolen Moments: Erotic Interludes 2; Lessons in Love: Erotic Interludes 3;* IPPY and GCLS Award winning *Extreme Passions: Erotic Interludes 4*; *Road Games: Erotic Interludes 5*; and the upcoming *Romantic Interludes 1: Discovery* (September 2008). She lives in the north woods of Michigan.

Xenia Alexiou is Greek and lives in Europe. An avid reader and knowledge junkie, she likes to travel all over the globe and take pictures of the wonderful and interesting people that represent different cultures. Trying to see the world through their eyes has been her most challenging yet rewarding pursuit so far. These travels have inspired countless stories, and it's these stories that she has recently decided to write about. *Lethal Affairs* is her first novel. She is currently at work on *Thief of Always*, the second book in the *Elite Operatives* Series.

Books Available From Bold Strokes Books

Falling Star by Gill McKnight. Solley Rayner hopes a few weeks with her family will help heal her shattered dreams, but she hasn't counted on meeting a woman who stirs her heart.(978-1-60282-023-4)

Lethal Affairs by Kim Baldwin and Xenia Alexiou. Elite operative Domino is no stranger to peril, but her investigation of journalist Hayley Ward will test more than her skills. (978-1-60282-022-7)

A Place to Rest by Erin Dutton. Sawyer Drake doesn't know what she wants from life, until she meets Jori Diamantina—only trouble is, Jori doesn't seem to share her desire. (978-1-60282-021-0)

Warrior's Valor by Gun Brooke. Dwyn Izsontro and Emeron D'Artansis must put aside personal animosity, and unwelcomed attraction, to defeat an enemy of the Protector of the Realm. (978-1-60282-020-3)

Finding Home by Georgia Beers. Take two polar opposite women with an attraction for one another they're trying desperately to ignore—throw in a far-too-observant dog—and then sit back and enjoy the romance. (978-1-60282-019-7)

Word of Honor by Radclyffe. All Secret Service Agent Cameron Roberts and First Daughter Blair Powell want is a small intimate wedding, but the paparazzi and a domestic terrorist have other plans. (978-1-60282-018-0)

Hotel Liaison by JLee Meyer. Two women searching through a secret past discover that their brief hotel liaison is only the beginning. Will they risk their careers—and their hearts—to follow through on their desires? (978-1-60282-017-3)

Love on Location by Lisa Girolami. Hollywood film producer Kate Nyland and artist Dawn Brock discover that love doesn't always follow the script. Romance. (978-1-60282-016-6)

Edge of Darkness by Jove Belle. Investigator Diana Collins charges at life with an irreverent comment and a right hook, but even those may not protect her heart from a charming villain. Romantic Intrigue. (978-1-60282-015-9)

Thirteen Hours by Meghan O'Brien. Workaholic Dana Watts's life takes a sudden turn when an unexpected interruption arrives in the form of the most beautiful breasts she has ever seen—stripper Laurel Stanley's. Erotic Romance. (978-1-60282-014-2)

In Deep Waters 2 by Radclyffe and Karin Kallmaker. All bets are off when two award winning authors deal the cards of love and passion... and every hand is a winner. Lesbian Erotica. (978-1-60282-013-5)

Pink by Jennifer Harris. An irrepressible heroine frolics, frets, and navigates through the "what if's" of her life: all the unexpected turns of fortune, fame, and karma. General Fiction. (978-1-60282-043-2)

Deal with the Devil by Ali Vali. New Orleans crime boss Cain Casey brings her fury down on the men who threatened her family, and blood and bullets fly. (978-1-60282-012-8)

Naked Heart by Jennifer Fulton. When a sexy ex-CIA agent sets out to seduce and entrap a powerful CEO, there's more to this plan than meets the eye...or the flogger. (978-1-60282-011-1)

Heart of the Matter by KI Thompson. TV newscaster Kate Foster is Professor Ellen Webster's dream girl, but Kate doesn't know Ellen exists...until an accident changes everything. (978-1-60282-010-4)

Heartland by Julie Cannon. When political strategist Rachel Stanton and dude ranch owner Shivley McCoy collide on an empty country road, fate intervenes. (978-1-60282-009-8)

Shadow of the Knife by Jane Fletcher. Militia Rookie Ellen Mittal has no idea of just how complex and dangerous her life is about to become. A Celaeno series adventure romance. (978-1-60282-008-1)

To Protect and Serve by VK Powell. Lieutenant Alex Troy is caught in the paradox of her life—to hold steadfast to her professional oath or to protect the woman she loves. (978-1-60282-007-4)

Deeper by Ronica Black. Former homicide detective Erin McKenzie and her fiancée Elizabeth Adams couldn't be any happier—until the not so distant past comes knocking at the door. (978-1-60282-006-7)

The Lonely Hearts Club by Radclyffe. Take three friends, add two ex-lovers and several new ones, and the result is a recipe for explosive rivalries and incendiary romance. (978-1-60282-005-0)

Venus Besieged by Andrews & Austin. Teague Richfield heads for Sedona and the sensual arms of psychic astrologer Callie Rivers for a much needed romantic reunion. (978-1-60282-004-3)

Branded Ann by Merry Shannon. Pirate Branded Ann raids a merchant vessel to obtain a treasure map and gets more than she bargained for with the widow Violet. (978-1-60282-003-6)

American Goth by JD Glass. Trapped by an unsuspected inheritance and guided only by the guardian who holds the secret to her future, Samantha Cray fights to fulfill her destiny. (978-1-60282-002-9)

Learning Curve by Rachel Spangler. Ashton Clarke is perfectly content with her life until she meets the intriguing Professor Carrie Fletcher, who isn't looking for a relationship with anyone. (978-1-60282-001-2)

Place of Exile by Rose Beecham. Sheriff's detective Jude Devine struggles with ghosts of her past and an ex-lover who still haunts her dreams. (978-1-933110-98-1)

Fully Involved by Erin Dutton. A love that has smoldered for years ignites when two women and one little boy come together in the aftermath of tragedy. (978-1-933110-99-8)

Heart 2 Heart by Julie Cannon. Suffering from a devastating personal loss, Kyle Bain meets Lane Connor, and the chance for happiness suddenly seems possible. (978-1-60282-000-5)

Queens of Tristaine: Tristaine Book Four by Cate Culpepper. When a deadly plague stalks the Amazons of Tristaine, two warrior lovers must return to the place of their nightmares to find a cure. (978-1-933110-97-4)

The Crown of Valencia by Catherine Friend. Ex-lovers can really mess up your life…even, as Kate discovers, if they've traveled back to the 11th century! (978-1-933110-96-7)

Mine by Georgia Beers. What happens when you've already given your heart and love finds you again? Courtney McAllister is about to find out. (978-1-933110-95-0)

House of Clouds by KI Thompson. A sweeping saga of an impassioned romance between a Northern spy and a Southern sympathizer, set amidst the upheaval of a nation under siege. (978-1-933110-94-3)

Winds of Fortune by Radclyffe. Provincetown local Deo Camara agrees to rehab Dr. Nita Burgoyne's historic home, but she never said anything about mending her heart. (978-1-933110-93-6)

Focus of Desire by Kim Baldwin. Isabel Sterling is surprised when she wins a photography contest, but no more than photographer Natasha Kashnikova. Their promo tour becomes a ticket to romance. (978-1-933110-92-9)

Blind Leap by Diane and Jacob Anderson-Minshall. A Golden Gate Bridge suicide becomes suspect when a filmmaker's camera shows a different story. Yoshi Yakamota and the Blind Eye Detective Agency uncover evidence that could be worth killing for. (978-1-933110-91-2)

Wall of Silence, 2nd ed. by Gabrielle Goldsby. Life takes a dangerous turn when jaded police detective Foster Everett meets Riley Medeiros, a woman who isn't afraid to discover the truth no matter the cost. (978-1-933110-90-5)

Mistress of the Runes by Andrews & Austin. Passion ignites between two women with ties to ancient secrets, contemporary mysteries, and a shared quest for the meaning of life. (978-1-933110-89-9)

Sheridan's Fate by Gun Brooke. A dynamic, erotic romance between physical therapist Lark Mitchell and businesswoman Sheridan Ward set in the scorching hot days and humid, steamy nights of San Antonio. (978-1-933110-88-2)

Vulture's Kiss by Justine Saracen. Archeologist Valerie Foret, heir to a terrifying task, returns in a powerful desert adventure set in Egypt and Jerusalem. (978-1-933110-87-5)

Rising Storm by JLee Meyer. The sequel to First Instinct takes our heroines on a dangerous journey instead of the honeymoon they'd planned. (978-1-933110-86-8)

Not Single Enough by Grace Lennox. A funny, sexy modern romance about two lonely women who bond over the unexpected and fall in love along the way. (978-1-933110-85-1)

Such a Pretty Face by Gabrielle Goldsby. A sexy, sometimes humorous, sometimes biting contemporary romance that gently exposes the damage to heart and soul when we fail to look beneath the surface for what truly matters. (978-1-933110-84-4)

Second Season by Ali Vali. A romance set in New Orleans amidst betrayal, Hurricane Katrina, and the new beginnings hardship and heartbreak sometimes make possible. (978-1-933110-83-7)

Hearts Aflame by Ronica Black. A poignant, erotic romance between a hard-driving businesswoman and a solitary vet. Packed with adventure and set in the harsh beauty of the Arizona countryside. (978-1-933110-82-0)

Red Light by JD Glass. Tori forges her path as an EMT in the New York City 911 system while discovering what matters most to herself and the woman she loves. (978-1-933110-81-3)

Honor Under Siege by Radclyffe. Secret Service agent Cameron Roberts struggles to protect her lover while searching for a traitor who just may be another woman with a claim on her heart. (978-1-933110-80-6)

Dark Valentine by Jennifer Fulton. Danger and desire fuel a high stakes cat-and-mouse game when an attorney and an endangered witness team up to thwart a killer. (978-1-933110-79-0)

Sequestered Hearts by Erin Dutton. A popular artist suddenly goes into seclusion; a reluctant reporter wants to know why; and a heart locked away yearns to be set free. (978-1-933110-78-3)

Erotic Interludes 5: *Road Games* eds. Radclyffe and Stacia Seaman. Adventure, "sport," and sex on the road—hot stories of travel adventures and games of seduction. (978-1-933110-77-6)

The Spanish Pearl by Catherine Friend. On a trip to Spain, Kate Vincent is accidentally transported back in time...an epic saga spiced with humor, lust, and danger. (978-1-933110-76-9)

Lady Knight by L-J Baker. Loyalty and honour clash with love and ambition in a medieval world of magic when female knight Riannon meets Lady Eleanor. (978-1-933110-75-2)

Dark Dreamer by Jennifer Fulton. Best-selling horror author, Rowe Devlin falls under the spell of psychic Phoebe Temple. A Dark Vista romance. (978-1-933110-74-5)

Come and Get Me by Julie Cannon. Elliott Foster isn't used to pursuing women, but alluring attorney Lauren Collier makes her change her mind. (978-1-933110-73-8)

Blind Curves by Diane and Jacob Anderson-Minshall. Private eye Yoshi Yakamota comes to the aid of her ex-lover Velvet Erickson in the first Blind Eye mystery. (978-1-933110-72-1)

Dynasty of Rogues by Jane Fletcher. It's hate at first sight for Ranger Riki Sadiq and her new patrol corporal, Tanya Coppelli—except for their undeniable attraction. (978-1-933110-71-4)

Running With the Wind by Nell Stark. Sailing instructor Corrie Marsten has signed off on love until she meets Quinn Davies—one woman she can't ignore. (978-1-933110-70-7)

More than Paradise by Jennifer Fulton. Two women battle danger, risk all, and find in one another an unexpected ally and an unforgettable love. (978-1-933110-69-1)

Flight Risk by Kim Baldwin. For Blayne Keller, being in the wrong place at the wrong time just might turn out to be the best thing that ever happened to her. (978-1-933110-68-4)

Rebel's Quest, Supreme Constellations Book Two by Gun Brooke. On a world torn by war, two women discover a love that defies all boundaries. (978-1-933110-67-7)

Punk and Zen by JD Glass. Angst, sex, love, rock. Trace, Candace, Francesca...Samantha. Losing control—and finding the truth within. BSB Victory Editions. (1-933110-66-X)

Stellium in Scorpio by Andrews & Austin. The passionate reuniting of two powerful women on the glitzy Las Vegas Strip where everything is an illusion and love is a gamble. (1-933110-65-1)

When Dreams Tremble by Radclyffe. Two women whose lives turned out far differently than they'd once imagined discover that sometimes the shape of the future can only be found in the past. (1-933110-64-3)

The Devil Unleashed by Ali Vali. As the heat of violence rises, so does the passion. A Casey Family crime saga. (1-933110-61-9)

Burning Dreams by Susan Smith. The chronicle of the challenges faced by a young drag king and an older woman who share a love "outside the bounds." (1-933110-62-7)

Fresh Tracks by Georgia Beers. Seven women, seven days. A lot can happen when old friends, lovers, and a new girl in town get together in the mountains. (1-933110-63-5)

The Empress and the Acolyte by Jane Fletcher. Jemeryl and Tevi fight to protect the very fabric of their world: time. Lyremouth Chronicles Book Three. (1-933110-60-0)

First Instinct by JLee Meyer. When high-stakes security fraud leads to murder, one woman flees for her life while another risks her heart to protect her. (1-933110-59-7)

Erotic Interludes 4: *Extreme Passions* eds. Radclyffe and Stacia Seaman. Thirty of today's hottest erotica writers set the pages aflame with love, lust, and steamy liaisons. (1-933110-58-9)

Storms of Change by Radclyffe. In the continuing saga of the Provincetown Tales, duty and love are at odds as Reese and Tory face their greatest challenge. (1-933110-57-0)

Unexpected Ties by Gina L. Dartt. With death before dessert, Kate Shannon and Nikki Harris are swept up in another tale of danger and romance. (1-933110-56-2)

Sleep of Reason by Rose Beecham. While Detective Jude Devine searches for a lost boy, her rocky relationship with Dr. Mercy Westmoreland gets a lot harder. (1-933110-53-8)

Passion's Bright Fury by Radclyffe. Passion strikes without warning when a trauma surgeon and a filmmaker become reluctant allies. (1-933110-54-6)

Broken Wings by L-J Baker. When Rye Woods meets beautiful dryad Flora Withe, her libido, as hidden as her wings, reawakens along with her heart. (1-933110-55-4)

Combust the Sun by Andrews & Austin. A Richfield and Rivers mystery set in L.A. Murder among the stars. (1-933110-52-X)

Of Drag Kings and the Wheel of Fate by Susan Smith. A blind date in a drag club leads to an unlikely romance. (1-933110-51-1)

Tristaine Rises by Cate Culpepper. Brenna, Jesstin, and the Amazons of Tristaine face their greatest challenge for survival. (1-933110-50-3)

Too Close to Touch by Georgia Beers. Kylie O'Brien believes in true love and is willing to wait for it, even though Gretchen, her new boss, is off-limits. (1-933110-47-3)

100ᵗʰ Generation by Justine Saracen. Ancient curses, modern-day villains, and an intriguing woman lead archeologist Valerie Foret on the adventure of her life. (1-933110-48-1)

Battle for Tristaine by Cate Culpepper. While Brenna struggles to find her place in the clan, Tristaine is threatened with destruction. Second in the Tristaine series. (1-933110-49-X)

The Traitor and the Chalice by Jane Fletcher. Tevi and Jemeryl risk all in the race to uncover a traitor. The Lyremouth Chronicles Book Two. (1-933110-43-0)

Promising Hearts by Radclyffe. Dr. Vance Phelps arrives in New Hope, Montana, with no hope of happiness—until she meets Mae. (1-933110-44-9)

Carly's Sound by Ali Vali. Poppy Valente and Julia Johnson form a bond of friendship that becomes something far more. A poignant romance about love and renewal. (1-933110-45-7)

Unexpected Sparks by Gina L. Dartt. Kate Shannon's attraction to much younger Nikki Harris is complication enough without a fatal fire that Kate can't ignore. (1-933110-46-5)

Whitewater Rendezvous by Kim Baldwin. Two women on a wilderness kayak adventure discover that true love may be nothing at all like they imagined. (1-933110-38-4)

Erotic Interludes 3: *Lessons in Love* eds. Radclyffe and Stacia Seaman. Sign on for a class in love…the best lesbian erotica writers take us to "school." (1-9331100-39-2)

Punk Like Me by JD Glass. Twenty-one-year-old Nina has a way with the girls, and she doesn't always play by the rules. (1-933110-40-6)

Coffee Sonata by Gun Brooke. Four women whose lives unexpectedly intersect in a small town by the sea share one thing in common—they all have secrets. (1-933110-41-4)

The Clinic: Tristaine Book One by Cate Culpepper. Brenna, a prison medic, finds herself drawn to Jesstin, a warrior reputed to be descended from ancient Amazons. (1-933110-42-2)

Forever Found by JLee Meyer. Can time, tragedy, and shattered trust destroy a love that seemed destined? Chance reunites childhood friends separated by tragedy. (1-933110-37-6)

Sword of the Guardian by Merry Shannon. Princess Shasta's bold new bodyguard has a secret that could change both of their lives: *He* is actually a *she*. (1-933110-36-8)

Wild Abandon by Ronica Black. Dr. Chandler Brogan and Officer Sarah Monroe are drawn together by their common obsessions—sex, speed, and danger. (1-933110-35-X)

Turn Back Time by Radclyffe. Pearce Rifkin and Wynter Thompson have nothing in common but a shared passion for surgery—and unexpected attraction. (1-933110-34-1)

Chance by Grace Lennox. A sexy, funny, touching story of two women who, in finding themselves, also find one another. (1-933110-31-7)

The Exile and the Sorcerer by Jane Fletcher. First in the Lyremouth Chronicles. Tevi and a shy young sorcerer face monsters, magic, and the challenge of loving. (1-933110-32-5)

A Matter of Trust by Radclyffe. When what should be just business turns into much more, two women struggle to trust the unexpected. (1-933110-33-3)

Sweet Creek by Lee Lynch. A celebration of the enduring nature of love, friendship, and community in the heart-warming lesbian community of Waterfall Falls. (1-933110-29-5)

The Devil Inside by Ali Vali. The head of a New Orleans crime organization falls for a woman who turns her world upside down. (1-933110-30-9)

Grave Silence by Rose Beecham. Detective Jude Devine's investigation of ritual murders is complicated by her torrid affair with pathologist Dr. Mercy Westmoreland. (1-933110-25-2)

Honor Reclaimed by Radclyffe. Secret Service Agent Cameron Roberts and Blair Powell close ranks to find the would-be assassins who nearly claimed Blair's life. (1-933110-18-X)

Honor Bound by Radclyffe. Secret Service Agent Cameron Roberts and Blair Powell face political intrigue, a clandestine threat to Blair's safety, and the seemingly irreconcilable differences that force them ever farther apart. (1-933110-20-1)

Innocent Hearts by Radclyffe. In a wild and unforgiving land, two women learn about love, passion, and the wonders of the heart. (1-933110-21-X)

The Temple at Landfall by Jane Fletcher. An imprinter, one of Celaeno's most revered servants of the Goddess, is also a prisoner to the faith—until a Ranger frees her by claiming her heart. The Celaeno series. (1-933110-27-9)

Protector of the Realm, Supreme Constellations Book One by Gun Brooke. A space adventure filled with suspense and a daring intergalactic romance. (1-933110-26-0)

Force of Nature by Kim Baldwin. From tornados to forest fires, the forces of nature conspire to bring Gable McCoy and Erin Richards close to danger, and closer to each other. (1-933110-23-6)

In Too Deep by Ronica Black. Undercover homicide cop Erin McKenzie tracks a femme fatale who just might be a real killer…with love and danger hot on her heels. (1-933110-17-1)

Stolen Moments: *Erotic Interludes 2* eds. Radclyffe and Stacia Seaman. Love on the run, in the office, in the shadows…Fast, furious, and almost too hot to handle. (1-933110-16-3)

Course of Action by Gun Brooke. Actress Carolyn Black desperately wants the starring role in an upcoming film produced by Annelie Peterson. Just how far will she go for the dream part of a lifetime? (1-933110-22-8)

Rangers at Roadsend by Jane Fletcher. Sergeant Chip Coppelli has learned to spot trouble coming, and that is exactly what she sees in her new recruit, Katryn Nagata. The Celaeno series. (1-933110-28-7)

Justice Served by Radclyffe. Lieutenant Rebecca Frye and her lover, Dr. Catherine Rawlings, embark on a deadly game of hide-and-seek with an underworld kingpin who traffics in human souls. (1-933110-15-5)

Distant Shores, Silent Thunder by Radclyffe. Dr. Tory King—along with the women who love her—is forced to examine the boundaries of love, friendship, and the ties that transcend time. (1-933110-08-2)

Hunter's Pursuit by Kim Baldwin. A raging blizzard, a mountain hideaway, and a killer-for-hire set a scene for disaster—or desire—when Katarzyna Demetrious rescues a beautiful stranger. (1-933110-09-0)

The Walls of Westernfort by Jane Fletcher. All Temple Guard Natasha Ionadis wants is to serve the Goddess—until she falls in love with one of the rebels she is sworn to destroy. The Celaeno series. (1-933110-24-4)

Erotic Interludes: *Change Of Pace* by Radclyffe. Twenty-five hot-wired encounters guaranteed to spark more than just your imagination. Erotica as you've always dreamed of it. (1-933110-07-4)

Honor Guards by Radclyffe. In a wild flight for their lives, the president's daughter and those who are sworn to protect her wage a desperate struggle for survival. (1-933110-01-5)

Fated Love by Radclyffe. Amidst the chaos and drama of a busy emergency room, two women must contend not only with the fragile nature of life, but also with the irresistible forces of fate. (1-933110-05-8)

Justice in the Shadows by Radclyffe. In a shadow world of secrets and lies, Detective Sergeant Rebecca Frye and her lover, Dr. Catherine Rawlings, join forces in the elusive search for justice. (1-933110-03-1)

shadowland by Radclyffe. In a world on the far edge of desire, two women are drawn together by power, passion, and dark pleasures. An erotic romance. (1-933110-11-2)

Love's Masquerade by Radclyffe. Plunged into the indistinguishable realms of fiction, fantasy, and hidden desires, Auden Frost is forced to question all she believes about the nature of love. (1-933110-14-7)

Love & Honor by Radclyffe. The president's daughter and her lover are faced with difficult choices as they battle a tangled web of Washington intrigue for...love and honor. (1-933110-10-4)

Beyond the Breakwater by Radclyffe. One Provincetown summer, three women learn the true meaning of love, friendship, and family. (1-933110-06-6)

Tomorrow's Promise by Radclyffe. One timeless summer, two very different women discover the power of passion to heal and the promise of hope that only love can bestow. (1-933110-12-0)

Love's Tender Warriors by Radclyffe. Two women who have accepted loneliness as a way of life learn that love is worth fighting for and a battle they cannot afford to lose. (1-933110-02-3)

Love's Melody Lost by Radclyffe. A secretive artist with a haunted past and a young woman escaping a life that has proved to be a lie find their destinies entwined. (1-933110-00-7)

Safe Harbor by Radclyffe. A mysterious newcomer, a reclusive doctor, and a troubled gay teenager learn about love, friendship, and trust during one tumultuous summer in Provincetown. (1-933110-13-9)

Above All, Honor by Radclyffe. Secret Service Agent Cameron Roberts fights her desire for the one woman she can't have—Blair Powell, the daughter of the president of the United States. (1-933110-04-X)